The Last Condo Board of the Apocalypse

Nina Post

A Division of **Whampa, LLC**
P.O. Box 2160
Reston, VA 20195
Tel/Fax: 800-998-2509
http://curiosityquills.com

Cover Art by Eugene Teplitsky
http://eugeneteplitsky.deviantart.com

ISBN 978-1-62007-016-1 (ebook)
ISBN 978-1-62007-017-8 (paperback)

For Jeremy

Chapter One

The Melancholy Cowboy Job

The Jackal was a high-maintenance client, prone to micro-management and fits of hysteria. He was also a resident of Amenity Tower, Pothole City's Finest Luxury Condominium Building. Two weeks earlier, the Jackal's estranged lover stole his favorite painting and sold it for a quarter at the building's annual tag sale.

The Jackal had little patience for local law enforcement, so he decided to bring in a professional to track down the beloved heirloom. His requirements were specific: he needed someone who could tolerate the eccentricities of working for an aardwolf—more commonly known as a gray jackal—and who could find their way around a high-rise populated with creatures that made him look normal by comparison.

A color copy of the insurance photo was folded away in Kelly Driscoll's jacket pocket. In the painting, a melancholy-faced cowboy wearing a Stetson hat and red sunglasses rode a roller coaster over an ocean, an opulent house in the distance. In one calloused, outstretched hand, the cowboy held a tiny walrus; in the other, a pink-frosted donut with sprinkles.

The cowboy painting job was an unwelcome reminder of the sorry state of her career. A year ago, Kelly had found the werewolf fugitive who became known as the Mennonite Butler, hiding in a Horse and Buggy Old Order Mennonite community in Lancaster, Pennsylvania, doing chores for a local family: carpentry, milking, buggy-driving.

When she confronted the Butler, he had a fruit flummery in the stove and politely requested that she wait until the oven timer went off. She agreed, and the oddly genteel and dainty sponge dessert was worth the wait. After the fugitive carefully put away the rest of the flummery, she collared him.

But she never got credit for the job. A vampire huntress in a luxury RV swooped into town and stole Kelly's thunder, garnishing accolades, media attention, and work. Lots of work.

"That was not fair play," Kelly said through her teeth as she stood on the roof.

She put the memory in a box, and imagined throwing the box off the roof until it smashed on the streets below. If there was one thing she was still skilled at, it was compartmentalizing. She needed all of her concentration to descend the granite flank of the sixty-floor Amenity Tower, wash some high-rise windows, and search for a painting of a melancholy cowboy.

What she wanted was a second chance, another fugitive to find.

The harness fit snugly around her chest and thighs as she strapped in, and she imagined what the great football coach Jay Vanner would say if he were on a seat next to her her, tan and focused: 'Kelly, we both know you'll be taking some hits while you chase down the big score. Just remember: your long-term performance is what really counts.'

She nodded as though in response, checked that her screw gates were tight and made sure that the ropes were attached to the eye bolt, then lowered herself in her hand-made boatswain seat, the wood cold against her backside. She pressed the handle of her chest harness to descend.

Kelly squeezed out each end of her mop into one of the buckets and ran it over the window in a square, leaving an overlap of dry glass at the edge.

February in Pothole City was aggressive, like the city itself held a grudge against its citizens. A frigid wind snapped around the skyscrapers, lashing Kelly like a bully-wielded gym towel, carrying the scent of agar, chocolate, and dust. A black watch cap covered her ash-blonde hair and part of her ears; tinted polycarb goggles kept her eyes from watering.

Grasping the squeegee with goatskin gloved hand, she started the blade at a forty-five-degree angle and turned the handle before it reached the right edge, skin crawling at the first squeak. She pulled the squeegee down at an angle to the left.

A hint of a smile creased her right cheek. A clean window gave her more satisfaction than any job she'd worked lately. On the boatswain chair, she felt free from the tentacles of her past, though they could reach all the way, if she stayed long enough. For the moment, she wasn't even afraid of the future.

To pass observational muster as a pro squeaker, she could take five minutes at each window. Even if louvered blinds were lowered and tightened, she could find an angle that gave her some visual access. She scanned the interior of an apartment with a weathered, yellow-taped spotting scope.

So far, no painting. She hoped that it was hanging on someone's living room wall, not accumulating dust under a bed. She needed this money, and preferred to break in through a window and not deal with going in the building otherwise.

Using the suction cup to stabilize herself, she moved to the next unit and saw a man in headphones hugging a roll of paper towels near the window. She stopped moving, stopped thinking about work, stopped thinking about her gray-toned life, and stared transfixed as he ran a hand through honey-colored hair, considering multiple backdrops he'd set up in his living room.

Ultimately—and she was completely absorbed in his decision, placing mental bets on which backdrop best suited that roll of paper towels—he placed the roll in front of a mountain range, compressing his tall and lean body into a crouch. A frisson of triumph went through her; that was her choice, too.

A white umbrella on a long stand glowed softly in the corner as he picked up a large camera and fiddled with the settings.

Time to make herself known.

She bounced lightly off the side of the building with the tips of her boots, and slapped her squeegee on his window. He jumped at the noise, holding the camera with a death grip. She slid the squeegee to the side, flashing a mischievous smile, and he went right up to the window. His widened eyes were the intense blue of a fresh *Lactarius indigo* mushroom, her favorite. She approved.

Kelly held up the squeegee in greeting.

After a moment, the man nodded, then returned to his work.

"What was it, the squeegee?" she muttered.

No painting, regardless. She finished his window and quickly installed a small plot watcher camera, which took a shot every eight seconds. Just in case.

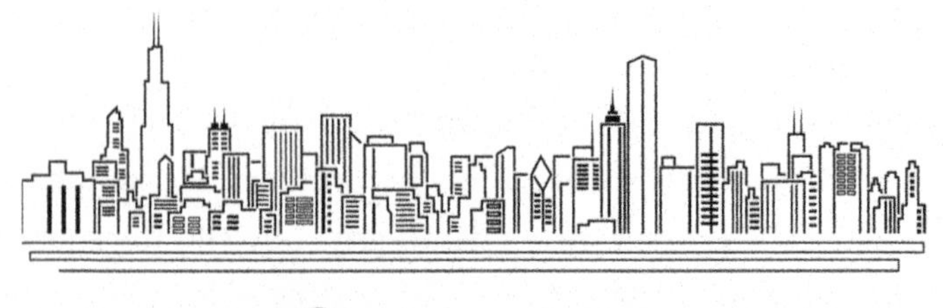

Chapter Two

This is a Terrible Idea

Murray used binoculars to watch Kelly assemble her equipment. It seemed easy enough at the time. But when he tried to do it himself, it was like watching traders in the mercantile exchange use those incomprehensible hand signals, then trying to trade on your own.

"Okay. Rope… feet… tighten these things… tools in bucket." Already, he wanted to throw up. He took a deep breath and counted to ten. "Be quiet. Be quiet. Calm down. No one is here to help you."

After some maneuvering, he stood up in the chair, put his wingtip shoes through, then lowered himself, slowly, onto the seat.

"This is a terrible idea," he muttered.

He looked down, in itself a terrible idea.

"Orangey handle," he whispered, hating his job, resenting his boss, and wanting to be safe in his apartment. Maybe Stringfellow had found his way home. "Okay, I think I—*Ow*!"

His hair was caught in the handle.

"Owww, dammit." He reached into his pocket for his multitool. After some fumbling, he managed to pry out the corkscrew, then the nail file and the screwdriver. Finally, he found the knife and cut his hair above his temple, releasing his head from the handle.

"Right," he said under his breath. "This rope to descend. It's just that easy! Or, I'll end up a puddle of goo on the sidewalk that people will step around with disgust."

His body felt leaden; he couldn't get enough oxygen; and despite the cold, he wiped the sweat off his forehead. Taking his hand off the rope, even for a second, almost made him pass out. He looked down without moving his head. "If this doesn't get me promoted—"

He stopped next to Kelly Driscoll, the one he was supposed to talk to. He had waited for her to come down, but she never did, so he went up. It was the last thing he wated to do, but he had other work to do, and his boss was insistent he get this done ASAP.

"Who the hell are you?" Kelly yelled over the howling wind. He presumed she was glaring at him, but couldn't tell through the tinted goggles.

"My name is Murray."

"Nice suit. Are you going to throw up?"

"Nope." He plastered a grin on his face, which he knew probably looked pained. "I'm great! This—yeah. This is just great."

She held still. "I'm IWCA-trained. Are you?"

Murray sensed her skepticism and tried to reassure her. "Yes, I run my own cattery, totally certified, very professional." IWCA sounded like it involved cats. International World of Catteries of... America. Wasn't that right? Oh, no. No, it couldn't be.

"Right." She smirked. He was as good as fired.

"Well, just be careful. I'd hate for all those cats to be left alone without their administrator."

"Oh, always. I am Mr. Careful." Murray almost bowed but froze just in time, his insides liquefying. It took a good minute of breathing exercises before he could talk again. "Listen, I'm here on the side of this building to talk to you on behalf of my employer, the Destroying Angel of the Apocalypse."

"Go on," she said.

"He's heard of your accomplishments—"

She laughed.

"And he would like to hire you to find a fugitive in this building. You would have two days to locate him and report back."

She bounced casually, especially considering she wasn't attached to anything, not really. He envied her ease with the terrifying wooden chair, and knew he would not sleep that night.

"How much?"

"$10,000, plus standard reimbursements."

She tacked an extra 70% onto the offer. "$17,000," she countered.

He desperately wanted this over with, but of course she had to be a savvy negotiator. He hated her for that. How many times would she counter?

"I can do $15,000, but that's the top of my budget," he said, knowing that his fear of heights compromised his negotiating skills.

"You got a deal."

"Excellent." He made the mistake of letting go and shaking her hand. Terrifying. "Not to be rude, but I'm going to get to solid ground now. Details later, OK?"

As he passed a fifth floor unit, he threw up, completely missing the bucket. A lizard-like creature on the sidewalk shouted and shook its fist. Murray mouthed "Sorry" and waved, but the lizard made a contemptuous and dismissive gesture in response.

Chapter Three

A Ferret, an Angel, and a Postal Worker

The Jackal, a diminutive four feet tall with thick, lustrous Andy Gibb-style hair, was delighted to hear that Kelly found his painting. He shrieked, tiny paw over his snout, then ran up to the apartment to repurchase the painting from its temporary owner.

She waited in the building's automat on the second floor. She dug in her pocket for some change, opened one of the little doors for a chocolate pudding, then poured a cup of coffee from the bird-head spigot on the dispenser.

The Jackal returned to the automat carrying the painting by the hanging wire, his little arms extended to keep it from hitting the floor. He paid her in full, and told her to take the painting.

"It's yours! Enjoy. Consider it a bonus."

"What am I supposed to do with this?" Kelly asked, still eating the pudding. "Strap it to my back like an apocalypse prophet?"

The Jackal put his hands on his hips. "You know how my partner sold the painting just to make me mad? If I give this painting to you, I can pretend I never found it, and then I can hold it over him for years."

Accepting the painting and her money, she went outside to the patio, leaned the painting against a tree planter, and packed up the gear she didn't leave on the roof. She crouched on one knee and put her lanyard, harness, goggles, and climbing helmet in her tackle bag, wondering when she'd actually have the time to buy some lumber and start putting her house back together. Right now it was a charred clearing with some random pieces of wood. Maybe after a few more random gigs she scraped up. Or a hundred.

Until then, she'd keep staying in hostels or empty houses, eating soup cups, and wandering the country by herself, doing the monster bounty hunter's version of ambulance chasing. She didn't want to admit it was lonely and empty, but it was. And she needed money.

When someone walked up to her and stopped a foot away, she raised her head and saw the awkward guy in the suit who had interrupted her window washing with a fairly generous offer.

"Nice painting," Murray said.

She grunted in response, then heard a sound and turned, noticed someone standing behind her: a small-framed, puffy-haired, placid-faced person wearing jeans with a large mirrored metal brand sign, a puffy black nylon jacket zipped up to the top, shiny black patent sneakers with a mirrored metal letter on the sides, and mirrored aviator sunglasses.

He moved closer and she looked askance at this stranger invading her personal space.

"Who's this, a lost extra from *Breaking Away*?"

"This is Tubiel. He doesn't speak," Murray said. "Most don't."

"Most what—most fashion victims?"

He laughed. "No. Tubiel is an angel in charge of returning small birds to their owners."

She looked at Tubiel, and back to Murray. "And I'm the angel in charge of good moods."

Tubiel put his feet up on the planter and showed Kelly his socks.

She ignored him and turned back to Murray. "You look a little washed out. Scared of heights?"

Murray scratched the back of his neck. "I'm just worried. Someone broke into my place and took my ferret, Stringfellow Hawk."

"Someone stole your ferret? Why, can he lead them to the Devil's Eye diamond?" She zipped up her bag.

"I can't believe they managed to take him," Murray continued, "because he's scrappy: he'll fight if he's taunted or condescended to or if he hears Grace Zabriskie's voice. I watched *Inland Empire* when it came out on DVD and he tore up the sofa."

She stood and stretched, twisting to the side to crack her back. "Tell me more about this job. The one that pays."

He gestured to the edifice she had just scaled. "This building, Amenity Tower, is a luxury condominium that's home to cast-out angels and interdimensional monsters."

She received the information with equanimity.

"The angels are bound to the building," he continued. "But eventually, if they figure out how, they'll escape from Amenity Tower and wreak destruction and chaos."

"That kind of sounds like your boss's job," she said. "Isn't that what the Destroying Angel of the Apocalypse wants—the apocalypse? That's a very specific title."

Murray scoffed. "What? No, he doesn't want that." He held up a finger. "More precisely, he doesn't want *these* angels to do it *now*. Regardless, your directive is to find this fugitive, an incredibly volatile and dangerous angel, and bring him in. Are you bonded?"

"Sure." Yeah right.

"Great! You have exactly two days to find the target."

She sighed. "Two days to find someone who could be anyone in a 500-unit building with high security?"

Tubiel gave her a small rock.

"I see your point, but do what you can. My employer will supply you with a case of glass vials," Murray said.

"I don't do urine samples."

"No, you would use the vials to collect and repatriate any suspicious monsters or fallen angels while you look for the fugitive."

"*Suspicious*." She cocked her head. "Like an angel who doesn't eat a breakfast that someone has prepared for him? Or who doesn't believe in regrets, or who doesn't like cheese, or who uses an alarm clock that requires you to solve an equation to turn it off? That kind of suspicious behavior?"

Murray shrugged. "Whatever you think looks suspicious. You don't have to do anything special; the vials do the work for you. I should also mention that anyone who works in medical office management, the dental profession, or the post office are invariably the lowest of demons. Just vial them on sight. No additional evidence needed."

"What, exactly, inspired them to find work in Pothole City?"

Murray cleared his throat. "We think they sensed the increasing activity at Amenity Tower. First the angels were bound to this building, then the cosmic detritus—"

"The what?"

"The interdimensional creatures. I don't know where any of them came from. Galaxy cracks? Your guess is as good as mine right now."

"Fine." She hoisted her bag over her shoulder and tilted her head toward Murray's friend. "Seriously, who is he?"

"He's a single-purpose angel." Murray opened his mouth to speak again but hesitated.

"Time is money." She made a winding motion with her hand.

Murray nodded then launched into it. "There's an angel for everything. There's at least one for every day and every hour of the day and night, at least one for every species, and at least one for every occupation. There's the angel of aquatic animals, the angel in charge of lumberjack sports and timber entertainment, the angel in charge of HVAC systems, the angel who protects commerce brokers—"

"Commerce brokers? What, like bankers?"

"And traders, yes."

"Yikes. Crappy gig."

Murray ran his tongue over his teeth. "That crappy gig happens to be mine."

"You're an angel?" She leaned against the planter.

"Yes."

Tubiel raised his hand for a high-five from Murray, who paused, bemused, then returned it with a tap.

"It's not as impressive as it sounds," Murray added. "Take my word for it: as much of a spaz as *I* am, I'm one of the few socially functional single-purpose angels—SPs for short. Most of us just, you know, do our jobs, and that's all we do. The fallens are like famous actors desperate for their next big role. That's partly why the fugitive you'll be finding for Don—"

"Don?"

"My employer, the Destroying Angel of the Apocalypse. That's partly why this fugitive is so dangerous. The fallens have an endemic sense of entitlement. This particular one is probably a raging diva. Look for grotesque displays of material wealth. They love that."

Tubiel pulled at Kelly's old rope bracelet.

"Why does Don want me for this job?" Her previous two jobs before finding the Jackal's painting were capturing over-breeding zombie bunnies on a college campus and tracking down a mysterious sulfurous scent. She hadn't exactly been a world-beater in the past few months.

"He's called some references. And they raved about your resourcefulness and your skill with disguises."

She was dubious, but wasn't about to argue. It was good money. "I'll get started this morning," she said, walking away.

"Wait!" Murray called out. "Where are you staying?"

"A hostel a few blocks away," she said over her shoulder. "They have free bananas and I tend to run low in potassium."

He patted his pockets and pulled out a set of keys. "I have a better place for you."

Chapter Four

Special Situations International

Murray showed Kelly the top two floors of a 1920s-era art deco building, the former headquarters of Special Situations International, a corporation of unknown provenance and purpose.

Murray, Kelly, and Tubiel went through a revolving door set between intricately carved stone panels. The gold-etched elevators inside weren't working, so they walked up the curving staircase of pink limestone to the top floor of the fourteen-story building.

"You can also use the fire escape at the back."

Murray opened the door with a large silver key in need of polishing, and Tubiel darted around and ran inside. Murray turned the lights on, revealing a long expanse of marble floors and high ceilings.

They continued into a long office area, where rows of desk extended inside an open perimeter like a corporate race track. Kelly dropped her painting, duffle bag, and doctor's satchel on the first desk she reached.

"I trust that a whole floor of 4,500 square feet is sufficient for your short-term stay." Murray signaled with his arms like a runway marshaller to indicate locations as he spoke. "Executive offices to your right. Conference room and kitchen at the far end. Bedroom and bathroom on the left."

He showed her to the first office on the right, at the fire escape end. The stenciling on the door read *Mr. Black*. A massive metal desk, the kind that could only be moved by a crane, hulked in the back of the room like a beast. She glanced at the walls, decorated with framed photos, evidently from Mr. Black's days as a orienteer.

She sat in Mr. Black's brass-riveted swivel chair, tilted back and surveyed the landscape of monogrammed memo pads, ballpoint pen holder, brass nameplate, and black push-button phone. A small part of her wished she could stay in this building longer than two days, take a break from the road, have some *space*. She could be completely alone, with no one around to bother her.

"Two of the offices are set up as bedrooms," Murray said. "The maid service took care of the sheets, so the rooms are good to go. You'll probably want to order some food and whatever else you need. There's a printer over there." He gestured to the south end of the general office. "For now, just order whatever you need to complete the job, and give me your expense reports. Don will quibble but he usually pays."

Tubiel padded through the door and went over to the huge desk where Kelly sat. He picked up the telephone receiver and put it up to his ear as though he could hear something on the other end. He nodded thoughtfully, hung up the phone, and gave her a curious look.

"OK." Murray headed toward the door. "I have to run. An orange juice futures trader invoked me to get him theater tickets, and I need to dissuade him from doing similar invocations in the future. Although—" He looked off to the left and chewed his lip. "He *is* more accurate than the city's meteorologists for anticipating the weather. So I won't be too hard on him. Tubiel?" Murray waited for Tubiel, who shook his head and crawled onto the desk and sat next to her.

Murray looked at Tubiel, then to Kelly as if to say, 'This all right with you?'

She shrugged.

"When are you going to start?" Murray asked.

"As soon as you leave."

"Oh." He waved his hand. "Good. Is there anything you need from me right now?"

"I have two days to find my high-value target in a condo building with 500 apartments. He could be a person, an animal, or a piece of furniture. You can just leave those expense reports. All of them."

Murray put a stack of them on the desk. "Follow me. I'll show you where to send them. And here's a corporate card." He paused to hand her a credit card with an absinthe-green glow, then went to a tiny room on the east wall next to the telephone closet. He reached into a shoebox-sized cubby in the wall, removed a capsule made of wood, and slid open a tiny window.

"This is the pneumatic tube system," Murray said. "Anything you put in this capsule and send will reach Don. But I have access to it, also." Murray placed the capsule in the wall, pressed a button, and the capsule whooshed away.

"When do I meet him?"

"I don't know if you will," Murray said. "He's agoraphobic."

"The Destroying Angel of the Apocalypse is agoraphobic?"

"Very much so. But I'll warn you: he tends to inconsistently micromanage. He'll want frequent updates, and then when you provide those updates, he'll ask why you're bothering him."

After they left the little room, she passed what looked like an old radio on the west wall. It was some kind of intercom system, with two rows of paper-labeled push buttons for each executive, and rows for the telephone room, conference room, tube room, and restroom. A spoon-shaped lever stuck out on the upper left side.

Next they went to the conference room at the front of the building, facing south. In the kitchen to the right, she spotted an electric kettle and a coffeemaker. Murray indicated for her to follow him back to the other end of the floor.

"I hope this is acceptable." He put on his coat. "Don used this place for out-of-town visitors, but doesn't anymore. Let me know if there's anything you're missing." He headed toward the exit. "You have my number, and you can always use the pneumatic tube."

After Murray closed the door behind him, she unpacked her bag on one of the general office desks, starting with transmitters, a pinhole video camera, a scrambled-band walkie, and some cheap baby monitors. On the next desk, she put her tracking supplies, paracord, duct tape, superglue, spotting scope, a few occupational uniforms, infrared goggles, and some snacks.

Finally, while Tubiel looked through the scope, she arranged her theatrical makeup kit, an extensive collection of dental apparatuses, and colored contact lenses, often necessary with her easily-identifiable eye color, not dissimilar from Max Headroom's. The lenses were non-prescription; her vision was 20/15.

From Mr. Black's office, she used her laptop and cell modem to access topographical, geographical, and seismic activity for Amenity Tower before pulling documents from Amenity Tower's website: elevator reports, operations logs, board meeting agendas, and management and engineering reports.

Tubiel wandered out of the office.

She ordered a high-resolution day/night camera. Finally, after some research into Pothole City, she ordered more uniforms and accessories.

Tubiel came back and handed her a stuffed albino peacock.

"Thanks. Who knows, I may need this." She glanced over Tubiel's outfit. "Are you staying?"

He smiled and shrugged.

"Can I buy you some pajamas?" After pulling up a few options, she angled the laptop toward him and he pointed to a set with a bird pattern. She bought two versions.

Back in the general office, she and rifled through the uniforms in her duffle bag, selecting a polo shirt and some things to go with it.

"Make yourself at home," she told Tubiel, who followed when she hurried into the kitchen. "I'll be back later. If you get hungry, grab one of those oatmeal packets." She waved a packet of a common brand of oatmeal in front of Tubiel.

He shook his head.

"Don't like oatmeal? Okay, what *do* you eat?"

Tubiel left the kitchen and went all the way back to Mr. Black's office, where he climbed up on the chair and typed something on her laptop.

She peered over his shoulder at the product page for a brand called Cluck Snack. "Knock yourself out. We'll get reimbursed later."

Before she left, she hung the cowboy painting on the south wall of Mr. Black's office.

Chapter Five

The Fallen Angel's Survival Guide

A**f worked alone in the Amenity Tower's club room.** The only sources of light were from his laptop screen and a table lamp. Outside beyond the floor-to-ceiling windows, illuminated snow fell onto the patio from a darkening sky, and a crab-like creature swooped into the beam of light cast by the tall lamp.

Now that he inhabited a mortal vessel, thankfully a serviceable and even attractive one, Af's conception of time had radically changed. Even if he lived a full life in the vessel, aged to its late thirties, he had a tiny speck of time to complete his current project, *The Fallen Angel's Survival Guide: Your Ultimate Handbook for a Bound Lifestyle*, and anything else he wanted to get done.

Sometimes, he woke in a panicked state over what a relatively short time he would have in a human vessel and his worry over why he was bound to Amenity Tower—had he done something wrong?

A flash, Fat Man bright, blew out to all corners of the room.

Af closed his eyes, then opened them in a squint. The light shrunk to a wavering corona that surrounded four figures standing on the long table in the conference room to his right. He sipped his tea and turned his focus back to the document as the newcomers spoke:

"Where am I?"

"What is this place? Sheol? Perdition? The Gates of Death? The Gates of the Shadow of Death? Silence? The Bilge? The lowest pit? *Where are we*?!"

"Will someone please set a nearby human on fire so we can see where we are?"

"Hold on, I have light burn-in. Ahh, crap, I'm in a mortal form factor. I can tell by the shoddy components."

One of the newcomers, who hadn't spoken, jumped off the table and left the room like a Fortune 100 CEO striding away from his private jet. The other figures stumbled off the table, blinked in confusion, then lurched in the general direction of the main club room.

"Well, look who it is!" The CEO-like newcomer stood at the head of the group and smiled at Af, his cosmetically straight and white teeth glinting in the dark. "Been too long, buddy."

"Not long enough, Raum." Af glanced over while typing. "But you look sharp."

Raum, in the vessel of a vigorously attractive man in his late fifties, looked down at his suit and clapped his hands on his chest. "I look good—and I feel good."

One of the new arrivals came closer. "You two know each other?"

"Get your head out of your ass, Forcas." Raum's tone sharpened, and he gestured to Af. "This is the Angel of Destruction and Anger." Raum raised his arms at Af as though to embrace him. "A Prince of Wrath!"

Forcas glowered. "Good for him. Can he tell us where we are?"

Raum chuckled. "Does it matter? Let's put some coffee on and figure it out later." He snapped his fingers a few times. "All of you, sit down at that table by the window." He smoothed the front of his jacket and went to the kitchen in the back room.

Af left his laptop on the next chair and joined him in the kitchen. Raum filled a drip machine with a full pot of water and scooped ground coffee from a plastic canister into the filter. As it brewed, Raum hung his head and exhaled in a shudder.

The other newcomers didn't fully realize what happened to them, but Af did, and he could see that Raum knew all too well.

"Tell me," Raum said, not looking at Af.

"You've been bound to Amenity Tower, a luxury condominium building in Pothole City. You have neglected your heavenly duties, have cast away your grace, and perhaps worst of all, now have to attend board and committee meetings. With that said, I have no idea why we're all bound to the same place. This is highly unusual."

Raum nodded and swallowed hard, taking it all in. "I was cast down, then. Is that different? Worse?"

"You're bound here, like the rest of us. And don't worry: you still have access to all the building amenities." Af's tone brightened. "We have an indoor lap pool, an automat, a fitness center. This club room."

"I was so angry." Raum pressed between his eyebrows. "You know? Resentful. Stubborn." He smiled, rueful, then snorted a quiet laugh. "I can't believe it worked out like this, but I suppose I'll have to make the best of it. In fact, I've written out a short bucket list."

Raum took a piece of paper from his jacket pocket. He cleared his throat. "(1) Mate with beautiful women and beget giants that will wreak ruin upon the human race, (2) Destroy whatever city we're in, and (3) Inflict bloodshed and destruction upon humanity and subjugate what remains. Not necessarily in that order." He winked at Af.

"What was that last one again?"

"Don't get your wings in a bunch, Af. That's what I do. I destroy cities. Which city is this?"

"Pothole City."

Raum grimaced. "That sounds terrible. Let's work on getting bound to a better-sounding city. Like... Sexy Mortal Lady City."

"Why don't you just enjoy our indoor lap pool for now." Af tilted his head in the direction of the pool. "It's soothing. Maybe you won't feel like destroying the city anymore."

In Af's opinion, destroying a city was small time, a mere warm-up, but he didn't want to be like that anymore. He considered his time bound to Amenity Tower as an opportunity to live his life in a different way. He didn't want to go back, not for a while. He didn't want Pothole City, let alone Amenity Tower, destroyed. And he realized that Raum and his followers were going to be a problem.

Chapter Six

The End of Days Sub-Committee

Forcas, Vassago, and Imamiah waited at a table by the window and stared, despondent, at a piece of paper in front of each of them. They greeted Raum's return with fretting hands and compulsive lip-chewing.

"Raum," Vassago said in a pleading tone. "Is this somewhere within the second Heaven where we're imprisoned awaiting final judgment in complete darkness?"

"No, it's happy sparkle balloon land, where dreams come true," Imamiah said, snarling at Vassago. "Get real."

"It seems to be somewhere between the two." Raum flicked his eyes down at the large table and picked up one of the copies of the paper. "What's this? Condominium Association Board Meeting." Then, still reading, "Agenda."

"Action Items," Forcas read, running a finger down the page. "Do we have to take action on all of these?"

"I don't care about the action items!" Imamiah pounded his fist on the table. "I'm confused, I'm depressed, I'm tired. I feel awful. The only action item I'm interested in is to sleep for a month so I don't have to think about what just happened."

"I think we're in a hotel." Vassago looked around.

The three-part club room was sleekly outfitted in dark wood and a color palette taken from a tapestry of *The Unicorn is in Captivity and No Longer Dead*. Overall, it looked like the lobby of a long-term, corporate-stay hotel.

Af kept working in the corner.

Forcas cleared his throat. "We've got to figure out where we are and what we're doing here. I think this agenda is a good start, so we should go over what it says, okay? Maybe they're instructions of some kind. Um, 'Homeowner Comments.'" Forcas looked up.

"Ah, call to order," Forcas continued. "Roll call/Establish quorum."

"We are definitely a quorum," Imamiah said. "Aren't we?"

Everyone at the table turned to look at Af, who raised his eyes from his laptop without moving his head. "What?"

"I pronounce us the new quorum of—" Raum started to say.

"Board," Af said.

Ram clutched his lapels. "I pronounce us the new quorum of board."

Af shook his head. "I pronounce us the new board of—"

Nothing.

Af leaned forward. "The new Board of Directors of Amenity Tower."

"What he said," Raum grinned. "I'll be the treasurer, because I'm humble and don't need to be in charge. Forcas, you know rhetoric and logic, so you can be president. Vassago, you find lost possessions, so you'll be vice-president. Imamiah, you supervise and control voyages, so you'll be secretary."

None of those assignments made sense, but he doubted it mattered. At the moment, the board was just him and a green darner creature. They didn't have specific roles, and left everything to Roger, who typed up the board agenda each month.

Af didn't want to have a fiduciary responsibility to protect the interests of the unit owners; he had a strong feeling it would be like standing in quicksand.

Raum wasn't the type of angel who liked to get things done, and he didn't fret over details. Af couldn't see any of them sticking to the tasks of the board, but they were more than welcome to try.

"What about him?" Vassago pointed at Af.

"Member-at-large," Raum said in a booming voice.

Af ran his tongue around his back molars. "Fine." Then under his breath, "As long as it's mostly 'at-large.'"

"Good enough for me." Raum ran his finger down the sheet and stopped at another point. "Approval of minutes."

"Approved!" Imamiah said, pumping a fist in the air.

They all stared at him.

"I'm feeling a little emotional right now."

Raum scribbled a note. "Imamiah, you humiliate and destroy enemies, so I want you to find out if someone is in charge here, then tell them they're not in charge anymore. If they give you any trouble, humiliate them, and then destroy them.

"The next item on the list is New Business: Pizza delivery. Vassago, why don't you look into that. We'll convene again tomorrow to strategize the End of Days."

"The board meets monthly," Af said, focusing on his screen.

"We'll meet daily. We have a lot to accomplish," Raum said.

"That's not tenable," Af said while typing, then added, "You can also hold committee meetings—operations, finance, community, rules and regulations." Not that he ever did. But theoretically, one could.

Raum rubbed his chin. "What if we wanted a different committee. One for bringing about the End of Days, for example?"

Af sighed. "If you, as the board, want to form a committee, say, End of Days, then you can make it a sub-committee under the purview of an existing committee."

Raum smiled. "Very impressive, Af. You've obviously been bound here for quite a while."

Af had been bound to Amenity Tower long enough that his quiet, comfortable life felt threatened, and he didn't like that feeling at all.

Forcas tilted his head. "The End of Days Sub-Committee. We can coordinate our escape and the End of Days at the same time."

"Let's stick that under Operations," Raum said. "Adjourned!" He paused at the door. "Wait, where's my apartment?"

Chapter Seven

Marmota Constant, Elevator Inspector

For her first disguised entry into Amenity Tower, Kelly entered the lobby in a brown wig, brown contact lenses, a dental apparatus, a baseball cap with a logo, a collared denim shirt, and blue khaki pants.

The shirt featured an embroidered logo of an eagle holding elevator parts in its claws over a map of North America. Underneath the logo was the phrase *In the Public Interest.*

In the lobby, she edged past a group of young Japanese guys wearing ski hats, pants cut off just below the knees, and flip-flops, went around a few medics, and finally passed two SWAT-type men wearing olive green jumpsuits, kevlar vests, and various weapons strapped to their legs.

A stocky man with an insulated pizza carrier whirled through the revolving door and charged a reception desk like he carried a beating heart for transplant, whereas the medics and the SWAT men seemed to be in no hurry.

After the delivery guy was buzzed in to the elevator vestibule, she approached the long curve of the reception desk. The nameplate on the desk said Clementine Jackson.

Kelly gave Clementine a close-lipped smile and flashed her credentials in a logo-embossed holder.

"Marmota Constant, Elevator Inspector and Supervisor with the National Association of Elevator Safety Authorities. This is a standard visit to ensure that all inspectors under my supervision in this jurisdiction are performing their duties in compliance with the requirements of the QEI-I Code of Ethics." She flashed a purposely reluctant smile that did not reach her eyes.

"I'll tell the manager you're here, but—" Clementine checked her watch. "He's just finishing up his show. And the show"—she winked—"is his priority."

Kelly waited close to the front desk in a stance that suggested she could stand there forever, and stood close enough to make Clementine uncomfortable.

It worked. "Oh, heck, just go on in. I've got enough to worry about. Like, do I do my job and let that delivery guy in, or risk losing my job and warn him that no one else delivering pizza has ever made it out?"

Once Clementine buzzed her in, Kelly went down a hall and into an enclosed reception area for the management office. A moment later, a man emerged from a glass-walled studio at her right. His dark brown hair was styled with claws, his over-ironed black suit would melt in the rain, and a cherry-red tie over a black shirt had her looking for a wand and white rabbit.

A small crowd followed him out of the studio, and one man hovered over the others, glowering. The man in the magician suit halted in front of him.

"What can I do for you, Dragomir?"

The tall man snorted. "Only five years ago, I was military's best engineer, and now I waste miserable life tending to impossible HVAC problems."

"I'm well aware of your previous employment history," the man in the suit said. "That darn air handler again, is it? I'll be right with you."

He pointed to her and snapped his fingers. She half-expected him to disappear in a cloud of fog. "Elevator supervisor, right? C'mon back." He gracefully evaded residents who all wanted a piece of him as he strode down another hallway to an office on the left.

He closed the door behind him and braced himself against it as if keeping out a zombie horde, then held out his hand for her to shake.

"Roger Balbi, property manager of Amenity Tower and host of *What's On Your Mind, With Roger Balbi*, the only local access TV show filmed in Amenity Tower and in front of a live studio audience."

Kelly shook his hand, noting his Casio Databank watch. "Marmota Constant." The sides of her nose and jawline were padded with theatrical putty, and an applique mole was stuck to her right cheek. Even just changing her eye color usually did the job, but she liked to be careful.

"Wow, firm grip."

"A firm grip for anyone, or for a woman?"

"A lot of men have weak handshakes," Roger said. "But I wouldn't shake their hands if I were you, because most don't bother washing after they use the john. Tell you what: let's make a pact right now to never shake hands again, with anyone. It'd be a shame if people didn't know about your firm grip, because that says a lot about you. But it's just gross, isn't it. Shaking hands." Roger scribbled something out on a piece of paper and signed it, then pushed the paper toward her.

The writing on the paper was indecipherable. She once spent three days trying to discern exactly what her doctor had written on the results of her annual physical. This was worse.

"It states that Roger Balbi and—"

"Marmota Constant," Kelly said.

"And Marmota Constant, on this date blah blah blah, swear to never shake anyone's hand again, and to always wash up in the john," Roger said.

Kelly looked younger than her age, she'd been told, but was no one's fool. Blah blah blah was ambiguous at best. Blah blah blah covered a multitude of sins. Blah blah blah said that the building would receive free elevator service for the next hundred years, with a twenty-minute response time.

"Nah."

"Fine, fine." He slapped his hand on the papers and dragged them away like a snake attacking a small rodent. "So what can I help you with?"

"I'm here to ensure that your Certified Elevator Inspectors are adhering to QEI-I compliance. I'll need to review the elevator inspection reports, complaints, and accidents for this building."

Roger didn't answer right away, and she wondered if she had accidentally worn her Department of Buildings shirt ("Where Building a Better Pothole City Begins"). No, she was more careful than that, but glanced at her chest anyway to verify the logo. Yep, eagle grasping elevator parts in its claws. Check.

"You bet," Roger finally said. "Let me get those for you." He turned his back to her and rummaged through part of his wall of file cabinets. He spun back around, wielding papers.

"You can keep this for your records," he said. "It's our elevator complaint log and some other stuff. We keep up with our annual inspections—which is not typical for Pothole City—and are up to code. Is there anything else you need?"

"I'd like to take a look in your elevator control room." This would take her two seconds, but the act of going to the room would make Roger impatient to get back to work, allowing her to slip away somewhere else. He would presume she could find her own way out.

Roger and Kelly passed an open elevator door on their way to the control room. Dragomir directed a hostile stare at the elevator's control panel, which was connected to a laptop on his metal tool cart.

"Are you working on that shaking cab?" Roger asked the engineer.

"A shaking cab?" Kelly said. "Could be a faulty drive system wiring or belt. Or it may just need a simple door adjustment. Is there any banging or scratching?"

Both men stared at her like she'd grown a second head. She stared right back. After all, she was Marmota Constant, elevator inspector. A little bit of homework could go a long way, and was usually a lot more than most people bothered to do. Marmota Constant knew her elevators. Marmota Constant graduated from Purdue. She, however, had a limited knowledge of elevators that would soon be exhausted.

"Uh, I don't—I don't think so." Roger flipped through his papers. "Maybe?"

"That's not good," she said. "Shaking *and* banging could indicate a broken hoist rope—"

"Or a relay needs replacing," Dragomir said, focusing on the control panel. "Or cables need insulating." He shot a territorial look of warning at her.

"Yeah. Or that." She shot a look back.

A tense moment passed. Soft jazz played through the speakers.

Roger was called away and said he'd meet them in the machine room.

"QEI?" Dragomir said in a kind of growl, as though challenging her.

"QEI supervisor," she corrected. "Periodic inspection on passenger and freight elevators."

Dragomir huffed with skepticism and closed the control panel. He packed up his cart and held the doors with a look that said, 'You getting in or not?'

They took the cab up to the second floor. Kelly watched Dragomir wheel his cart into an unmarked door down the hall. He had evidently honed his wiry physique with a combination of fuming, seething, and building engineering.

Once he was gone, she took the stairs up to the other floors to look for her fugitive.

Chapter Eight

The Seventy Holy Pencils

Kelly took the stairs two at a time to the next floor. She practiced whenever she could in the city, often carrying a twenty-pound bag of bird seed. One day, there would be a very hungry, very large bird and a non-functioning elevator. On that day, she would be prepared.

She crept through the hallway. Smelling. Listening.

An apartment door ahead of her cracked open and a face peered around the edge. When she reached the door, she opened it wider and stepped in.

A small figure who reminded her of Tubiel sat cross-legged on a hardwood floor surrounded by pencils that had scattered to the walls. A concentration of furniture and towering stacks of papers and magazines completely dominated the wall near the window.

A big pop art pencil the length of a swordfish took up the space on one of the walls, and old pencil advertisements papered the other walls.

The small figure wiped his nose on his sleeve and emitted a half sob, half hiccup. She approached and crouched in front of him. His purple irises had tiny gold petal shapes in a daisy pattern from the pupil, and his pale skin was slick with tears. He scribbled on a drawing pad and handed it to her.

"'I dropped the seventy holy pencils," Kelly read off the paper. "I must find all of them before the Senior Reconciler comes back. If the Senior Reconciler finds out that I lost the holy pencils—"

His eyes widened and glazed over in terror.

"No wonder you look freaked out. I'd hate to work for someone with *that* title." But then she remembered that she was working for the Destroying Angel of the Apocalypse.

She reached out and patted the side of his arm, even though she always felt awkward trying to reassure anyone, and often thought that a robot would do a better job. "When is he coming back?"

He sketched a clock.

"An hour?"

He swallowed hard and nodded.

Kelly scratched her neck and stood. He must be a single-purpose angel like Tubiel. She would help him out, but needed a more exact time. "How about forty-five minutes to round up the pencils?"

The angel studied the large clock on the wall like it didn't make any sense to him. After a moment, he held up some fingers.

"Twenty-seven minutes," she said.

He nodded.

"How did this happen?"

The angel scribbled something down and she read it out loud again: "'I got nervous and I threw the box in the air and pencils went everywhere.'" He rocked back and forth, hugging his knees.

"Okay, I got it. You just hold tight." She noticed a small refrigerator under the wooden pencil. It contained small cans of coffee drinks in one brand: Cluck Snack. She took out a Cluck Snack P'nut Butt'r Koffee Drink and handed it to the angel against her better judgment.

He scrawled '70' across the entire surface of the pad and circled it several times.

"Yeah, I got it, don't worry." Kelly started to gather the pencils. "And you're welcome," she muttered under her breath.

Twenty-four minutes later, after searching around stacks of *Carbon Fancy* magazine, Faberhardt-Castel catalogs, Eberhard Faber Mongol boxes, colored 'Hard Blue' pencil boxes, guides to the Dewey Decimal System, taped-up cardboard boxes, and other crap, Kelly held a full box of seventy pencils.

She presented the box of holy pencils to the angel in the manner of a Chinese businessman handing someone his business card, but he curled up on his side in some kind of fugue state, his purple and gold eyes staring blankly at nothing in particular.

She waved her hand in front of his face. "Hello? You've got about a minute before the Senior Reconciler shows up, and I don't even want to be here for that." She slapped him, gently. He drooled. She slapped him again. Finally, he blinked.

Forty-one seconds. "I have the pencils."

He took the cigar box and opened the lid, then tentatively rolled the pencils with his fingertips. He seemed to like the sound the pencils made when they rolled against one another, so he kept doing it until she put her hand over his.

"I'm gonna go now. OK?"

Twelve seconds. The purple-eyed angel could count the pencils if he wanted.

She had no desire to run into the Senior Reconciler, so she jogged down the hallway to the stairwell, but the elevator arrived with a "*ding*" before she reached the door. She ducked behind the wall and peeked out at the elevator.

The elevator doors opened and swamp-gas green flames flickered out. A yellowish, bioluminescent blob with horn-rimmed glasses crept out of the cab. It made a guttural, phlegmy, harrumphing sound as it oozed across the carpet. Somehow, it wore a tie with a Windsor knot.

Moments after the Senior Reconciler egressed the elevator cab, a hand reached out and held one side of the doors as they started to close. An orange moth-like creature—distracted by the glow of his mobile phone—left the cab and stumbled down the hallway, seemingly unaware of the hulking blob in front of him.

The moth creature was in the wrong place at the wrong time.

The Reconciler sprayed a corrosive toxin from two acid glands, advanced on his immobilized prey, and oozed right over him. He emitted a dainty belch, and continued down the hallway to his home office.

Kelly waited until the door down the hallway had opened and closed before she took the stairs.

This was one weird building.

Chapter Nine

Pestilence Should Take the Cargo Elevator

Af headed toward the elevators and joined Roger in the vestibule.

"What's up, Af?" Roger flexed his neck until it cracked, smoothed his hair back, then hunched his shoulders up and down like he was struggling under a yoke.

Af wanted to know what Roger knew about the situation, and if Roger had something to do with all of the fallen and cast-down angels getting bound to the building he managed. If Raum and the rest of the board escaped, there would be a precipitous rise in assessments for those who stayed.

"Going down?" Roger gestured to one of the elevators. The other high-rise elevator was out of order and barricaded with yellow tape.

Af nodded and got in with Roger. They went to the first floor. Roger started to go toward his office, then paused mid-stride. "Sorry, Af, did you have something to tell me?"

"What do you make of this escaping business?"

"What do you mean?"

"Have you heard about it?"

Roger gave him a sly grin. "I'm the manager. I know everything."

"Do you think it's a good idea?"

"Well, I can't stop them from planning the End of Days or from leaving, if that's what they want to do."

"And the assessments for the rest of us?"

"Painful." Roger winked. "Sorry, Af, but I've got some things to finish up in the office." He started toward the office and added, "Stop by later and pick up a copy of my new CD, *Morning Energy with Roger Balbi*!"

Arlene, who resembled a slender armadillo, but in a shade of lemon yellow, stepped out of the elevator, purse and sunglasses in hand.

"Oh, hello, Af. Long meeting, wasn't it?"

"Long? It's like a memory of an entire summer spent somewhere."

Arlene tittered and headed to the door.

Imamiah walked at a competitive-level speed into the elevator vestibule.

"Imamiah," Af called out, and the angel spun around, his heel squeaking on the polished granite floor. "Have you or the other board members reviewed the historic board minutes from before you and the others took over?"

"Well, no, why?"

"Just curious. Don't you have access to them?"

"Yes, we do. I guess we didn't think they were important. We have so many things to work on, you know? Planning the End of Days, figuring out whether we should purchase the ab machine that the Jackal wants in the fitness center, whether we should add a security camera to Roger's living room so we have a better idea of what's going on in his life, whether we should change the automat's coffee brand to Cluck Snack. So busy, especially with so many board meetings."

Imamiah's answer was just as ambiguous as Roger's, which made Af worry. Imamiah seemed to be spending his time on trivial matters, but that didn't mean he was against trying to escape—it only meant that he wanted to make sure the building was maintained and the reserves bolstered until they did manage to escape. Or was he being too optimistic?

If Raum and the rest of them managed to escape their prison—and he considered Amenity Tower a prison, as much as any brass vessel at the bottom of the sea or Ms. Pac-Man game in Erie, Pennsylvania—why would they care what condition the building was in after they left?

At a loss, Af pressed the up elevator button and waited as he considered the situation. Some of the fallen angels physically bound to Amenity Tower had probably been cast down at some point, but they were all mysteriously bound to the same place. In some cases, both, and in every case, they left angry.

They were resentful and stuck in a perpetual angel adolescence, and would almost certainly want to raze their condo prison behind them as they left. What was one more bridge burned? They'd have to keep burning things behind them over and over in the vain hope that it would assuage the pain of irrevocable loss.

But it couldn't. Only amenities could do that.

The elevator arrived, he stepped in, and the doors closed with inches to spare when a white hoof insinuated itself between them. The doors reopened and revealed a jackal with the feathered blond hair of Andy Gibb, on a white horse the color of Af's favorite paper towel brand and coconut sorbet brand.

"Forty-eight, please," the Jackal said with a mellifluous, smoky voice. The horse clomped on the granite floor.

Af pressed forty-eight, one of the penthouse floors, and kept as much distance as possible between him and the horse. He wondered where Tom the giant water scorpion was. Maybe it was his day off.

"Nice day, isn't it?" The Jackal tossed back his shiny hair. "Pestilence and I were just out enjoying the snow."

"Pestilence should take the cargo elevator," Af said, a tad churlish.

"I will do that in the future," the Jackal replied politely.

The elevator stopped and opened the doors. The Jackal kicked the side of the horse, which neighed and tossed its head and pranced into the hallway.

"Ta." The Jackal waved.

Af continued to his condo, where he called the front desk to report a horse using the high-rise elevator. He was fairly certain that horses or their variations like Pestilence weren't allowed; they should have taken the cargo elevator at the very least.

He figured that the Jackal got sucked in through the air handler on the roof, found a unit, and hadn't bothered to read the rules and regulations yet. But the Jackal did have a lovely voice and lustrous hair.

Af put the kettle on and made a sardine sandwich, which he ate at the counter. Then he tended to his laundry, safety-pinning his socks before putting them in the washer.

Chapter Ten

Handy Invocations for the Troubled Banker and Trader

M**urray called and asked Kelly to come back to the** apartment to take Tubiel on a run. She was checking units on the sixteenth floor and took her call by the window.

"Tubiel doesn't seem like the running type," she said.

"No, a run to return a small bird to its owner. There's no actual running involved."

"How has he managed to return them before?"

"I'm not the boss of him," Murray said. "Can you do it?"

"I'm only on my first disguise, and I'm not even close to checking all of the units," she said, not bothering to mention she had no idea what she was supposed to be looking for and that maybe Don should have been more specific if he wanted to find this target. "I can't leave now. Can't you take him?"

"I'm on a job, too." He sounded petulant.

"Why is your job more important than mine? I only have two days."

"Mine is about to jump off a building. But I'm going to drop off a vehicle for you," Murray said.

"I'll be right there. But if Don gives me crap about this, you're covering for me. By the way, an acid-shooting fungus in a paisley tie dissolved a moth monster in the hallway with its corrosive juices."

"I love our talks."

Kelly sat on a stone ledge next to her building and chewed some red string licorice.

A few minutes later, Murray pulled up in a black sidecar motorcycle and listed severely to the left as he braked. Another smaller sidecar swiveled off to the side of the sidecar like a tray table.

"What is that thing?" She had to yell over the engine noise.

"It's your outfit. But you'd better hurry," he yelled. "It tends to stall."

"Where did you get this?"

"A commodities trader who invokes me every time he gets a panic attack. When he goes to the sand dunes, he takes his pet bobcat and the bobcat's pet chinchilla, hence the second sidecar. He let me borrow his hack for the day. He lets me borrow anything I want."

Murray stepped out of the main car in his ever-present brown suit, and fell. He popped up behind the motorcycle and waved.

She climbed into the car and adjusted the goggles he handed her.

"You look like Snoopy on the Red Baron," Murray said.

Tubiel came running out to her, wearing his usual clothes.

His pale arms were wrapped around a birdcage with a small blue bird inside. He hovered nervously for a moment before attempting to get in the main car with her.

She pointed to the sidecar. Tubiel nodded and climbed in, holding up the cage with a questioning look. She gestured to the third, smaller sidecar, and he placed the cage there. She gave Tubiel goggles to wear and assessed the four-speed gearbox.

"Patience is a virtue here," Murray yelled. "Don't rush the gears."

After expending considerable effort to release the clutch, she put the bike into gear and listed to the right as she gave it gas, leaving Murray behind on the sidewalk.

At the next block, Tubiel pulled on her sleeve.

Steering felt like pushing a mastodon. She turned right, pushing hard on the left grip as she pulled up to the curb. Maybe this would be

Tubiel's only task, and she could go right back to the job.

A cab driver stuck his head out his window as he waited at the nearby light. "What is that thing?"

"It's my outfit," she said.

Tubiel scrambled out, ran to a tree, and captured something in his hands. After running back to the bike, he opened the door to the cage and put the small yellow bird in with the small blue bird. He scribbled something on a sketch pad and showed it to her, a downtown address.

"You were invoked again?" she asked, taking off again.

He nodded.

"How do you normally get around?"

He shrugged. She suspected this task would take much longer than she expected or wanted.

They made four detours, collecting a dozen small birds on the way to the downtown address. They rode through alleys and parks, delivering the birds to a firehouse, a horseman of the Apocalypse working in the police's mounted unit, a sandwich maker, and the president of an insurance company.

On the way to returning a chickadee in the middle of nowhere, the bike started to leak fuel.

Kelly pulled up to the curb by a park, pushed up her goggles, checked out the carburetor gasket, and clenched her fists. It was late. She already lost hours from her job. She gestured at Tubiel to get out of the sidecar and he carefully set the cage in the seat.

"Find me a large frog. But don't go too far." Tubiel headed into the park. Several minutes later, he returned with a large frog. "Go wait for me in that bus stop." He did. "But don't get on a bus!"

She held the frog with her left hand. With her right hand she took out a knife. "Sorry, frog," she said quietly. "I need your help." She killed it humanely with her thumb then skinned it. She put the frogskin on the hot carb gasket and the skin adhered to the metal pores, stopping the leak.

After she plugged the leak, they drove home, plowing easily

through high drifts of snow. Tubiel pointed to the soda fountain across the street.

"You want to go there?"

He smiled and nodded.

Kelly parked and called Murray from a phone booth to let him know they were back.

In the booth, Tubiel held the cage with one hand and drew a frog and a question mark on the glass.

"He was a great frog." She waited for Tubiel's expression to change. "He'll be remembered, out of all of those other frogs."

Tubiel nodded, reassured.

They went inside the diner and ordered. The birds chirped and sang until she put her jacket over the cage. Nearly ten minutes later, Murray rushed in through the door.

"Sorry it took so long." He dropped his bag on the seat and a book, *Handy Invocations for the Troubled Banker and Trader*, on the table.

"Local outreach," he said. "Getting the word out, building my brand."

Kelly sipped a vanilla milkshake while Murray and Tubiel shared coconut cream pie. Tubiel took out a miniature bottle of Cluck Snack Top'n ("Makes Anything Taste Like Cluck Snack") and dribbled it onto his slice of pie. He glanced questioningly at Murray, who shook his head. Tubiel gave him a 'you don't know what you're missing' kind of shrug.

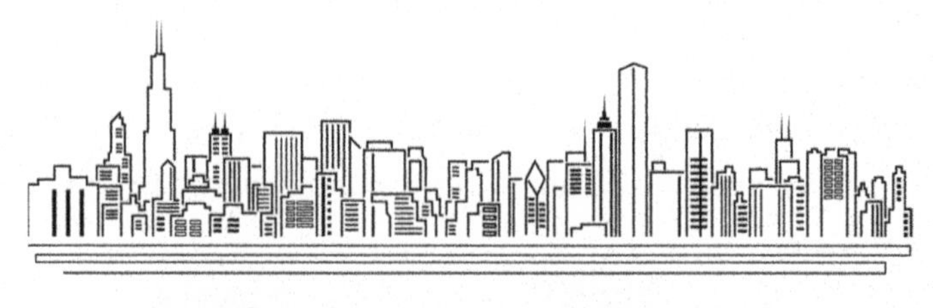

Chapter Eleven

Death Worms Don't Add to the Feng Shui of Your Life

Af's board position, Member-at-Large, was a title for the commitment-phobic. He sat in the front with the board, because it was expected, but put his chair as far to the side as he could get away with. The board meetings took hours now, and were held weekly, a compromise Af negotiated with Raum. Af opened his notebook and started writing his review for a new brand of copy paper.

Forcas, the board president, cleared his throat. "Do we have any comments from homeowners? No? OK. We have a quorum with all five board members present. Approval of minutes from the previous meeting."

The board approved the minutes then moved on to the agenda item of the death worms. It hadn't escaped Af's attention that more residents were adopting death worms. He'd seen one that was five feet long, like a large tube with silken fur and unnerving jaws at one end.

"This is an abstract quality of life issue," Imamiah, board secretary, said. "Allowing tenants to keep death worms, to allow them to take them down in the elevator and through the lobby—well, it would be like death by a thousand cuts. It doesn't add to the feng shui of your life."

Forcas agreed. "We would have to change the Building Declaration Grimoire, and that requires a majority diabolical signature from the owners."

"Forget it," Raum said. "That sounds like way too much work."

"Fine with me. Next item: club room furniture," Forcas said. "Roger?"

Roger cleared his throat. "We recently cleaned the club room furniture at an expense of $750. But we need to replace three coffee tables. They were danced on during the last party. Danced on hard."

"Which party?" Imamiah asked. "'Unbound' or 'Bound But Proud'?"

Roger checked his clipboard. "The former."

A resident raised his hand and Roger called on him.

"Replaced for how much?" the resident asked.

"No more than $1,500," Roger answered.

"You know what, piss on the new coffee tables," Crocell said.

"Crocell!" Vassago said.

"Well, who cares about the damn coffee tables? Don't you want to get out of here? Because I do, and I know a lot of you do, too," Crocell said, turning and addressing the residents who attended the meeting. "We're all bound here. OK, *some* of us are bound here. We should be using this time to figure out a way to escape, not to worry about the contracts or common element repairs or a tree rental!"

"Crocell is right. Let the building rot and the death worms roam free. Forcas sat forward in his chair and put his hands on the table. We're going to find a way to get out of here—with the reserve money—and then what does it matter if we don't have a landscaping contract, or a scavenger contract, or a plant in the lobby?"

Vassago, board vice-president, glanced at Forcas. "If I may say something." Forcas nodded.

"We don't know *if* we can escape, and we certainly don't know when. We need to maintain the building in the meantime."

"It's a quality of life issue," Imamiah repeated.

"Yeah, right," Crocell said, sneering. "Quality of life."

"Oh, you don't think so?" Vassago said. "Do you have any idea how much garbage this building produces? If we let the scavenger contract lapse, and you couldn't escape yet—well, this would be a hell you *wouldn't* like."

Roger held up a finger. "On that topic, the second installment of the Scavenger Rebate has been received from Pothole City. These funds have been deposited into the Association operating account."

Raum grinned and tapped his hand on the table. "Perfect. Bringing about the End of Days is not inexpensive."

Vassago put a finger on the table as though to hold it down. "Crocell, you used the pool yesterday. Did you benefit from the non-slip pool deck material? Or the well-balanced chemicals?" He lifted his finger and made circles toward Crocell as though he were mixing the chlorine with it.

Crocell scowled. "I suppose."

"And I saw you using a treadmill this morning," Forcas added.

Vassago wasn't done yet. "Do you like the view from your window, Crocell? Or making your famous chicken pot pie in your kitchen? Or walking out on the patio without chunks of the building falling onto your head? How about being able to drop off your trash and have it taken out of the building? Do you like how the trash doesn't build up in the chute?"

Forcas leaned over to look at Crocell. "Do you enjoy watching cable TV, Crocell?

One of the residents shouted, "How about discounted movie tickets?"

Forcas glared at him. "We're *bound* here, idiot!"

Af glanced up from his notebook and stretched his neck. In the seat next to him, Murmur, a Fallen whom Af sometimes saw in the elevator, was knitting a scarf, or maybe a death worm sweater.

Crocell stood. "But we ought to be using at least half of our time every meeting to figure out a way to escape from this—this *prison*! Because that's what it is. A prison, with a pool and a hot tub and a sauna and a library—"

"And our own luxury apartments," Af said. "Some on the penthouse floors. The horror."

"Well, I want to get the hell out of here," Crocell muttered.

Forcas agreed. "As much fun as I'm having, I believe that we're not fulfilling our purpose as long as we're bound to this building."

After a brief silence, Vassago jabbed a finger on the table. "As long as we're bound here, we need to run the building along with Roger. And we need all of this time at our weekly board meeting to do that. So I propose that we officially form a sub-committee."

Raum clapped his hands and rubbed them together. "Yes! Let's form a sub-committee so we can really focus on our escape plan. Great idea, Vassago."

"Uh, we already formed that committee, Raum," Vassago corrected. "I'm proposing that you move your escape business to the End of Days Sub-Committee, and let the board work with Roger to manage the building."

"Our business," Crocell said. "Just to clarificate, escaping is all of *our* business. We should be working on it together, not in some radical splinter group."

Af made a face. *Just to clarificate?*

"*Hello*?!" A sea cucumber-like monster gestured at the board. "Could we get back to the rest of the management report, please? I'd like my floor construction approved before the End of Days. Not the meeting of the sub-committee, but the actual event. You've put it off for two meetings and I need my floors redone!"

"We'll get to that next week," Forcas said, and the infuriated cucumber-monster made a face and extruded his guts all over the floor.

Forcas rolled his eyes. "If you show up next week, I'm going to wrap you in duct tape before we form a quorum."

Roger cleared his throat. "OK, let's table the sub-committee issue. We have an air handler project update. Our engineering consultant is continuing to review the velocity data as well as photographs of the mesh performance during the last few snow storms. We anticipate a full report at the next board meeting."

"What are you *talking* about?" A humanoid swamp monster tossed up his hands in exasperation. "Can we see some slides or something?"

Af had no intention of joining the End of Days sub-committee or whatever they called it. He had come to accept and even enjoy his situation, while many of the others couldn't. He would really just prefer to do quiet things indoors that didn't involve massive destruction or the deaths of humans.

Sure, they were angry, Raum and the others, the ones who wanted to escape. And normally, he would be the angriest, on a professional level, or at least the one wreaking epic-scale wrath on a professional level, but not now.

Af knew that clinging to his past, tempting as it was, stole from his present and future. He had to move on, as much as he wanted to go home. Instead of wasting his time wallowing in things that couldn't be fixed, he'd rather use the amenities and focus on writing his book and his product reviews.

Yes, he was bound to the building and had no idea why, but he wanted to make the most of it.

While he thought about this, the agenda continued.

Roger cleared his throat. "Be it resolved that the board approves expenditures totaling $2,312 authorized by the property manager for various common element repairs. We have $400 in hot tub repairs, from when a resident drained the water and replaced it with gravy."

"But we need gravy to breathe!" Twin amphibious fishes with bulbous eyes protested from the back row of chairs.

Af didn't think that was strictly true. He figured that they could breathe through their skin when in a moist environment, but didn't require it. Otherwise, they'd be dead right now.

"And to lay our eggs!"

A shocked murmur rippled across the room. Roger scribbled down a quick note.

"Regardless," Roger said in his reasonable tone. "It's not fair for the residents who *don't* need gravy to breathe and who restrict their egg-laying to their own apartment. Until we can update the rules and regulations to prohibit residents from filling the hot tub with a non-standard material, or laying eggs anywhere in the common areas or outside a resident's own unit, I will make a plea for you to be neighborly.

"Moving on, ah, treadmill repairs, $220, because the Anakim giant tried to use it despite the sign on the door expressly discouraging use by Anakim giants; and club room furniture cleaning, $750, from the 'Unbound' party."

A bound angel in front of Af leaned toward his seatmate and whispered, with precise diction, "Worth every penny."

An Anakim giant huddled in the back raised his hand. "Can the board consider adding a giant-rated treadmill in the fitness center? Any giant-rated cardio machine would be great."

"We'll add that to the agenda for next week," Forcas said.

"We'd have to replace three weight machines to fit in a giant-rated cardo machine," Vassago said. "Plus, the vibration would affect the other machines."

The Anakim giant started to get up from his chair.

Roger put out a hand. "Watch the ceiling! We'll see what we can do. The next item on the agenda: Be it resolved that the Board approves a $120 fine assessed to an owner for excessive shrieking."

"Yeah, what the hell is that?" Crocell said. "I can hear it five floors up."

"I believe it's the resident's death worm," Roger said.

"Wait, are we even allowed to have those?" asked a beetle resident with overlarge red eyes who joined the meeting late.

"Technically speaking, yes," Roger said. "Though admittedly, the building wasn't designed for death worms. There's not enough space for them to play outside, there's not a special death worm elevator, and we've had a number of noise complaints. Also, a fine was assessed last month when a resident took his death worm through the lobby. As you all know, death worms are only allowed to go out the side door."

"Residents shouldn't be allowed to have death worms," a marmot-porcupine monster said. The marmot had been annoying Af for some time, sitting on the floor sprawled out like a small bear, eating flowers with his mouth open. "They're a menace!"

Af put down his pen and spoke up. "I agree that short-term tenants, bound or not, should not be allowed to have them. Death worms are a violation of our right to quiet enjoyment."

"Imamiah, what are you for?" Raum asked.

"I'm for whatever makes this meeting over," Imamiah said.

"We should vote on forming a death worm sub-committee under the aegis of the rule and regs committee," Forcas said.

The vote passed.

"This brings up another matter," Raum said. "Where are these monster things from? I see them coming in through the gas lines and living in the stairwells. I have to sprinkle salt in front of my stove."

"And I had to stop stair-climbing for exercise," Gaap said.

"Roger, are there any nearby buildings with a similar profile to ours?" Vassago asked. "Maybe they've done something with their monsters that worked."

"Are you joking?" Roger said, letting his diplomatic facade slip for a rare second. "This is the only building with monsters, let alone cast-down angels. And Raum, you'll have to talk to the building engineers about your gas line problem. I'll check with Dragomir and bring it up at the next meeting, but in the meantime, fill out a maintenance request."

"Do these monsters pay assessments or are they just squatting?" Crocell asked.

"They're residents," Roger said, rubbing his eyes. Af thought he looked exhausted.

Af didn't have any interest in the remaining agenda items, so he quietly snuck out to the open patio for some fresh air. He pulled the edges of his leather jacket closer in the dry cold and watched people walk around their lit offices in the surrounding buildings.

He knew Raum was determined to get out, even though this prison had to be the best one in their experience—better, for example, than Raquia, where fallen angels were imprisoned waiting final judgment in complete darkness, without the benefit of a backup generator or a grocery store on site that sold rotisserie chickens.

A thousand years in one place rarely included maintenance, services and amenities, let alone company, though Af could often do without that.

Chapter Twelve

Hamster Memorial Service

I**'m here to facilitate the hamster and hermit crab** memorial." Kelly told the woman behind the front desk.

The memorial notice on the Amenity Tower website gave her the info. For the occasion, Kelly wore a badly-cut brown suit in a fabric apparently sourced from tree bark, an auburn wig styled in a long braid, green contact lenses, and padding in her chest, which came across as maternal and comforting.

The woman behind the desk seemed to serve as a gargoyle or chimera, with a stout body, mercilessly ponytailed hair, and cold FARC eyes.

"Hello," Kelly tried. This could be a while.

"Oh, she's on the cleaning crew," said Clementine, walking out of from the mail room in back. "What's that you're carrying?"

Kelly held up the object. "It's a car for hamsters. I find it helps with the grieving process."

She was buzzed in.

On the second floor, she found the club room, closed for the hermit crab/hamster memorial. Somber-looking angels and monsters sat quietly in lined-up chairs, listening attentively to an angel who looked as though he didn't care abut things like eating or showering anymore.

"Then I found out that Mr. Cromwell's sweat gland got infected. A doctor picked him up for an operation, but he never woke up again, and when he came back to me, it was in a box. It's not easy being physically bound to anything, and Mr. Cromwell was my best friend. I took him with me everywhere in Amenity Tower."

She shut the door.

Since she didn't have an electronic fob, she had to wait by the fitness center until a resident opened the door, then went in behind him. It was empty, but she took a quick look around and walked by the magazine racks on the way out. Residents could read *Revelations*, *Lodge & Camp* ("For demons or fallen angels interested in time-sharing any of the seven lodges of Hell"), and *Other People's Success*, which she took with her.

She returned to the memorial. A different angel was addressing the group. He held his note cards with shaky hands and read, "I'm so sorry, Edgar. I should have written a better checklist or flowchart in case you molted. My partner thought you were dead, but you were just molting." He couldn't hold in a hitching sob. "I'm just a dumb, cast-down angel incapable of caring for anything with a beating heart. Please forgive me."

The angel sat down. "This is too hard. I don't like being quasi-human."

On the other side of the H-shaped floor, past the elevators, she found a long beige hallway. On the door was a sign, 'Angry Dance in Progress, Do Not Disturb.' She opened the door.

The room was much bigger on the inside than it looked from the outside, with big oil drums, ductwork, a cement floor, and dripping roof. An angel contorted himself and leaped and jumped in what appeared to be the middle of an angry dance.

Just before she closed the door, she reconsidered. Did he really need to stay here, just doing an angry dance? Opening the door all the way, she held out a vial and the fervently dancing angel was sucked into it just as he jumped on one of the barrels. After all, he could be the fugitive Don was looking for. But then, anyone could be.

Just down the hall, in a small library, two angels played cribbage, but the game had turned violent. Blood had spattered in dots and pools over the books, the walls and the table.

Kelly dug two more vials from her pocket. "Time to go home, boys," she murmured, and within seconds, the vials filled with a carbonated green foam. "Calm down," she told the foam in the vials. "You can finish your game later."

At this rate, she would need more vials, but she couldn't wait for her target to go into one of the common areas, and couldn't canvass every apartment in Don's insane timeframe.

A pudgy maintenance engineer walked by and paused as his radio crackled. Her voice distorted by static, Clementine said, "Bogdan, one of the residents is trying to give me a dead dove he found. Do we still accept those without a pre-filed maintenance request?"

Bogdan rubbed his forehead and grimaced.

She took the radio from him. "Clem, get some paper towels and a brown bag. Take the dove from the resident using the paper towels and put the dove in the bag. Then call wildlife rescue to pick it up." It was too large a bird for Tubiel, and probably didn't have an owner.

Bogdan smiled and nodded (it wasn't far from a curtsy) when she handed back the radio. Dragomir interrupted and started arguing with him in Romanian and English, with the odd interspersed Anglo-Saxon curse word.

From what she could gather, a plumbing situation was festering on the fifty-eighth floor—one of the penthouse units. Dragomir gave a frustrated gesture and stalked off. And while Bogdan had his back turned, she slid up behind him and applied pressure to his carotid artery until he passed out.

Chapter Thirteen

Another Satisfied Customer

Kelly gripped Bogdan's short body under the arms and dragged him to one of the doors in the hallway, hoping no one was looking at the footage from the hallway camera. She clipped his two-way radio and key set to her belt, then put on his shirt with the sewn-on Amenity Tower decal over hers. Bogdan was an unflattering name for a female, but ambiguous enough, she guessed.

"Bogdan," Clem said over the radio. "Can you go up to 1204 for a plumbing call?"

Making her voice low, Kelly clicked the radio and said "Got it."

Keys jangling and radio constantly chirping—these guys didn't suffer from a lack of work—she took the stairs to twelve. The resident who called in the maintenance request was a lanky angel with an impressive parachute collection hanging on the walls.

He pointed to his toilet with a grimace of derision. "That device is leaking! I hate the requirements of this mortal substrate."

A simple problem to fix. She flushed the toilet, and water leaked over the basin by the flush valve. She put the top of the basin back on, turned a valve by the wall, and flushed it again. "You're all set, sir," she said, handing him a maintenance receipt.

"What, uh... what was the, um..."

"Your water pressure was set too high. The water actually sprayed up in a fountain when you flushed it, which caused the leaking. I lowered the water pressure just enough and the leaking stopped. It shouldn't happen again."

Another satisfied customer.

Her radio crackled.

"Can you check out a noise complaint concerning unit... 4102?"

Kelly confirmed that and took the stairs two at a time to the forty-first floor. She vowed to throw the radio down the trash chute or leave it on an elevator floor after doing this task.

4102's music reverberated all the way down the hall. Kelly knocked.

When the door opened, she stuck her foot out. A puffy toad monster opened the door with a beer in his hand and she caught the resident in a very painful arm lock.

"A society," she said, "like this building, operates on rules. What most of those rules boil down to is: don't be a selfish d-bag. Are you aware that other people live in this building, some just down the hall?"

He didn't respond. She made the lock even more painful.

"Yes, yes!"

"Do you want to see me at your door again?"

"No!"

"Then have a nice day."

Chapter Fourteen

Ukuleles and Margaritas

Kelly set Bogdan's toolbox down on the alcove window by the elevators and sagged against the wall, worried that she was actually terrible at hunting monsters for bounty and at finding fugitives and at everything else.

The legendary coach Jay Vanner would understand: it's discouraging to discover that what you do well isn't what's needed to get the job done.

She could get into the building, sure, but didn't know how to find something that could be anything. Vanner would remind her to adapt and be flexible, even when that meant you couldn't use your strengths.

Grabbing the toolbox by the handle, she leaned over and pressed the button for the elevator. She didn't have the energy to take the stairs, even if it was only twelve floors going down.

When the doors opened, she was surprised to see an elevator attendant, a giant water scorpion holding a ukulele and a bottle of margarita mix.

"Which floor?" It reached out one of its six limbs to hold the door. After a moment, the elevator made an insistent beep.

"Quickly, Miss—holding the door could cause a malfunction."

Kelly stepped into the cab just as the attendant poured tequila, lime juice, orange liqueur, and ice into a blender using his topmost two limbs.

When the elevator stopped at the first floor, she looked down. One of the scorpion's arms shined her shoes while he kept working the elevator buttons and the blender.

A man who seemed familiar stepped in after a polite wait, when he determined that the passengers inside were not getting out.

"Which floor, sir?" the scorpion asked.

"Forty-two, please, Tom."

The man glanced at Kelly then did a double-take, then a third take at her shirt and toolbox. "Aren't you the window washer?" He snuck a glance at her shirt. "Er, Bogdan? That sounds like my favorite brand of paper towels: Brobdingnagiany Towels."

"Right," she said. "I saw you photographing those paper towels, in front of a Swiss Alps backdrop."

He wrinkled his forehead. "What are you doing here, again?"

"I'm looking for a job at the World Wicket Company," she said.

He tilted his head and gave her a hint of a smile. "You're in the wrong place. This is Amenity Tower, Pothole City's Finest Luxury Condominium Building."

She took a map from her pocket and unfolded it. "No wonder. This is a map of Copenhagen."

"My name is Af. I live here."

"Nice to meet you." She held out her hand for him to shake. Several seconds passed.

Finally, with a shake of his head, realizing, he took her hand.

"Kelly." She closed her eyes, wishing she hadn't screwed up like that. But he had this amused, kind expression, like he was naturally empathetic, like they were in on a joke together, and it just slipped out. She wanted to be honest with him, and thought she *could* be honest with him.

"Not Bogdan?" He smiled.

"Mm, no."

"I won't tell."

She tried to force-calm the fluttering warmth in her chest, but Tom and his table dominated the right side and much of the center of the elevator cab, so they pressed up against the left and back wall. One more resident could get in, but at the expense of close personal space.

"Margarita?" Tom poured ingredients into the blender. At her nod he pressed the start button.

"I don't understand," Af said, still shaking her hand. "Are you a window washer or a maintenance engineer?"

"Neither. I'm looking for someone. But he's proving hard to find. He could be anyone in this building."

She accepted a salted glass from Tom and reluctantly let go of Af's hand.

The elevator stopped on floor forty-two, but no one got out.

"Which floor, sir?" Tom asked.

Af gestured to indicate any floor.

Tom pressed the second floor button and when the elevator started to move again, handed Af a margarita and strummed his ukulele. "I take requests. Song, not drink."

She tilted her head to look at Af. "You're bound here, aren't you?"

Af deflected his gaze. "How did you—? You make it sound so—"

"No, no." She held up her palm. "I just meant—"

"It's true. I am one of them." He cleared his throat. "Fear not."

"Requests?" Tom asked again.

"What are you in charge of?" Kelly asked Af. "Whole grains? Men's ties? Card games? The protection of jockeys?"

"I'm in charge of this vessel." Af swept his arms down the front of his broad shoulders and lean legs. "And barely keeping up with that."

"Obviously." She turned to Tom, who was delighted at the prospect of providing another service, possibly a song.

"You have a request?" he asked, black eyes blinking.

"Do you know the theme to *Ultraman*, the 1962 version?"

Tom clacked his claws a few times in thought. "No."

"How about the vocal theme to the *Six Million Dollar Man*? The Dusty Springfield version?"

Tom looked physically pained. "No."

An awkward moment passed. "I'm out of songs with 'man' in the title. What *do* you know?" Kelly asked.

Tom brightened. "I'm Happy to Be Your Manager," by Roger Balbi."

Chapter Fifteen

An Over-Active Cloaca

The elevator stopped at forty-two, where a gelatinous green sea slug, taller than Kelly, squeezed into the limited space on the side against the wall. It faced Af and somehow gave a cold shoulder to Tom at its left.

"Afternoon, Elysia," Tom said to the slug in a tight voice.

"Tom," the slug replied, with a nod.

She did not want to think about the subtext in *that* little exchange.

Af touched her, arm to arm, out of necessity. Kelly started to feel flattered he would rather be pressed up against her than a gelatinous slug. She reconsidered and wondered if she should be annoyed instead. Finally, she settled for flattered.

Af met her eyes briefly. "Close quarters in here."

The slug snorted with derision. "At least *someone* is getting something out of it." It came up with a cheese puff from a hidden pocket and inserted it into its mouth. A moment later, what little was left of the cheese puff oozed from its cloaca onto the floor.

Af and Kelly watched the slug, eyes wide, though they politely kept their heads faced toward the digital screen. Eventually, they looked away and read the notices for the upcoming pizza delivery sub-committee, the cowboy song workshop in the club room, and a reminder to not feed the dragonflies in underground level five.

The screen updated to show Roger's quote of the day: "It is better to have a good neighbor than a friend who's far away."

"Unless that neighbor has a death worm," Af muttered.

"How are you enjoying your vessel?" Kelly asked Af. He must be in love with a mortal female, she guessed. Isn't that always why angels walked the earth?

"It's fine," he said. "I mean, I've inherited a few minor physical ailments from—"

"The poor bastard's body you stole?"

"I didn't steal it," Af said, affronted. "We take whatever form suits our needs. To be honest, I have no idea how it works."

She was thinking how his form would suit her needs.

He hesitated. "And I miss some things, of course."

"Sure," she said. "Power, immortality, wings. Who needs it? Be human and suffer."

The slug shifted position and rubbed against Af's arm. Af discreetly wiped the residue off on the back of his shirt.

"I haven't seen you in a while," the slug said, presumably to Tom. "You look good."

Kelly thought the slug was staring straight ahead, but it was hard to tell, especially from the back. The scorpion used one of his left limbs to shine Af's shoes.

"You too," Tom said gruffly.

"Is this a new service?" she asked Af.

Tom spoke up. "I live in the building, but needed the health care. The union has great coverage."

"You mentioned suffering," Af said to her. "Is that what it's like?"

She sipped at the remnants of her margarita and nodded to Tom, who started the blender again. "Let's see. Losing people you love, not knowing if you'll ever be with them again. Tyrannized by what you said or didn't say, what you did or didn't do. Lugging our pasts behind us like mace balls from a chain. Decisions we've made mauling us day after day. Our grief like murderers, jumping out to stab us with a dagger when we don't expect it. The worry. What's not to like?"

"That sounds so violent," Af said.

The elevator stopped at two and the slug glided out. Over what might have been its shoulder, it said, "I'll be at the pool, if someone cares to join me."

Tom handed Kelly her second margarita.

"Seriously, what are you in charge of?" she asked Af.

"Wrath. Destruction. The death of mortals."

"The death of mortals."

"Mm-hm."

"You say that like you're ordering a sandwich. Does that mean you can tell me what happens to mortals when they die?"

"I don't really know," he said. "It's beyond my purview."

The elevator stopped at floor one and she pressed the button for fifty-seven herself, making a conciliatory gesture to Tom. The doors closed and the elevator went back up.

"You don't know what happens after?"

Tom picked up his ukulele. "'Let's Be Neighborly,' by Roger Balbi." He softly strummed a song. "Let's just all be civil, let's be neighborly..."

"Look, um—"

"Kelly."

Tom strummed as he sang softly, "Let's meet in the common areas and share our common dreams..."

"Our bureaucracy is vast and dense," Af said. "Layers upon layers upon layers of administrative subgroups."

She pictured a napoleon with layers of pastry and custard. A flaky biscuit. A lasagna. She dug around in a pocket and found only an unwrapped stick of gum covered in lint.

"There is so much granular specificity with our positions. Each layer is very protective of what it does. There's very little inter-agency communication. I do my small part, and then someone else takes over. Trust me, no other angel would be surprised that I don't know. What happens to mortals after they die? Only a few at the top know that kind of thing."

The elevator stopped at fifty-seven. Tom didn't even ask; he just pressed floor two.

"I'm sorry I don't have anything better," Af said.

The digital sign promoted Roger's latest show with his featured guest, the band "Föhnkrankheit."

"So am I," she said.

Chapter Sixteen

She Wasn't About to Explain That to the Angel in Charge of Water Insects

That night, the angel in charge of the protection of water insects, also known as Dave, invoked Tubiel to find and return his canary. Kelly was surprised to discover that one SP could invoke another SP.

After some tree-climbing with a flashlight, Tubiel found the chirping yellow bird. She expected to see someone like Tubiel—placid and silent—but Dave looked like a guitar player for Föhnkrankheit.

And Dave, like Murray, talked.

"What is this, a bed and breakfast?" Kelly asked, looking around.

"It's a grant-supported communal living home for retired showgirls," Dave said. "Similar to a B&B, but with all the televised roller derby, dense smoke, and butterscotch candy you can eat. Anyway, thanks again for finding Pearl."

She presumed that was the last she would see of Dave. But a few minutes after she stopped in to check on Tubiel, Dave showed up in the ground level camera feed at her building. He found the outside intercom and pressed the button.

"Hey, uh, Kelly? It's Dave, from earlier. I have the canary, Pearl?"

She shot a dubious look at Tubiel as he ate a Cluck Snack Steak-

Flav'r Pudd'n cup. "You know anything about this?"

He shook his head.

"Then how does he know where I live?"

Tubiel set down his pudding and scribbled a business card on his sketch pad.

"You gave him my card? The one I don't give to people?"

He nodded, proud.

"Why do I even have those cards?" she muttered, and pressed the intercom. "Dave, I'll meet you in back, by the fire escape."

Tubiel's pudding consumed, he padded over to the kitchen and poured a bowl of Cluck Snack Krispy Baked B'nana Bitz for Dogs and Ferrets ("Can Be Used As Cereal!").

She took the fire escape down to the last rung and stayed perched there. It was hard to see Dave with all the black until he smiled and his white teeth flashed.

"Fear not," he said.

After jumping to the ground, she approached Dave with a large flashlight.

"Legs apart, hands on your head. Do it."

He did it. She patted the sides of his legs and torso.

"What are you doing here?"

"One of the girls started thinking I was her least favorite ex-husband and then they all turned against me," Dave said.

She patted down the sides of his shirt and jacket.

"I sort of brought someone," Dave turned his head to the dumpster. "That's Kermit. He's in charge of three o'clock a.m."

She waved the flashlight over him.

Kermit, who was skinny, with longish dark hair and as wide-eyed as a lemur, wore a red race track helmet with a lightning logo and ear flaps. He inexplicably did a brief tap dance.

"Why?" she asked Dave, her arms folded.

"He loves to tap dance," Dave answered. On her expression, he corrected himself. "Oh, you mean, why do I have Kermit with me?"

"I don't care why he's with you. Why did you bring him here?"

"I ran into him at a convenience store." Dave held his hands out defensively.

"So you don't even know each other?"

Dave laughed. "Of course we know each other—he's in charge of my favorite hour! Also, it turns out we're both in the Small Birds Club." At her look, he elaborated. "For the encouragement of the propagation of small birds."

Kelly considered the two angels in front of her and wondered how she got into this nutbar situation. Her job was supposed to be to find the high-value target for Don, and to vial any angels or supernatural creatures along the way to be, as Murray put it, repatriated. The job was not to let single-purpose angels stay at her place and place absurd demands on her time.

She considered living in the stairwell of Amenity Tower so she could get some work done.

At this rate, she would never sleep. Then she would collapse. Then all the money she earned from this job would get sucked into her blindingly expensive hospital stay. Then when she was still recovering, she wouldn't have any time to work more jobs to pay for her electrolyte drip or whatever because she would spend every available minute on the phone with the insurance company arguing over duplicate billing and incorrect procedure codes. But she wasn't about to explain that to the angel in charge of water insects.

"It would be for just one night," Dave said. "Please?"

She let out a breath.

"Isn't it kinda strange that all of us are in the same city?" Dave asked.

"What do you mean?"

He unsnapped the collar of his leather motorcycle jacket and put his hands in the side pockets. "Our kind—single-purpose angels—are usually much more scattered. Mobile. I've never seen this many of us in one place. I guess we all sensed it was a hot spot." He shrugged. "Lucky you."

Kelly met eyes with both of them.

"We heard one of us was killed," Dave added in a low voice. "By someone who obviously knew how to do it. Majorly disconcerting."

"Why me? Why here?"

Dave gave her a half smile and a shrug. "Just a feeling?"

"One night." Her reputation for getting a job done was being compromised, but she suspected her fugitive could be a certain mild-mannered fallen angel with honey-colored hair—just a gut feeling. But she wouldn't say anything for now, at least not until she learned more about Don's real agenda.

Dave gave Kermit a high-five. Kermit ran back to the dumpster, grabbed a duffel bag, and walked back toward the fire escape with a loping gait, arms dangling awkwardly at his sides.

She got them up the fire escape and into the top floor and tossed their bags on a desk just before the intercom rang again. More SPs.

She made a quick stop by the pneumatic tube room, where she jotted down a message:

M, Need reinforcements! Come over now!

As she popped the latch and sent the tube on its way, she wondered if Murray would misconstrue that request.

Chapter Seventeen

I Would Prefer You Not Secrete Enzymes Into My Rhubarb Pie

As a former Angel of Anger and Prince of Wrath, Af tried to stay calm and bend like the willow, but often found mortal and condo life to be a series of affronts.

The first thing that annoyed Af that day was the drip coffeemaker, which leaked from the carafe every time he poured it. After that, it was the uncleanable ceramic stovetop and the cabinet knobs that caught the fly in his pajama pants.

Af poured his coffee and wiped off the coffee puddle from the carafe with a rag.

Earlier in the week, he researched how people got through the days. In something called summer camp, young humans had blocks of different activities, then lunch, then more blocks of activity, and a group event in the evening. They woke up and went to bed at the same time every day. In human prisons, schools, and monasteries they did very much the same thing. Af based his schedule on this model, with specific times every day for eating, exercise, hobbies, and leisure. He didn't need much sleep, but liked to try, or pretend.

Every day at 9:00 a.m., he spent thirty minutes in the fitness center. Every day at 4:30 p.m., he went downstairs to check for mail and packages. (He subscribed to a wide variety of publications, including *Turkey World*, *Rock and Dirt*, *The Lancet*, and *Tugboat Review*.)

He liked being able to schedule things. He had spent thousands of years bound to a gold urn at the bottom of the Gulf of Mexico. Then another thousand years bound to the Ms. Pac Man game in Erie, Pennsylvania, where that jerk Abaddon inadvertently released him. He made a mental note to send Don a gift basket.

Since Af's release from the Ms. Pac Man game was an accident, no one noticed. He took advantage of the mistake and did some traveling, but after a few weeks, he found himself inexplicably bound to a luxury condominium high-rise in downtown Pothole City.

Amenity Tower lived up to its name, though Af sometimes marveled how he was doing activities profoundly unbecoming to an angel of his stature. Riding the elliptical machine. Attending board and committee meetings. Making his own food. Having a death worm in the elevator sniff his pants.

Af was one of many angels in Amenity Tower, but didn't associate much with the others outside of the meetings. They would nod in the hallway and in the fitness center and around the pool. And every day, new monsters that left behind bioluminescent smears and weird little adhesive hairs and bizarre scents moved into the building. And, of course, everyone had to have their own death worm.

On any given day, Af had a new neighbor of indeterminable provenance. Earlier that morning, he opened his door to a beetle-monster holding a rhubarb pie with serrated, whiskery arms.

"Hey, neighbor," it said, trying to ingratiate itself. When Af reached out to take the pie, the beetle-thing sheepishly admitted that on the way over, he pierced the pie with his beak and secreted enzymes into the filling. "I just couldn't help myself."

And what could Af say to that? 'I would prefer that you not secrete enzymes into my rhubarb pie?' It was a nice gesture, after all.

"That's very kind of you," Af finally said, accepting the pie. "But you'll have to excuse me; I need to finish some minor home surgery." He gently closed and locked the door to a bemused but sympathetic expression on the beetle-monster's face.

Af wondered when he would see Kelly, the window washer/maintenance engineer/fugitive hunter again. Because even though he was stuck in a small enclosed space with a giant ukulele-strumming, margarita-mixing water scorpion and a green blob with an over-active cloaca, he was happy to talk to her, and didn't think he had ever enjoyed himself as much. Her strange pale eyes reminded him of his favorite facial tissue line, 'Sky Expressions.'

Chapter Eighteen

It's Kind of the Opposite of the Deal

Two hours later, Dave, Kermit, Tubiel, and half a dozen other single-purpose angels were devouring Cluck Snack toaster oven pizzas in the conference room.

"What's going on?" Murray asked.

In Mr. Black's office, Kelly checked the plot watcher feeds for the cameras she had installed in Amenity Tower, which took an image snapshot every eight seconds.

"The angel of water insects, the angel of the three o'clock hour, and the angel in charge of returning small birds to their owners and who knows who else are watching a romantic comedy in my conference room." She closed her laptop.

She and Murray went past the general office area toward the kitchen and lingered in the door to the conference room, where the SPs watched the movie.

Dave said, "I don't understand why she believed he was a good choice for a mate. He lacks manly features. How can he be expected to exact blood vengeance for her kin?"

A ding indicated something set off the motion detectors, and she walked back to Mr. Black's office, murmuring, "What now?"

On the monitor, three angels wandered around the front revolving doors in a confused way. Two of them bumped into each other while the third leaned against the stone and seemed to instantly fall asleep.

Murray stopped in the door. She swung her arm at the monitor. "Go downstairs and bring them up before someone sees them. They think this place is a safe house."

Murray raised an eyebrow. "Isn't it?"

"Providing lodging to every single-purpose angel in the city wasn't part of the deal."

"You have the whole building. Put them on the next floor."

"This is not the end of it, Murray. More SPs, maybe all of them for all I know, are going to want to come here, through angel telepathy or Dave's blog or courier birds or however they operate. Don is already on my back for not single-handedly rounding up his target. I should be at Amenity Tower 24/7, but I keep getting pulled away."

She leaned back in the swivel chair and closed her eyes. "Also, I don't like people."

Murray sat on the edge of the desk. "These aren't people."

She gave him a skeptical look. "You're right. They're angels, with a single-minded focus on water beetles or tree frogs or clowns. I wasn't going to tell you, but—"

"What?"

"I dated an SP once. Didn't know it at the time. He was in charge of the protection of jumping spiders and ship's husbands. The second job was one he took over for someone else. Eventually I got tired of his work schedule and the spiders he was always leaving around my apartment and the ship's husbands he'd bring over."

"What is a ship's husband?"

"Never mind. My point is—never mind." She waved it off. "It's fine. I'll take care of it." She opened her laptop.

"Okay, because I—"

"Look, they need supervision, not to mention bedding materials and food, and that is definitely not something I'm good at."

"Well, I don't need supervision, and I'm an angel," Murray said.

"Oh, a sample of one to represent many. Q.E.D., then."

"Don't worry. We'll fill out reimbursement forms for any supplies."

"Bring another stack. And don't think I won't vial the lot of them. I'm in enough trouble as it is."

Murray snorted. "Ironic that they think this is a safe house."

"Okay, bring them up. We'll need more food. I wouldn't have expected they would eat at all, let alone as much as they do."

"They acclimated."

"And they won't eat anything but Cluck Snack." She let out a breath. "You may as well tell me who the rest of them are."

"I have no idea. But they're wearing ID bracelets."

They walked through the apartment from Mr. Black's office, down the open hall to the conference table, where she checked bracelets. Each bracelet told her what they were in charge of and their favorite Cluck Snack product, like Ilaniel, angel with dominion over fruit-bearing trees; favorite food: Cluck Snack Frozen-Like Dess'rt Bars.

"Good to know," she said, then lifted a bracelet to show him what it read. "Return to Cluck Snack headquarters."

"Return what—the SP or the bracelet?" Murray said.

"Both? And where are the headquarters?"

"I don't know."

Murray went out to buy sleeping bags and Kelly placed orders for delivery. She put the SPs up in the offices and general office areas. But they didn't like to stay put, unless she was nearby.

That night, while she was reading in bed, something in the book made her think of her mother, and her grief hit her fast and hard. She didn't notice the door open, or the soft sound of feet on the floor. Tubiel climbed up on the bed, turned on *The Cluck Snack Network* and sat there watching cartoons until she was asleep.

Chapter Nineteen

Bureau of Rodent Control

Kelly arrived at Amenity Tower with blonde hair, blue contact lenses, and padding on the upper part of the body, including the arms. She wore a long-sleeved polo shirt featuring Pothole City's logo—a pothole—along with a rat that seemed to gnaw at the red circle and angled slash. She carried a metal toolbox and that universal all-access pass, the clipboard.

"Pothole City Bureau of Rodent Control," she said to the front desk employee. "We have a report of a wasp nest the size of a party balloon up on your roof. Is the manager available?"

Kelly liked to be the first to mention the manager. But this employee—Josh, according to the nameplate—looked at her as though he only expected good things from people: kindness granted, efforts rewarded, treats given.

"The manager is recording his show. He does a local access interview and variety show here in the building." Josh beamed.

"Sure. *What's On Your Mind, With Roger Balbi*. It's my favorite."

"Is this going to take long?" Roger squinted into the wind sweeping over the roof. "Because Biofilm is going to be in my office in exactly six minutes and they're surprisingly punctual."

"Biofilm?" Kelly pretended to look for the wasp nest with a stick.

"An all-giant jazz band here in the building."

"Well, I don't see a problem here." Kelly tapped the stick on a ledge. "Sometimes we get false reports, but we have to take each report seriously. OK, you're all set. You'll be receiving confirmation from the city in eight to ten days, though it could be up to twenty-four weeks. Feel free to phone our office, but only two people work there and they don't answer the phone."

Roger squinted. "Wait, confirmation for what?"

"Confirmation that the nest has been eradicated."

"But there is no nest, you said."

"Sir, I'm not in charge of Pothole City's Streets and Sanitation Department. I just remove or eradicate the nests and issue rat stoppage tickets. Did you want a rat stoppage ticket? I think I have a whole stack of them on my clipboard."

Roger knitted his eyebrows together and squinted. "I'll just wait for that paper in the mail, then."

"That's best. Well, you're all set, Mr—" Kelly pretended to check her clipboard. "Mr. Balbi. On behalf of Pothole City's Bureau of Rodent Control, I thank you for your cooperation."

They headed back to the stairs. As she expected, once they got close to the manager's office, Roger ran off like a mongoose to continue with his show.

Using the security fob she pocketed while in the guise of an elevator inspector, she summoned the high-rise elevators and went to the top penthouse.

Once she covered the top ten floors, she took the stairs down and walked right into an apartment that had somehow been constructed inside the forty-fifth floor stairwell. She leaned over the metal railing and looked down at the fuzzy pink caterpillar-monster in the hanging bubble chair.

The space was configured unlike the small landings of all the other stairwell floors: with its high ceiling and generous space, it looked like a high-priced industrial-style loft.

The walls of the stairwell were a blush pink, the stairs a glossy white—but only on that floor. A huge painting of multicolored swirls and bubbles covered the east wall by the door to the hallway. Two smaller paintings of general-store candy added pops of color to the darker west wall.

A blonde realtor with a briefcase bag stood in front of the caterpillar swaying in the bubble chair.

"You told me that I would have access to utilities," the caterpillar said, and ticked off the list on a tiny proleg. "Water, power, bathrooms."

"You have power." The realtor waved at the lights overhead and the table lamp by a hanging bed in the corner, on the other side of the stairs.

"Fine," the caterpillar-thing said, "but if I have to use the bathroom, I have to go all the way down to the second floor. The photos you showed me misrepresented the space. You said this was, and I quote, 'a gritty urban loft in a full-service building.'"

The realtor shook her head and held her briefcase in front of her. "It's not my fault if you assumed the unit had a bathroom."

The caterpillar stood and paced the long side of his apartment toward the door, his tubular body elongating and contracting. As he returned toward the bubble chair and the realtor, Kelly admired the colorful, beetle-style elytra covering the creature's hindwings.

"The photos showed a bathroom and shower."

"Located in the second floor locker room," the realtor said. "Why do you think you were able to get this price? This is Amenity Tower, Pothole City's Finest Luxury Condominium Building. You have full access to all of the amenities, as long as you pay your rent. Look on the bright side: you have no neighbors on either side of you."

The caterpillar crossed several of its prolegs in a huff, using one to point accusingly at the realtor. "I have very poor vision and more than six times the number of muscles you have—nearly 300 in just my head segment alone. Do you have any idea how much time and physical effort it would take to get to the second floor bathroom?

We're talking an epic-scale challenge—if one of my neighbors doesn't eat me first."

Kelly descended the rest of the way, rounding the corner until she was in the middle of this creature's apartment.

"Excuse me," she said. "Just, you know, taking the stairs."

Chapter Twenty

Makes Anything Taste Like Cluck Snack

During a brief stop at her apartment, Kelly lugged the last of a dozen boxes from the building's entrance into the general office area. She tore off the packing tape and folded open the box flaps. Inside, as she ordered, were smaller boxes containing the entire Cluck Snack product line. The return label said 'Clucking Along Holdings,' with no indication of the street address, city, or state.

She removed and stacked box after box of Cluck Snack Krispy Baked B'nana Bitz for Dogs and Ferrets ("Can Be Used As Cereal!"), Cluck Snack Cereal ("Can Be Used As Cereal!"), Cluck Snack Top'n ("Makes Anything Taste Like Cluck Snack"), and more.

More than a dozen SPs ran up to the boxes and tried to get them open.

"Cool your jets," she said. "I haven't even started on the salsa or the chewable vitamins."

The SPs ran off again with their favorite products and traded the stickers and tiny comics using thick photo albums.

She took one of the books from them and looked through it, running her fingers over pages full of meticulously-placed puffy stickers, holograph stickers, and scratch-and-sniff stickers for every Cluck Snack product. Many of the stickers looked old, and Kelly wondered who the Cluck Snack company was and just how long the product line had actually been around.

Kelly handed Tubiel the sticker book then brought an armful of boxes into the kitchen. Tubiel ran up to the table with a beer stein.

"Bar's closed." She took out some non-perishable nonfat milk containers and set them on the table.

Tubiel tore open a box of the Cluck Snack Krispy Baked B'nana Bitz for Dogs and Ferrets ("Can Be Used As Cereal!"), poured the bowl close to full, then ran into Mr. Orange's office.

She peeked in around the door. In a moment, to Tubiel's delight and apparent expectation, a dancing chicken head filled the screen and said, "Try Cluck Snack Krispy Baked B'nana Bitz for Dogs and Ferrets ('Can Be Used As Cereal!')" Then the chicken sang:

"Cluck cluck cluck cluck cluck cluck snack
Snack snack snack snack snack snack cluck
Cluck snack cluck snack cluck snack cluck
Snack snack snack snack snack snack cluck."

Tubiel clapped to the song, thumped his hand on the desk on the last "cluck," then picked up his bowl to continue eating. Kelly entered the room and sat in Mr. Orange's swivel chair.

"This is all you guys will eat? Cluck Snacks?"

Tubiel nodded, his mouth stuffed full of Krispy Baked B'nana Bitz.

"You like that as cereal?"

He nodded, eyes wide, milk dripping down his chin. Kelly rose briefly from the chair to wipe off the milk with the back of her hand, which she brushed on her jeans. "Okay, Tube. I'll see you later. Refer to the lists if you need to."

Tubiel nodded again to indicate that he knew all about the lists and how to use them. The lists gave a process for what to do if someone or something showed up on the surveillance cameras, or if they needed food or assistance, or if they were under attack.

As Kelly locked up the apartment and climbed down the fire escape, she started to sing the Cluck Snack jingle. "Snack snack snack snack snack snack cluck. Damn, that's catchy."

Chapter Twenty-One

I'm Just That Popular

The top two floors of Kelly's building were full of single-purpose angels, leaving twelve empty floors below. Later that day, four more votaries arrived, bedraggled, each with a bag: the angel in charge of the protection of wrestlers, luchadores and luchadore mask makers; an angel in charge of facial hair; and more angels of the hours and days.

When the single-purpose angels weren't returning small birds or protecting water insects or growing fruit or dispensing dreams or overseeing a particular hour or protecting oceanographers or bike messengers, she had to give them things to do. If she didn't, they would just group around her.

She taught them how to make pictorial maps and sketches, identify footprints, track down monsters, and impersonate city officials. Her only skills.

Murray had paper cuts on his hands, tape on his face, and sponge moistener in his hair from filling out so many forms. "Tell me again why they're all here?" he asked her, pressing on his temples.

Kelly poured herself some coffee. One of the SPs walked in holding a pineapple and sat in the corner of Mr. Black's office. He held it in front of him and stared at it.

"I'm just that popular." She set her mug on one of the stacks. Murray winced, picked up her glass, and moved it to a coaster. "Or it's you."

"What's me?"

Murray shrugged. "Maybe they're coming here because you're one of them, and you look like you can protect them."

Another SP wandered in and climbed up on Mr. Black's desk to play with the adding machine. He was delighted when it spit out a thin strip of paper with a *chchchchchrrr* sound.

"Looks can be deceiving," Murray said. "Okay, let's test your hypothesis and move to the general office area."

Kelly shrugged and guided the angel with the pineapple and the one at the adding machine into the general office area.

"I'll be right there," Murray said, and went somewhere else. In a minute he returned, but stood a few yards away.

"Now what?" Kelly asked.

"Just wait."

Gradually, all of the angels in the top two floors gravitated to Kelly, and within a few minutes, they clustered around her.

"You're like the coach of an overly clingy little league team," Murray said. "You know what—you do kind of remind me of Walter Matthau."

Chapter Twenty-Two

I Rammed My Aedeagus Into Her Ovipore

A**f went to a workshop in the library where residents** learned how to be more creative with the diabolical seals they used to sign pacts. He left early, since he didn't have much use for one anyway, went to the fitness center at exactly 9:00 a.m., and settled into an exercise bike with a copy of *Lodge & Camp* magazine.

A yellow locust squatted hundreds of pounds on his small frame at the Smith machine. Another locust, black and yellow in color, spotted him, applying a featherweight touch with his tiny forelegs under the bar.

"C'mon Aldo, c'mon! One rep at a time!" the spotter yelled. "What's the word, buddy? What's the word?"

The weight-squatting locust exhaled forcefully through his palps. "Swarm!" Then he hissed out an alternating sequence of sounds: "Sssss! Thhhwwwwew! Sssss! Thhhhhwwwwew!"

"What is the word!" the spotter yelled.

"Dammit, Tim," Aldo said.

"What is it, Aldo?"

Swarm," Aldo said, weakly.

"*What is the word?*!" yelled Tim.

Aldo struggled with his last rep. "Swarm!" He dropped the bar on the floor, denting the rubber tiles with a loud thud.

On the bike, Af seethed. In his apartment it was easy to be the new, calm Af: just a normal, easygoing quasi-human, doing a crossword with a cup of coffee. But when he left the sanctity of his home, he opened himself up to external stimuli like these obnoxious locusts. Their mandibles hadn't stopped flapping since he got there, and Af wanted the common areas to be quiet.

"This is our year, buddy." Tim threw a small towel over one of his wings. "We're gonna get so much ovipore we'll barely have time to strip fields."

"Yeah," Aldo said. "I hit one last night, a nymph. I bent her over, gripped her with my valvae and rammed my aedeagus into her ovipore, like, a hundred times."

Af waged a small internal struggle. Be like the willow, he told himself, closing his eyes. The bending willow. He tried so hard to picture himself as the bending willow, but it was almost impossible in the face of grunting, serotonin-drunk locusts.

Tim helped Aldo place the bar on the stops. Aldo sat up and they both scarfed two large pizzas resting on a nearby weight bench, followed by a bag of chocolate cupcakes and a quart of fruit punch each.

Af cringed at the sounds of mandibles gnawing through big pieces of food. He wanted to rip off those muscular locust legs and watch locust juice squirt all over the floor until their creepy eyes clouded, because every time he tried to get a peaceful workout, there were these two lunkhead locusts in their gregarious phase making all this noise.

Af couldn't take it anymore. He got off the bike and went over to the locusts as they devoured the last of the food.

"Would you locusts mind keeping it down?"

Tim rose from the bench, hunching his wing buds up under his yellow-spotted thorax. He tilted his head and considered Af through half-closed lids as he rubbed his over-muscled hind femora against his under-developed abdomen, puffy from too much beer.

Their color turned dark as Aldo finished off another pizza. Af wished he could temporarily shut off his overwhelmed human sense receptors, busy processing the food, talcum powder, and weird locust sweat that reminded him of old dish sponge.

"You got a problem, old man?" Tim asked, rhetorically.

"Yeah, I have a problem," Af said. "I can't hear my podcast over your macho posturing."

Tim and Aldo focused their reddish-violet eyes at Af, antennas quivering.

"We don't think we're being loud," Tim said.

"Yeah. If you don't like it, go somewhere else," Aldo said.

"Do you know what I like to have for dinner once in a while?" Af casually leaned an arm on the Smith machine. "Roasted locust with olive oil, crushed garlic, fresh ground pepper and rosemary. 375 degrees for thirty minutes. If I'm out of the apartment, I like bags of hot-boiled locusts. And then for dessert, I like to take a locust, pound it into a mash, then mix it with flour, water and sugar. It makes a nice little cake. Sometimes I even use a madeleine pan."

Tim lunged at Af, his bulging femora flexing, but Aldo held him back.

"Lemme go!" Tim yelled.

"Dude, don't you know what he is? It's not worth it. He's not worth it, okay? Let's go do some plyometrics outside. We gotta focus on the training."

Tim threw his damp towel on the weight bench. With that final exhibition of petulance, the two locusts stormed out of the free weight area, leaving pellet droppings, torn *Locust Fitness* magazines and damp weight benches in their wake—but they didn't make it to the door. Af finally lost his temper.

When Pedro, a member of the building's cleaning crew, entered the gym to replace the sanitary wipe canisters, he found a gory scene: segments and antennae, scraps of membranous and leathery wings, and body fluid coating the floor and equipment.

"*Dios mio*," he whispered.

It took Pedro twenty minutes just to fill out the maintenance checklist. More than once, he regretted leaving his storied trapeze family for a job in Amenity Tower.

As he mopped up the last locust part, Pedro regretted that the locusts weren't smaller, because then he would take them home. His wife Maria would wash them and toast them on the *comal* with a little lemon juice. They would eat them as a crispy *botana* while watching his honored namesake, Pedro Infante, in their favorite movie, *Los Tres Huastecos.*

As he mopped the floor, Pedro thought about picking up a bag of *chapulines* at the market for Maria.

Chapter Twenty-Three

Fiend-Smiter

Before she put on her next disguise and headed over to Amenity Tower for another futile stint looking for Don's fugitive, Kelly stopped by the tube room to check for messages.

Incident at post office in bowels of HVT's condo bldg. M

She pulled on jeans and a sweater, then grabbed her tool bag and some extra vials on her way out the window.

In the post office under Amenity Tower, the employees—foul and demonic on any given day, even in their thin human facade—had transformed to pure demon, a trifling difference in temperament, yet worthy of urgent action. Kelly didn't know what triggered them to return to their original form (job stress?) but it was unpleasant.

A postal demon scuttled forward with a horseshoe crab body, looking in all directions from three slug heads on a long scaly neck. One of the heads shot out a tongue, tipped in a suction cup and coated with yellow mucous. The suction cup stuck to a postal scale and the demon yanked it into its mouth.

The second demon sounded a warning croak from its giant toad head, cracking its skin and activating pus eruptions. It reeked of rotting potatoes. Claws punctured out of toe pads at the end of turtle legs.

Fetid drool oozed and sizzled onto the counter, setting the stamp book on fire.

Murray walked up behind her. "Where to start, right? I hope you brought some of the bigger vials. You're going to need them."

Kelly rummaged through her bag as the slug-head demon spewed chartreuse-colored vomit, which instantly eroded a black-rimmed streak in the floor, toppling the entire series of queue barricade poles.

A third demon emerged from the package processing area. "Another Richmond in the field." She recoiled from the giant wasp body with twelve long-necked heads.

The wasp-demon's faces morphed from the postal employee facade, to the customers it probably ate, to random celebrities it had probably read about in magazines. Most of the heads spat or drooled green foam as it reached toward Kelly and spoke in a voice that sounded like a wood chipper.

"Fiend-smiter!" the wasp-demon said.

"I guess that's me," she said to Murray. "Can you get that embossed on one of those metal nameplates for my desk?"

"You don't have a desk," Murray said.

"For now, I do."

"Fiend-smiter!" the wasp-demon shrieked again and flew at her, knocking her down with surprising heft, and she pushed away the tiny, snapping, sharp-toothed heads. Green foam dripped onto her jeans and burned away the cloth until she frantically wiped off the residue with a Priority Mail envelope.

Two of the heads clasped on to her upper arm and her hip and wouldn't let go. Its saliva burned through her shirt and tiny serrated teeth hooked into and pulled her skin.

Murray pulled at the largest section of its wasp body and some of the heads that weren't already attached to her. Some of the heads whipped around to bite at him and one sank its multiple rows of pointed teeth in Murray's arm.

He yelled and she reached down to her right ankle under her jeans, past the head gnawing on her hip, and pulled out one of her knives, a true switchblade. She pressed a button and the knife sprang out.

She seized one neck a time, slicing back and forth, then scrambled backward to avoid the darker and more viscous green slime spurting from the necks like arterial blood.

"These post office employees are the worst," Kelly said.

She cut off the rest of the heads, took a bigger knife from a sheath on her left calf, tossed the knife to Murray, who thrust it into the back of the wasp with a dry *crunch*.

The twelve decapitated heads on the floor writhed and shrieked and she grabbed one of the large vials from her bag and held it out. The vial sucked in the postal worker, severed heads and all.

"One down, two to go." Kelly secured the still-shrieking, green foam-filled vial into her bag. "Try getting *that* through airport security."

She faced the remaining two, who were still digesting their meal but no longer distracted with eating. "C'mon."

The slug-demon hissed.

"Big deal," Murray said. "A post office employee did the same thing when I defaced government property one time."

"What'd you do, piss down a mailbox?" Kelly asked.

"No, I adhered stamps over other stamps, but she treated me like I humped the President's leg at a press conference, so I'm really enjoying this."

The postal demon came towards them following the slime trail the other one left.

"We'll show her how defacing really works." In one deft movement, she lunged forward with her right leg, fencing-style, and sliced downward with the knife. The slug body waved and clicked its claws.

A woman opened the door near them and walked in with a package.

"It's closed." Kelly gestured her off, but her face and shirt was coated in demon viscera and vomit, so the woman recoiled anyway.

The customer made an exasperated sound. "Can't I just get some stamps?"

Murray took the customer by the shoulders and guided her out, locking the door behind her and ignoring her look of affronted surprise. He turned around and tried to wipe some of the viscera off his face with a package insurance form.

Kelly held out a vial and it sucked in the slug-demon. "Just one more, then we go get some lunch."

"Nothing takes away your appetite, does it?"

"Not really."

The toad-demon slithered down the counter, stopped to regurgitate a shoe, jumped onto the floor, and threw up more chunky chartreuse-colored barf.

"Even now?"

"Nope." She kicked the demon the front, embedding her sneaker in a bubbling pus sore, and when she pulled back, her shoe stayed. "I'm submitting an expense report for that."

With all three postal demons dispatched, she wiped the sweat off her forehead and leaned against the forms counter to rest a momen, then hoisted her bag up to the counter and made sure all the vials were secured in their pockets in the bag.

"Those vials should blow sunshine and rainbows up Don's butt," Murray said. "But what do we do with the... uh... *that.*" He gestured at the pile on the counter.

"There's only so much room." She took a sweeping glance around. "This'll take just a minute."

She snapped on a rubber glove and scooped the postal demon pile into a UPS Express Flat Rate envelope. She handed the envelope to a grimacing Murray to hold while she yanked open the bottom door to a copy machine, which beeped loudly in protest.

"Envelope, please."

Murray held the envelope by his fingertips and she stuffed the envelope into the copy machine and called the number on the copier. "I'd like to report a broken copier."

She finished the call then put her phone back in her pocket.

"That's nice, make it the copy tech's problem," Murray said.

"He's got the easy job."

Chapter Twenty-Four

Training Montage

Af stepped onto the building's patio for his midday walk. The perimeters of the invisible prison extended to anything on the property, which included the patio, the outdoor area at the front of the building, and the small grocery store, accessible from inside the building.

Gaap, a fallen angel with huge bat wings, a purple sweatband, and mesh shorts, jogged around the patio, just inside the bound zone, and punched out jabs and hooks. Almiras, the master of invisibility, popped in and out of vision while doing jumping jacks and pushups, and Purson, who could discover lost treasure, pulled comrades in a wheelbarrow using heavy-duty rope.

Af was soon in the midst of a large-scale training exercise.

Roger was outside in his usual black suit, red shirt and black tie, holding up a boombox. Over a rousing song evidently titled "Teeth of the Smilodon," Roger led dozens of fallen angels, giants, locusts, scorpions, worm and moth creatures, wasp-things, and unidentifiable blobs in a series of warmup exercises.

"Well, screw this," Af muttered, going back inside.

"No backing out of this class," Roger said through a bullhorn. Right everyone?"

Af paused, hand on the door.

"Right!" the residents yelled.

"Teeth of the Smilodon!" Roger yelled.

A worm-thing said 'Teeth of the Leopard' instead, which Af thought was perfectly understandable.

"Got the guts?" Roger asked over the music.

"Not really," Af said. He wanted to set up the lighting for a hand sanitizer photo.

Whatever his fellow fallens and those monsters were up to, he didn't want any part of it. He was still getting acclimated to the building and didn't want anything to upset his delicate equilibrium.

Af liked exercising well enough, but thanks to those locusts, he never wanted to use the fitness center again. Not worth the hassle. But before he even knew how it happened, he was doing jumping jacks in the third row of the bootcamp class .

"Teeth of the Smilodon" ended and an upbeat instrumental started.

"OK everyone—grab one of those sacks of fertilizer from that pile and run sprints from the door to that patio umbrella, five times. Let's go!"

Af wondered why the property manager was trying to kill them. He snuck back inside and watched the melee from the safety of Amenity Tower's automat.

Roger spurred the residents into jumping up like frogs then throwing heavy balls to the resident across from them. Some of the resident monsters who didn't have any appendage capable of catching just let the ball hit them or drop in front of them.

Exhausted just from watching, Af went back to his apartment and made a yogurt from his soft-serve machine while reading a few hard-hitting articles from *The Amenity Tower Bulletin* ("East Stairwell Vs. West Stairwell: Which is Better?" and "What's That Thing Delivering Our Mail?")

Later, he took the elevator back to the second floor and stopped by the automat to check the status of the bootcamp. He found Roger looking out the floor-to-ceiling windows at the bootcamp participants, still working in teams.

"Isn't it great?" Roger didn't turn around when Af approached.

"The building's cleaning company wants all this extra money for 24/7 service," Roger said, "*Triple* the cost compared to regular business hours, can you believe it? So I'm training the residents to do all the after-hours work, which saves me the money for after-hours service."

"Is that legal?"

Roger ignored him and continued. "Not only that, but I told the janitorial service that I'd get the residents to eventually do *all* the work, and they quaked. Amenity Tower is a big contract, so this will give us huge leverage when the next renewal comes around."

Af didn't think this was a good idea.

Roger cocked his head at the residents on the patio. "During this morning's bootcamp, they've already completed the landscaping replacement, cleaned the grill heating plates, applied the concrete sealant, power-washed the deck, cleaned the patio furniture, repaired the granite, and finished the caulking and patching, without knowing they were doing any of those things. With some plyometrics in between. You were smart to leave early."

Chapter Twenty-Five

Cream of Kate

The postal demon bite on Kelly's upper arm needed attention. Using his first-aid kit, Murray cleaned the wound and sterilized a one and a half inch needle.

"Go faster, I'm hungry."

Murray pulled black thread through the edge of her skin. "I'm not going to go faster. This is precision work, and I want to minimize scarring, if that's okay with you."

He tied a knot, cut the thread, then applied an adhesive strip.

"Tinkerbell couldn't use that as a panty liner. Get me a bigger one."

Murray pressed on the adhesive. "Keep those in for two weeks and don't remove them even a minute sooner. Keep it dry for the next twenty-four hours and dry it off when you shower. Try to avoid getting it wet, if you can."

"Thanks. Can we get some dinner now?"

"Dinner?' Murray asked.

"Lunch."

"Then what's dinner called?"

"Supper, at least where I'm from. Can we just eat, please?"

At the soda fountain across the street, they took seats at the counter.

"Also," Murray said, "try not to, you know, block someone's punch with your wound. Stuff like that."

"Got it."

Overhead, a tube similar to the one in her building moved transactions from the cash register to an unknown place that returned change and a receipt.

She ordered eggs, toast, and pancakes. Murray ordered the special. "I'll have the sweet potato fries and the cream of kate," he said.

The spider-cat server raised a questioning brow at them from behind the counter. "Cream of kate?"

Murray nodded.

"You mean the cream of kale?" the spider-cat said.

"Ha! Right. Sorry. That's what it looks like on the specials board. A bowl of that, please."

The spider-cat went over to the specials chalkboard and redid the 'l' in 'kale.'

"Cream of kate? Really?" Kelly said while she played with the table jukebox.

"That's what it looked like on the specials board!"

She chose a song by The Specials on the jukebox and a new set of customers entered: giants. Four of them attempting to fit through the front door, which they finally just removed, knocking over the gumball machines at the entrance on their way in.

"I've seen them in Amenity Tower. They can leave?" She asked Murray in a whisper.

"Only the angels are bound there. Anything else is free to leave and eat in the soda fountain or stop by the pharmacy or the museum or get jobs or whatever else they want to do."

The rest of the customers threw down their papers, sloshing their coffee over the rim as they hastily put down their mugs and hurried out the back. Kelly and Murray exchanged glances and hoisted themselves over the counter.

The spider-cat ran out the side door.

The giants ripped out the tables and sat in the booths, their knees tucked up against their chests and touching the opposite giant's knees.

"First, how are they going to eat, sitting like that? Second, who's going to serve them?" Kelly asked in a whisper.

"Pothole City wasn't designed with giants in mind—and I guess *we'll* have to serve them."

"Sure, I've got loads of free time."

The giants, four in all, at adjacent tables, sat patiently, but looked around for the server.

"Yeah, why not," she said. "Giants have to eat, too."

Murray tied a white apron around his waist.

"You first."

Murray nodded and crept over to the tables. "What can I get for you?"

The giants responded with various buzzing sounds at different tones and pitches. Murray scribbled something on the order pad and went back to the counter.

"What did they say?" Kelly asked.

"I have no idea. Let's just give them whatever we can actually make and hope they don't get mad."

They made grilled cheese, egg salad, BLT, and chicken salad sandwiches, reasoning that the giants could swap if they didn't like it. Kelly made iced teas and ice cream sodas. Murray got servings of fries from what the cooks left, and some pickles. They brought everything to the two tables then waited at a safe distance.

The giants leaned forward and moved hands the size of cast iron pans over the food like they were reading auras. The bald one with the orange Swatch chose the egg salad sandwich and slid the sandwich and fries off the plate into his mouth with one gulp.

The giant with the bushy hair and an arm tattoo of a horse riding a skateboard followed suit with the grilled cheese and drinks and ice cream sodas. The giant wearing a t-shirt with something written in Swedish took the BLT, and the fourth giant, the one in pink headphones and a bathrobe, took the grilled cheese.

Then all four of the giants turned in creepy unison to stare at Kelly and Murray, standing ten feet away.

"We're gonna need more sandwiches," Murray said under his breath to her.

She wheeled around to go back into the kitchen. They carried out sandwiches and ice cream sodas piled high on three successive platters. The giants, buzzing with apparent impatience, devoured everything on the table in under a minute.

"I'm not staying here all night."

"Wait," Murray said. "Look."

The giants unfolded themselves from the booth benches. Their buzzing took on a lower, calmer tone.

"Are they leaving or are they coming to kill us?"

"I think they're leaving."

As a tip, they each left a giant coin, which wasn't acceptable as currency anywhere. Except with giants.

Chapter Twenty-Six

I Will Say It as I Spit on Your Grave

Dragomir, Traian, and Bogdan, Amenity Tower's full-time engineers, skulked into the mechanical room, which spanned an entire floor in the penthouse section. An engineering consultant, holding a clipboard like a shield, followed them into a cavernous room with high ceilings, brown walls, and insulated pipes, and where a motor emitted a continuous muffled roar.

Traian took a broom and cleared snow from the mesh filter. Dragomir and Bogdan peered closely at the primary filter bank and heating coil behind the louver.

"The opening clogged from the snow." Dragomir gestured to the louvered vent. "We clear out, but pressure readout too high again."

The consultant stepped over to the stack and waved his hand in a circle around the vent. "The gauge isn't designed for this equipment. It reads like it's too high, but it's fine how it is."

Dragomir turned from the vent to the consultant.

"Oh no," Bogdan said under his breath.

Traian froze in position with the broom and muttered a Moldovan Orthodox protective blessing. Bogdan took a few cautionary steps toward the door, shaking his head at the consultant's foolishness.

"Is fine how is?" Dragomir glowered at the consultant. "Is fine how is? Do you lose job if pressure gets too high and breaks? You have other jobs, soft, squishy American! Our building just one of many for you, like loose woman is to sailor."

The consultant folded his arms, looked down and chewed on his lip as though to gather his patience. "Look, Drago."

Bogdan clapped a hand over his mouth and gaped at Traian, who warily resumed sweeping, head tucked down.

"My name is *Dragomir*." The engineer thumped his chest once. "I will say it as I spit on your grave."

The consultant put up his hands, acquiescing. "Dragomir. Well, I have to say, this is the most unusual situation I've seen in my whole career."

"I vomit on your career."

"Well, notwithstanding your, ah, feelings," the consultant said, "this is a highly unusual situation. You have a lot of turbulence here, and I don't know why. The filters only function when there's a certain velocity flowing over them, and you often have excess velocity."

Dragomir wandered off near the motor.

"The velocity is often excessive," the consultant raised his voice toward Dragomir, "because of the continuous turbulence. Problem is, you're challenged by the original design of the building."

"You are challenged by the original design of your brain," Dragomir said, returning. "The air handlers, filters, building—our responsibility. Residents complain wind too loud in lobby, then manager complains because we turn down gauge, slow the air handler when heavy snow happens. Then, doors not work, elevators not work, and alarm goes off outside door."

Dragomir flicked his arm at the door with the precision of a j'ai-alai player. "There is no way to win; we lose both ways!"

Bogdan tried to steer the consultant back to the door, but the consultant brushed him away and focused again on Dragomir.

"During certain snow events," the consultant said, "the mesh filter gets overwhelmed."

"The mesh is not always clogged with snow events," Bogdan muttered.

"Now, you or I or Bogsnatch here—"

"Er, Bogdan," Bogdan said.

"Bogman, sorry. Any one of us could come up here during these events to brush the snow off the mesh, but maybe there's a better solution," the consultant said.

Dragomir, Bogdan, and Traian huddled briefly to discuss the inter-dimensional monsters coming in through the air handler, and how you couldn't just brush the monsters off the mesh. They argued, in urgent whispered tones, about the likelihood of the handler clogging with the monsters, then the whole thing exploding and taking the building with it. Dragomir turned back to the consultant.

"If we reduce the velocity of the stack during big snow—if we slow the air handler—there is impact to building. "Then there is violent crap storm."

"Unless you also slow the exhaust," the consultant said.

"And aggravate building's odor migration?" Dragomir said.

"Yes, the make-up air side is challenging" The consultant stroked his chin.

Bogdan exhaled. It was near the end of a very long day of dishwasher and hot tub repair. He just wanted to go home to his small apartment and work on his scale circus model, especially the reptile show banners, but now they would all be delayed until Dragomir won.

Dragomir spoke in the tone of a dictator woken up too early. "Do you know what happens if stack clogs?" He took slow steps toward the consultant like a panther cornering an animal before eating it. Soon, he violated the consultant's personal space with prejudice.

Bogdan could see that the consultant was not accustomed to confrontation, nor to Dragomir's high-revving territorial drive.

Behind Dragomir, Traian shook his head at the consultant as though to say 'Stop now and give in.'

"Well, you would probably have to replace the parts—"

Dragomir barked a laugh. "Do you know what happens if stack clogs?"

Again, Traian shook his head for the consultant, this time in a more exaggerated manner, so even a thick-headed fool like the consultant would know to also shake his head no. Bogdan did the same.

The consultant glanced at Traian, then reluctantly met Dragomir's eyes.

"Um... no?"

Dragomir scoffed and dismissed the consultant with a gesture that made Bogdan and Traian gasp, but which meant nothing to the consultant.

"A lot more happens if the handler breaks than just having to replace parts." Traian cleared his throat in a self-conscious way.

"Like what?" the consultant asked.

Bogdan stepped off to the side and conferred with Traian in Romanian as Dragomir stalked back and forth in front of the air handler, cursing.

"If we tell him situation, maybe he would"—Traian paused to think of the colloquialism—"get off Dragomir's back."

"If Dragomir is unhappy, we are more than unhappy," Bogdan said.

"No, better if the consultant does not know," Traian said. "This building is not like others."

"Agreed. Consultant must not find out," Bogdan said. "What if the city also found out? We could be fined, and out of our jobs."

"We put up with the consultant as we brush aside a mosquito at our ear," Traian said. "But it is up to Dragomir."

"Look. Guys." The consultant waved his file folder. "I have another building to get to, so maybe we could wrap this up."

Dragomir lost his last scrap of patience and self-control, which Bogdan thought were stronger than others realized. "Oh, you like to wrap this up? We are up here to do nothing?"

"No! No," Traian said to Dragomir, eyes wide.

"We are done. Is not your job on the line, and is more than our jobs on the line. Okay? You go now," Dragomir said with contempt.

The consultant put his palms up to Dragomir. "Fine, fine. I've done my part."

"You do nothing," Dragomir said. "Your part is as a pebble in my shoe. An owl pellet I kick in the barn."

The consultant rolled his eyes and muttered "Whatever, buddy." He opened the door back into the building. Dragomir, Traian, and Bogdan remained in the mechanical room.

"The foolish man is right. The gauge is not, ahm, designed for equipment," Bogdan said.

Dragomir rested a hand on the vent. "Is OK for now."

Chapter Twenty-Seven

Binding a Fellow Ruler of Destruction to an Arcade Game Just Wasn't Good Sportsmanship

After the bootcamp in the patio, Af showered and made a marshmallow and mozzarella panini. Though his day-to-day tasks seemed mundane, being bound to Amenity Tower was actually a huge improvement, compared to his previous situation.

Just before he arrived at Amenity Tower, Af had 1,003 years left on his sentence. The King of the Demonic Locusts—occasionally known as the Angel of the Bottomless Pit, the Destroying Angel of the Apocalypse, the Angel of the Abyss, the Destroyer, or Don, depending on his mood or whom he wanted to impress—wanted to put Af out of commission, and kept finding ways to bind him for long periods of time.

They had never gotten along. Af considered Don both indolent and competitive, a dangerous combination, and knew Don thought of him as a threat to his position. But Don screwed up when he bound him to a Ms. Pac-Man game at a run-down AMC movie theater in Erie, Pennsylvania.

The game was unwinnable, or so Don assumed. But then some metalhead kid in the AMC beat the high score, reached the kill screen, and inadvertently released Af from his prison.

Hubris. Gets you every time.

As a direct result of what everyone in the know called "The Shirley Temple Incident" or "The Don Knotts Incident"—in reference to the other famous bow-wearers aside from Ms. Pac-Man—Af was free under a loophole in his contract.

Binding a fellow ruler of destruction to an arcade game just wasn't good sportsmanship. It told Af that Don couldn't compete on a level playing field. Don lacked the discipline and intelligence of his more savvy peers, and compensated by lying and cheating his way up the totem pole.

Af had spent his whole existence being wrathful and destructive. It was his job, his purpose. He operated with a wide swath of autonomy, but the bureaucracy wore on him and he found it difficult to work alongside the same people over such a long period. Even though they were angels, his colleagues' negative attributes became more pronounced over time.

Within a vast structure of variably-ranked angels, at least a few were keenly interested in Af's position. As for how well another angel could do his job, he didn't much care anymore if they did, or if they handled it poorly or superbly.

It pleased him that he wasn't constrained to an identity that was many millions of years old or limited by anyone's perception of him—with the exception of Raum, who wouldn't shut up about it. It wasn't Af's concern. He just wanted a quiet life of cooking, exercising, reading, and his favorite activity: photographing products he liked and posting reviews of them online. Maybe he would start writing longer essays about some of the products he reviewed.

His former more volatile self would have invaded nearby buildings, the city as a whole, and other towns and cities, all before lunch, if directed to.

He laughed, thinking of his old friend Temeluch, his colleague to whom souls were delivered at the death of the body. Temeluch resented the huge workload he faced after Af went on a tear.

"Well, they're going to have to wait," Temeluch would say, referring to the souls awaiting transfer. "I have a daughter to raise, paperwork to do, dinner to make. I have three dozen cupcakes to make for those terrorizing, cupcake-extorting demons at the PTA."

But Af was different now, to his own amazement. Not only did he refrain from laying waste on a wide scale, he sat and discussed agenda items like the lobby tree, the scavenger contract, and whether or not a resident could use the regular elevators with his or her pet death worm.

Af thought about his conversation with Kelly in the elevator and wondered why he didn't tell her about Temeluch. Perhaps he assumed it would sour her opinion of him.

As he set up a paper carton of tomato sauce to be photographed, it occurred to him that he might have to fight to stay in Amenity Tower.

Chapter Twenty-Eight

Or Should I Call You Bogdan?

Kelly swaggered in to Amenity Tower wearing a brown wig, mustache, and a black baseball cap embroidered with "FDA" in red letters. Her dental tray featured large front teeth.

"FDA Criminal Investigations." She showed her badge to Clementine, who apparently worked most shifts. "We have a report of an unlicensed banana farm in unit 4202. I need to get up there right now."

Clementine was breezy and friendly, but Kelly had seen her rip into people for violating process before.

"I didn't know the FDA had a criminal division." Clementine raised one brow dramatically.

"Yes ma'am, they do," Kelly said briskly. Clem didn't have to know that they investigated mostly corporate executives.

"Well, I guess I don't call up to that unit, considering. Let me ring the manager." Clem picked up the phone.

She smiled. Roger was probably busy interviewing a pigeon breeder or a bioprocess engineer. He wasn't going to blink an eye at an FDA investigator.

Clem mumbled into the receiver and hung up. "Okay. You can go on in."

She followed a resident who looked like they were made entirely of rubber, then got into the next open high-rise cab with a short toad resident and his leashed death worm. Tom the giant water scorpion wasn't there, so she pressed the button for forty-two. Af's floor. As they rose, the toad hummed a Roger Balbi song and she could swear the worm was looking at her funny. She shifted a sideways glance to it.

She walked to the end of the hall, smelling toast and eggs from much earlier that morning, along with fabric softener, a new piece of luggage, orange juice, and at least a few things she didn't recognize at all. Also, someone had printed out a stack of paper.

Kelly placed her head up to a doorjamb five units down from Af's apartment.

Af found her on his way to go for a swim. "It's good to see you again, Kelly. Or should I call you Bogdan?"

She smiled at him and felt stupid (it wasn't even her smile—the dental tray made her lisp a little). They looked at each other awkwardly. Af was dressed for the pool in board shorts, an old Howard Jones t-shirt, flip-flops, and goggles perched on the top of his head.

"Well, I was going to go down for a swim, but I'd rather have you over for coffee so you can tell me why you're wearing that horrible thing," Af said.

"Can't." She pressed her lips together with some effort over her dental tray. "Working."

"I can tell by your teeth."

"The teeth draw attention," she said. "Obviously."

"Well, come down to the pool when you're done." Af flashed her an irresistible grin and went over to the elevator, carrying his large towel. "I look forward to seeing you as you one day."

Kelly didn't know if there was much left.

She skulked back down the hall and checked out another unit. Whiffs of something strange blew gently out of the door frame. After sniffing around a few more doors, she couldn't take it anymore.

She found Af on the edge of a lounge chair at one end of the pool, looking like someone stole his balloon and let it go. The pool was full of lap-swimming angels, all bumping into one another.

Af waved, a half-hearted gesture, and she walked down the length of the pool toward him. "I was really looking forward to a swim," he said when she got close enough. "This is the time when I swim. My whole schedule is off now."

She sat next to him. "Why are there so many in the pool?"

Af shook his head. "I created my schedule based on the least populated times in each place, but then everyone in the building started to train for something. Don't know what. Don't care. I just want to swim."

She stood back up and checked her pockets, starting with the back, pulled out an empty vial from her front right pocket, and sucked in everyone in the pool.

"Wow," Af said. "You can fit all of them into one vial?"

"Not really," Kelly said. "If I'm feeling generous later, I'll transfer some to another vial."

"Where do they go, and should I be worried?"

"They're repatriated, as far as I know. Why, did I vial one of your friends?"

"No... but should *I* be worried?" Af asked again.

"Nah."

Af smiled, basically making her day all over again. "Thank you." He descended into the water and adjusted his goggles.

She loved that he had the whole pool to himself.

Kelly went back to Af's floor. The first apartment she checked was redolent of toast and piperine, and the resident was watching what sounded like a repeat of *What's On Your Mind, With Roger Balbi,* one with Roger talking to a ninja with unceasing hiccups.

She shrugged and made a notation in her notebook. The fourth apartment smelled like horseradish, spikenard oil, and peaches. The sign on the door read "134th Anniversary Annual Meeting and Dinner."

"Anniversary of *what*?" she said.

At the doorjamb of the fourth apartment, Kelly detected eucalyptus shampoo and formic acid (probably a death worm bath), as well as voices from a radio show.

At the fifth, she smelled ambergris tincture and new furniture.

Kelly tucked her notebook in her pocket and rested against the wall by the window, feeling her mother's absence from the world, which made her want to vial every single angel she saw. None of them had any answers.

Her hand tightened around one of the vials. Maybe she should sweep this whole building right now and be done with it. They could sort the HVT out later. Or is that what Don hoped she would do?

The elevator stopped on the floor and the doors opened. She pocketed the vial and nodded politely to a locust with a fidgety young worm on a leash. Tapping the vial in her pocket with a fingernail, she paused, then took the elevator back to the first floor. The worm shrieked the whole way.

Chapter Twenty-Nine

The Geranium of the Bottomless Pit

Kelly stopped at her building to check on the SPs and swap some gear. Murray was there waiting for her, dressed ominously well. She dropped her bag on the floor. "Is it time for the spring ball already?"

His charcoal gray wool suit and four-in-hand tie knot made her nervous. He had shaved, perhaps seconds ago, and his hair had been cut by someone licensed.

She took a guess about his formal attire. "Am I meeting Don? Can I call him Don?"

"Today's the day."

"I'll get dressed." She emerged five minutes later in a midnight blue dress, black flats, and a gold locket.

"It's my 'Lady in a Bag' kit," she said.

"As opposed to the 'Bag Lady' kit?" he asked.

"I use the Bag Lady Kit a lot more."

They took a cab to the train station and got on a biomorphic tube that contracted to a stop and gave them an opening. Murray gestured her in.

The inside looked like a 1930s lounge car, silver and scrupulously clean, outfitted with cherry-wood paneling, leather seating, and two dining tables. A fresco painting of a forest scene covered the ceiling. On every table, a set of playing cards in leather cases sat next to backgammon boards with solid wood pieces.

"Can I live here?" she asked Murray.

"Your place not big enough?"

Kelly and Murray didn't have the car to themselves: a man with a red plaid shirt, a chew tin imprint in his front pocket, and tin belt buckle gave them a slow nod. Otherwise, the man looked out the window until he got out at the next stop.

Murray mixed a drink at the bar using liquid in crystal decanters.

"How did you end up with this lousy handler gig?"

Murray stared at his drink for a few seconds before glancing sideways at her. "Tribal sorcerer curse."

"Typical."

"I've worked for Don a long time. Too long." Waving off the conversation, he went back to the bar to refill his drink.

She leaned back in her sleek, curvy chair and crossed one leg over the other and stared at the painting. In the distance was a small wood-frame cabin. "Holy crap," she said, her voice higher from her stretched neck.

"What? What is it? Did you forget your third backup switchblade?"

She pointed up. Murray came around from behind the bar and stood next to her.

"What?"

"That's my cabin."

"Huh?" He looked up.

She stood on the chair for a closer look. "Why is that painting there?" she asked in a demanding tone, like he'd been keeping something from her.

"You built a cabin?" Murray asked.

"Answer me."

"When was this?"

"I started it when I was eleven and finished it when I was twelve."

"Not by yourself."

"Yes. By myself. I didn't have a place to live. It took a really long time."

"This type of train can show its passengers scenes from their past. It's probably trying to make a point, but no one can ever tell what they're supposed to take from it."

The train came to a stop so smoothly they wouldn't even have noticed but for the appearance of a tall man with red hair and a vest uniform who announced their arrival at the last stop.

"Who's that?" she asked.

"I've heard him called the majordomo, the avatar, the persona. I don't think he has a name, otherwise."

They entered an arched vestibule and continued on to a short hallway. A hen with a coin insert stood on the left side of the vestibule. Kelly put in a penny and held out her hand under the metal chute.

"What did you get?" Murray asked.

She rolled the object in her palm and picked up the round object, a small tin egg. Unscrewing it revealed a bonbon, which she popped in her mouth.

"Praline," she said. "Want one?"

"If you have another penny. But I want to get my fortune told," he said. An automata fortune-teller on the right side of the vestibule stamped Murray's name and fortune on a tin band.

He held it up to show her.

"Your car is waiting," she read out loud.

"Look," Murray said, pointing.

A man with gigantic aquamarine wings sat in a military-style jeep playing a hand-held video game.

"Are you Kelly and Murray?" he called to them.

"Yes," Murray said.

"Get in," he said, without looking up.

Kelly exchanged a look with Murray, and they got in the jeep.

They drove over sand until they reached a modest-sized bungalow with a potted red geranium on the front porch.

"The Geranium of the Bottomless Pit," she muttered.

Chapter Thirty

The Pizza Situation Can't Get Much Worse

That night, Af attended the Pizza Delivery Sub-Committee Meeting, which was assembled to solve the problem, once and for all, of finding a pizza delivery vendor for Amenity Tower. Four other residents attended: Vassago, Crocell, Imamiah, and Roeled, a fallen angel who caused stomach trouble.

"The last nine or so delivery people never actually made it out of the building," Roeled said. "They keep getting eaten. No one will deliver here anymore, and the residents are up in arms about it. The suggestion box—it's like ballot stuffing, with all the vitriolic comments. Amenity Tower needs pizza delivery and that's all there is to it."

"Why is it so important to have pizza delivered?" Gaap asked.

"This is Amenity Tower!" Roeled said. "We lack an important amenity!"

"We should have as many amenities as possible," Vassago said. "Hello, we're physically bound here!"

"Is pizza delivery considered an amenity?" Crocell asked.

"Only if the building provides delivery as a service," Af said without looking up from his notebook.

"How can we turn it into an amenity?" Crocell asked.

Af chimed in. "I've been making my own pizza. I get the supplies delivered to me and make it myself. I think it's better. You can also get frozen pizza delivered."

"I'm happy for you," Roeled said, "but most residents want it brought to their door, hot and fresh."

"And so did I." Af raised his pen. "But I realized that in the time it takes to have a pizza delivered to your door, you could have made a pizza for less money."

"Well, what do you want from me, Af?" Roeled said. "You want to do in-depth psychological testing disguised as a resident survey to determine why people like pizza delivery?"

Af tilted his head. "Maybe."

"We're not going to do that," Vassago stated. "Does anyone have any ideas of how to turn pizza delivery into an amenity?"

No one said anything. Crocell started to talk, then changed his mind.

"Anyone?" Roeled said.

Af sighed. "They're afraid to say something you may not like."

"What? Why?"

"They think you'll cause them stomach trouble, obviously," Af said.

"But it's a relatively small thing, stomach trouble. Why not let me have a little fun?" Roeled said with a smile. "It's not like I'm, oh, I don't know, an angel of destruction. For example."

"It's actually worse," Af said, "because though most people have only an abstract realization of their own mortality, and don't have any personal experience of wide-scale destruction, they know only too well what a little stomach trouble is like. It's very real to them, and they're justifiably wary of it. One of the many little drawbacks of the mortal form."

The other residents nodded.

"Fine," Roeled raised a hand. "I promise not to cause anyone stomach trouble during the sub-committee meeting. How about that. Everyone happy? Can we move on now?"

Crocell cleared his throat. "If any of us could leave, we could use one of us to make the deliveries. Like Gaap."

"Those bat wings of his would come in handy for delivery," Vassago said. "But even if he weren't bound to Amenity Tower, like all of us, he's too busy. I think he's training for some kind of triathlon."

Af snapped to attention. "Did Gaap tell you he's training for something?"

"I just inferred he was," Crocell said. "He's always running or jumping rope or boxing. But no, I haven't talked to him. I haven't even seen him in the elevator. Why?"

Af shook his head to dismiss the topic. "Just curious."

Roeled put his palms up. "C'mon, people. I'm not going to keep you up worshipping the porcelain god, remember?" He held up a copy of *Pizza Today* magazine. "I've been looking through this for vendors, but every one I call just hangs up on me."

Af raised a finger. "I did see a flyer for a cockatrice promoting his delivery services."

Roeled laced his fingers. "A cockatrice."

"Yes," Af said. "There was a poor-quality image of him on the flyer, but it was definitely a chicken-headed serpent. I presume he can fly."

A murmur swelled among the sub-committee.

"I have some experience with the cockatrice," Roeled said. "Pros: the cockatrice can fly, and won't get robbed. Cons: it is impervious to charm, it's a biter, and it lays poisonous eggs."

Imamiah put his hand up. "I'm concerned that if he's not tipped well enough—and who knows what that arbitrary amount would be—the cockatrice would retaliate. Its breath and even its look can be fatal, so woe to the ungenerous or displeased resident."

"The pizza situation can't get much worse," Crocell said. "No one will deliver here."

Af sighed. He hated to get involved. "Why don't we ask Roger to work up a contract with the cockatrice to provide pizza delivery and catering. The cockatrice would handle the whole process. Maybe Roger could arrange a weekly pizza night." He looked back to his notebook and tapped his Amenity Tower floaty pen on the paper. He glanced back up at the silence.

"That's a great idea, Af," Imamiah said.

"The cockatrice would deliver *and* cater?" Roeled asked.

Af tapped his pen in a rhythm against the paper. "Hypothetically, the cockatrice would provide a mix-and-match service, where he delivers other stuff, too."

"Like babies? And guitars?" Roeled asked.

"Maybe," Af said carefully. "And he could provide credit accounts through the building."

"Are there any security risks?" Crocell asked.

"Well, the bite of the cockatrice is no small matter," Roeled said. "But we can just warn the residents, through flyer postings in the mail area and bulletin board, and with the digital sign in the elevator, to avoid eye contact with the cockatrice when it delivers their pizza."

"I think it's worth the risk," Vassago said. "If the cockatrice is our only viable option for pizza delivery, I say we seriously consider it."

"Great!" Roeled said. "Af, set it up with Roger. Let's adjourn this dog and pony show."

Af stayed to get some writing done, but wondered what Kelly was doing.

Chapter Thirty-One

Angel of the Apocalypse, 1625-1989

Kelly and Murray sat in front of Don's desk. Four rotary phones, three black and one red, lined up on the side by a gold statuette encased in a block of lucite. She picked up the statuette.

"Angel of the Apocalypse, 1625-1989," she read.

"365 years is an Angel-Year," Murray said, "so it's not as impressive as it seems."

Minutes passed as they waited. "I guess he's late," Murray whispered, head tilted towards hers.

She sat straight, tense. "So where is he?"

"His other office, downtown. He takes his own train; he's never actually outside. He'll be tellied in for the meeting."

"He'll be what?"

A telepresence robot rolled out from the back room. Its video screen showed an image of an omelette and hash browns.

"What the—?" Kelly turned to Murray and whispered, "Is this normal for him?"

"Your directive, Ms. Driscoll," Don said to her through the speakers on the robot, "was to find the most dangerous angel in existence, who could be any one of the residents living in a 500-unit condo building, and to vial any troublesome supernatural beings you saw along the way. I generously gave you two whole days to accomplish this simple task."

Don's robot rolled behind the desk in a rocking motion. The screen changed to an egg sandwich.

She twitched.

"But I have been so overwhelmed by this inundation of requisition and reimbursement forms that I had to get an intern to process them."

The screen changed to show a baby penguin with a clip-on badge that read 'intern'. The penguin waved a flipper at them. The screen changed to a birthday cake and she drummed her fingers and winced. How did the Angel of the Apocalypse know her weakness for breakfast foods, birthday cake, and baby penguins?

"If these tiny angel mechanics, angel traffic controllers, whatever you call them—" Don started.

"Single-purpose angels," she said. "They only keep the whole universe running."

The image on the robot screen flashed to a biscuit with gravy and a side of egg yolks. Kelly recoiled, and the image flashed to a bowl of oatmeal with fruit, as though to placate her and show a breakfast she liked better. But what was Don's game with this, to distract her?

"If the angel janitors aren't making trouble, fine. But must I pay to house them? I mean, really, look at this." The robot's screen showed a stack of expense reports. "Sleeping bags, pillows, bulk grocery, office supplies."

"They're in danger," she said. "One of them was killed. And Murray gave me a credit card."

The penguin popped onto the screen and changed into some kind of fractal screen saver.

"Word got around that Kelly could protect them," Murray said.

"And the beer? You think you can construe that as a legitimate business expense? Are you trying to get me audited?"

"One of the angels needs it for his roof garden," she said.

"She's right," Murray said. "It keeps the slugs away."

"Are slugs a problem in winter?" Don asked. "How does this angel have a rooftop garden in the Pothole City winter, anyway?"

Don's robot rolled across the room and stopped by the window.

"The angel in question has dominion over fruit-bearing trees, so I suppose he can grow them in any climate."

Don remained silent for a moment. "OK."

"OK?" Murray asked.

"I'll approve these," Don said in a cautionary tone through the robot's speaker as it rolled around in a half circle and back to the desk. The screen showed a waffle with a side of crispy bacon. One of her favorites. She looked away.

"It's not the money. I've got more than this in my rounding errors account. Just don't go crazy."

"We'll cancel the order of Jet-Skis and hot air balloons," she said. "Sir."

"Sarcasm does not become anyone, Ms Driscoll," Don said through the image of a plate of Huevos Rancheros.

"Noted."

"You're dismissed." Don rolled out of the room.

On the way out, she asked, "Why do we have to come all this way to talk to Don's telepresence robot?"

"He likes in-person meetings," Murray said.

Chapter Thirty-Two

What's On Your Mind, With Roger Balbi

Kelly gained access to Amenity Tower by claiming to be a member of PCPD's Fugitive Apprehension Task Force. This time, she wore green contacts and a crooked teeth dental tray.

Roger cornered her near the elevators.

"Are you SWAT?" Roger swiped at the light sheen of sweat on his forehead and pulled at his tie knot. "I want to interview you for my show, *What's On Your Mind, With Roger Balbi.*"

"I'm not SWAT." She flashed her badge. "Harmony Mongol, Fugitive Apprehension Task Force."

It felt like her eightieth disguise, and time was running out. Jay Vanner knew this situation well. "Kelly, it's not a single moment. It's a collection of moments, a season. If you're developing your skills and learning from your missteps, winning will naturally follow."

She was probably developing her skills, but didn't even know what her missteps were, and as she was finding out, the job involved more than just vialing supernatural creatures while searching for her HVT—especially considering how the SPs came to her for protection. What would winning even look like? She didn't think she would recognize it anymore.

A resident accompanied by a jaunty, happy-go-lucky death

wormpassed by Roger, who shifted his shoulders as though wearing a shirt lined with horsehair.

"Great, great," Roger said. "Well, if you haven't apprehended anyone yet, I just want five minutes of your time. I'm sure the fugitive can wait."

The fugitive isn't going anywhere, she thought.

"We're just finishing up one thing," Roger said. "Sometimes I bring employees in for an interstitial between segments."

Kelly entered the studio behind Roger. A surly Dragomir, as happy as a wet cat and swigging from a bottle of Tuica, hunched over a microphone in front of the large camera, and performed a joyless, spoken-word rendition of "Neutron Dance" by the Pointer Sisters.

Dragomir finished the song with a final, deadpan "whoo-hoo." He tossed the microphone on a chair and stalked out of the studio, muttering curses as he walked past her. He pushed up wire-frame glasses with a machine oil-greased finger and fired off a few select insults at Roger before he left.

Roger seemed used to it. He cleared his throat and picked up the microphone with a big smile.

"And we're back. I hope you enjoyed our chief engineer's interpretation of a song I know none of us can resist dancing to."

Kelly took the seat next to Roger.

"Building engineers are under a lot of pressure," Roger said to her. "Anyway, I'm very pleased to have with us today a warrior for the public in Pothole City's own Fugitive Apprehension Unit. Welcome to the show. Can you tell our audience what that job entails?"

She tried to look capable and sound appropriately brisk. "We coordinate and streamline the efforts to address the continuous flow of warrants received by Pothole City's sheriff's office. We maintain active files for wanted subjects and we work closely with other law enforcement agencies."

"Very good," Roger said. "And how would you define a 'fugitive?'"

"A fugitive is any wanted person whose whereabouts are unknown."

"After I was ten years old, I would have considered my father a fugitive," Roger said. "And probably officer Mongol here would, too.

Am I right?" He looked at Kelly like he knew all about her, and that kind of thing was annoying.

"I didn't grow up with you, Roger, so it's hard to say if I would consider your father a fugitive." She flashed a broad smile at the camera.

Roger put on a show of pondering, then tried again.

"I get the feeling that you never really knew your father. But who did, am I right?"

"You're right, I never knew my father." Her expression clearly communicated a threat, to be delivered at some later time.

Roger quickly switched to "What sort of training do members of your unit receive?"

"We receive instruction in fugitive investigations at training facilities," she said.

"Now, this would be after your mother, a masterful thief, taught you how to track in the forest."

Kelly sprang out of her chair. "What—"

"Think about it: what better training could there be?" Roger asked, now perfectly calm and composed, his facade of neurotic anxiety gone. "Of course, now you're in an urban environment," he said. "That must be quite different from what you're used to, all concrete and skyscrapers, which could put you at a disadvantage. Come on, sit down."

Her pulse quickened. How could he possibly know this about her? Roger always seemed so scattered and distracted—did this mean he was also aware of every time she was in the building?

"Getting back to the matter at hand." He smiled, addressing the audience. "Forgive me for getting a little personal. What would you say is your biggest challenge at the Fugitive Apprehension Unit?"

It took her a few seconds to get back in the groove of the interview and try not to think about what just happened. "I'd say that our biggest challenge is personnel and resources." Not to mention a floor full of angels who have the appetite of bears and refuse to eat anything except Cluck Snack products. Not to mention the thing trying to kill them.

"That's funny, isn't it?" Roger said.

"What do you mean?"

"Well, considering you don't have either one."

She just looked at him. What the hell was he talking about?

"What I'm talking about, officer, is your almost total lack of personnel or resources. On the one hand, who is more resourceful than you? But on the other hand, no man is an island. You're being asked to accomplish so much on your own. On top of that, you're being pulled in divergent, often contradictory directions, aren't you?"

She pinned Roger back with an intense, unwavering stare.

"I'm putting you on the spot," Roger said, backing off with palms held out. "Let's table that. Tell me, how do you go about catching a fugitive?"

Whatever Roger's game was, she could play it.

"Good, old-fashioned leg work, Roger." She leaned forward and put her hands together. "We use the information we collect from surveillance and intelligence gathering to pinpoint a fugitive's location."

"And what happens then?" Roger asked.

"We turn the fugitive over to the appropriate agency," she said. In a transparent vial, like they're a urine sample at a doctor's office, she thought.

"The appropriate agency," he repeated.

"That's right." She leaned back in her chair and crossed her legs.

"What does this agency—whichever agency it may be—do with the fugitive?"

"Your guess is as good as mine." But considering the supernatural beings were converted to a gaseous substance in a vial, maybe they were used as a new kind of fuel.

"You don't know?"

"It's beyond my purview." That's what Af had said to her.

"You're not interested in what happens to them?" Roger asked. She wanted to punch him in the face.

"That's beside the point," she said, in a warning tone.

He glanced at the camera again. "Don't you have any concern for what it's like for the fugitive after that point?"

She dropped the glibness and pictured Tubiel. And Af. "Yes."

"Maybe they're a fugitive for a good reason," Roger said. "If they're returned to wherever they come from, and don't receive the support they need, maybe they'll leave again, and by the time they show up in your radar, they're damaged." He looked at her with a squint, like he was trying to determine if she understood him.

"Damaged."

"Yeah."

"Maybe they're damaged in the first place," she said.

Af rewound the building manager's show on his DVR. He missed the first ten minutes owing to the excitement of unboxing his new professional-grade soft-serve machine, which he bought to replace the puny consumer model that leaked all the time.

Taking to the sofa with his peanut butter ice cream, he almost did a spit-take when he saw that Roger was interviewing Kelly. And why was Roger glancing so surreptitiously at the camera?

Af abandoned his food on the tray table and ran out the door.

"So perhaps, officer Mongol, you are all too willing to compromise what scraps of ethics you have left in order to achieve your goals," Roger said.

Kelly saw something in her peripheral vision and looked out the studio window. Af gestured frantically at her to leave. She gave the smallest of shrugs. He rolled his eyes and paced the reception area, hands on his head. Finally, he just opened the door to the studio.

Roger pointed to the *Filming* sign on the other side of the door then flicked his hand at Af, mouthing, "Go away."

"Please forgive the intrusion," Af said. "But I think there's a fugitive in my kitchen making soft-serve ice cream."

She sprang out of the chair. "My fugitive loves soft-serve."

"Yes, he's really making himself at home in there. So if you would come with me, I would be most grateful."

With a curt nod to Roger, she left the studio with Af, who, when they reached the safety of the elevator, exhaled like he'd been holding his breath for minutes.

"That was close. I might've had to sing 'Let's Be Neighborly.'"

Chapter Thirty-Three

Grace Zabriskie Sings the Ferret Hits

Kelly climbed in through the fire escape window at the back of her building, and dropped her bag on the floor. "Hello?"

She walked toward the conference room on the south end, looking into offices on the side. None of the SPs were there.

"Murray? Tube?"

She stopped at the window in the conference room and looked down at the street, noticing the bright soda fountain sign and a Cluck Snack mobile food truck on the street.

She called Murray, but it went to voice mail.

"This is Murray. If you're a warrior of the trader pits and need help or protection, please leave your name and address and a brief description of your problem. If this is an operative, I cannot immediately requisition whatever piece of equipment you are invariably demanding to have right this minute, so just tell me what it is and I'll get back to you."

Beep.

"It's Kelly. The SPs aren't here. Call me."

She snapped the phone shut and looked down the main hall through the door. She considered the possibilities. (a), Murray didn't want to leave them here alone so he took them on one of his jobs. (b), Every SP was out on their own job. (c), They got bored and left en masse to get food or wander the streets. (d), They were in the proverbial ditch. (e), They had the power of invisibility.

She settled on the option that Murray didn't think the SPs were safe in the apartment, scribbled a note and left it on her bedroom door, then wrote the same note and sent it through the pneumatic tube.

That done, she slung her bag over her shoulder cross-wise and put together a large bowl of cereal, using an old shaving mug and her titanium spork. Holding the mug, she went down the fire escape and grabbed her bike.

Tailed by taxicabs, cars, and buses, she kept up her speed as she rode hands-free down the busiest street in Pothole City, eating cereal from her mug using the spork. She drank the sweetened milk at the bottom after she sped through the yellow light adjacent to a Cluck Snack delivery truck.

After turning left, she headed south a few blocks and came to a halt in front of Murray's apartment—a former toy company building, judging by the faded stenciling. Wood slats covered the door and first-floor windows. Weeds stuck out of the cement around the front entrance in their intent to claim the entire structure.

She knocked hard three times, waited, then three more times, and called him again. "Murray, get your hedge-fund trader-protecting ass over to your phone now and tell me where my damn SPs are, because I rode my bike all the way to your place."

It took several minutes to jimmy the door, but she got through. Though the off-putting exterior promised only the rejected flotsam of a long-departed toy business, the interior was a loft with red brick walls, concrete floors, and a modern kitchen.

"Nice." She turned in a circle. Kitchen on her right and TV area on her left, with flat-screen display, a worn sofa the color of an old man's hat, and cabinets full of record albums.

Something rubbed against her ankle. A long-haired black and white cat sinuously threaded itself through her legs.

"Where's your food, Yvonne?" Kelly asked, naming the cat after

Yvonne De Carlo. She went back to the kitchen and opened cupboards until she found some cat food. She peeled back the lid on the can and emptied it into one of the cat's bowls. The other bowl she filled with fresh water.

She opened the freezer door and took the lid off a pint of lemon sorbet. Murray had carved the top of the sorbet so flat it looked like a tiny Zamboni had gone over it. When she put it back, she noticed an opaque plastic container with a label on the front.

"'Prairie Dog Heads.' Gross."

The refrigerator's double doors opened out like the suicide doors on an old car. Inside were towers of plastic containers with leftovers and two-pound plastic tubs of Cluck Snack P'nut Butt'r Chunks ("For Ferrets, Not Dogs").

"I thought he was kidding about the ferret." She took the P'nut Butt'r Chunks and switched their location with the similarly-packaged yogurt.

In the cupboard, she found dry milk, olive oil, sardines, and stacks of canned beans and boxed grains, all neatly lined and stacked. She took out two boxes of hot cereal and held one in each hand. "Bear Mush. Germade. Huh."

On the middle shelf, she found a row of Cluck Snack brand vitamin supplements, and selected a bottle from the middle. "Contains thirty billion active bacteria."

Kelly headed to the opposite side of the loft and picked up two books from the coffee table: *Managing the Strong-Willed Operative* and *The Stick or the Carrot: 115 Strategies for Motivating the Stuck Operative.* She put the books down in the most messy arrangement possible, turned her attention to the record albums at one end of the storage unit, and perused the selection.

Shaking her head, she moved to the next cabinet and looked through the albums there. In stunned disbelief, she rapidly flicked through the albums in the remaining three cabinets. There were hundreds of copies of the same album.

"*Grace Zabriskie Sings the Ferret Hits.*" On the cover was a sly, impish

Grace Zabriskie, accompanied by three ferret friends. She opened the hinged top of the record player, slipped the record over the silver knob, and positioned the needle.

The moment the sound came out of the speakers, a white ferret scrambled out from under the sofa and faced Kelly. The ferret, outfitted in a purple walking vest, hopped from side to side, back arched, tiny jaws wide open.

It turned its head and varied its movement with short backwards hops as it made a hissing sound. When the song ended, the ferret pounced on her shoe.

"Hey!" She shook it off. The ferret ran into a far corner of the room and burrowed into a tiny tent, and then rolled something back to her that looked like the droppings of a small woodland creature.

"No thanks," she said, but the ferret was insistent, pushing whatever it had up against her shoe over and over. It finally resorted to holding the object in its mouth and digging into her jeans with its claws.

"All right, keep your vest on." She reached down and put out her hand. The ferret placed a hard, engraved pellet the size of a large marble on her palm. She held the pellet under a lamp so she could make out the lettering. "Custom Ferret Food," she read, rolling the pellet around in her palm.

The ferret made a strange sound, probably in impatience, but he could wait. She chewed on her lip. After a moment, she reached into an inside jacket pocket and took out another pellet identical to the one the ferret had just given her.

"What do you know." She rolled a pellet in each palm. "Wait, didn't I see a container of this stuff?" In the kitchen, she opened a cabinet and took out a metal canister. Something rattled inside. She held it over her hand and let another pellet fall into her palm, then read the front and back of the canister.

"This Ferret Food is prepared especially for Murray by The Ferret Purveyors, and is known as Whole Small Prey Multigrain Blend. 1984. Ingredients include fresh meat protein, organs, bones, skin, feathers, fur, dried porcine blood meal, barley, oats, papaya, spices."

She held a pellet in each hand. In her right, the pellet she had carried for years, a hard, round ball the color of liver left behind by whoever sent her mother, five others, and their cabin up in a tower of fire.

Hearing a sound at the front door, she stood and shoved the food pellets in her pocket. With careful steps, she crept to the door and put her nose up to the doorjamb. She remembered the scent: cedar and furfural. The person on the other side of the door was the man she had been following ever since the day she found the pellet.

One solid knock. "Murray!" A man's voice, clipped and irritated. "Murray, open up." He started to pick the locks.

She pulled her larger knife out of its sheath and held it with a loose grip. She backed away out of sight but kept him in sight.

A few minutes later, the man jimmied open the locks, swaggered into the apartment and went right for the kitchen, searching through cabinets and the fridge, inadvertently mirroring her movements. With a frustrated sigh, he ran a hand over his bald head and then wandered over to the sofa.

Moving closer, she watched him pick up a copy of *Modern Handler Magazine*, flipping through the pages until he tossed it back on the table.

With a yawn, he leaned back, switched on the TV, and watched a few minutes of a recorded episode of *What's On Your Mind, with Roger Balbi*—then deleted everything Murray had stored on his DVR.

Cold, but something a friend would do, too. What if they were friends, he and Murray? Maybe Murray recruited her on the bald man's orders and she had been working under the bald man's control this whole time?

Having wreaked havoc on the DVR, the bald man wandered over to Murray's clothes rack and messed up the precisely-spaced hangers, spacing some far apart and some too close together. She poised to strike, but the bald man rushed out the door, pulling it shut behind him.

She took the new pellet and rolled it between her fingertips.

Chapter Thirty-Four

I've Got a Death Worm to Feed

"I found a loophole."

Raum burst into the conference room, where the five bound angels on the End of Days Sub-Committee were eating food from the automat. They stopped mid-chew.

"A loophole for what?" Crocell asked, a noodle sticking out of his mouth. "Also, you're twelve minutes late."

"A loophole for *what*?" Raum bellowed, incredulous. "Only the most important thing to all of us." He touched two fingers to his chin and looked up. "Gosh, what could it be possibly be?"

"Oh, you found a loophole for that short-term occupancy thing?" Gaap asked, his bat wings folded around him like a shawl sweater. "It's about time. There have been no fewer than four short-term monster occupants in the unit next door during the past month, including a Gorgon, can you believe it? I can't keep living like this. And why is it so cold in here?"

"I'm not talking about short-term guests," Raum said. "I'm talking about the loophole I found for escaping this prison."

Gaap put his palms up and reared his head back. "Whoa there, Raum. Slow down."

Raum sat on the edge of the table and took a carton and a pair of chopsticks. "Did I short out your single synapse path, Gaap?"

"Where did you find this loophole?" Crocell asked.

Raum rolled his eyes. "*The Journal of the Contemporary Bound Angel, Western Canada Edition.*"

"Wait, you're talking about getting out of this building?" Forcas said.

"Yes," Raum said. "Is there a gas leak in here? Why are you all so obtuse tonight? Maybe I should draw you a picture?" He lunged over to the whiteboard and grabbed the black marker. The marker squeaking, he sketched a building with windows, then an arrow and the words 'Amenity Tower Prison.'

He swept a pointed look across the room to make sure everyone was paying attention before sketching stick figures with wings outside of the building.

There was no reaction.

Raum tossed the marker on the conference table. "The wheel is spinning but the hamster is dead. I want you all to listen to me very closely. We no longer have to be bound to Amenity Tower." He clearly enunciated each word.

"Where would we go?" Gaap asked.

"Yeah, is this a timeshare type deal?" Forcas asked.

"Are we going to a different building?" Crocell asked. "I'd like one where the fitness center is higher up, like in the middle or even the top of the building. And I'd like more amenities. Maybe a death worm run and a fire pit? I'm thinking of getting a death worm."

"Ooh, I want a climbing wall!" Gaap said.

Raum paced on the far side of the room, hands on his head. "More amenities. Unbelievable," he muttered. He turned back to the group, voice firm. "We are going to our freedom, you dunces. There's no pool. There's no fitness center. There are no meetings. You can, however, utterly destroy all these things and more, with fire or plague or sword or wrath. You can do whatever you want. Bring about the end of days." He laughed. "Wouldn't that be—" He pressed his hands together in a steeple and put them up to his lips. "Deeply satisfying?"

The residents murmured, then a lull of silence.

Crocell raised his hand. "Will there be a shuttle bus?"

"There is no shuttle bus." Raum picked up the marker and stabbed the table with it. "Don't you understand that you would be free? Isn't that what we all want? We just formed this sub-committee a few weeks ago. I was sure we were all on the same page."

After a moment, Forcas raised a finger. "Raum, I'm still not sure where we would be going, or when we'd be back. I can't just up and leave without notice. I've got bills to pay, a backlog of shows to watch, plants that need watering—"

Raum slapped his palm onto the table and everyone jumped. "Do you want to stay here for the next thousand years, until 'they' allow you back?"

Shrugs. Glances. Eating.

"And if they deem you worthy," Raum said, "then you're just thrown back in without any support: no mentor program, no communication, no process. The last time I was sent back, I was exhausted, I was depressed. I was angry—"

And sad. Raum knew he would never be accepted again, not really. He was done with going back. It was too hard. "I'm sure at least some of you felt the same."

Forcas sighed. "Tell us about this loophole."

"The loophole is that we can leave the building *passively*, in some kind of container. We cannot actively leave the prison of our volition but—*but*—we *can* leave in a container that is brought out of the building by a third party."

"Like a giant bus?" Crocell said.

"Or a double-decker trolley?" Forcas said.

"No." Raum rubbed his eyes. He was mentally exhausted, and felt his loss all over again. He wanted to give up, just go back to his apartment and try again the next day—or leave them behind. "A thousand times no." His voice was a tired, beaten down imitation of what it was earlier. "We leave in a dumpster."

"No way," Gaap said. "Adenovirus from bats!"

Forcas barked a laugh. "You should talk. And there aren't any bats in the dumpster."

Gaap rolled his eyes and continued, ticking off each item on his fingers. "*Bartonella rochalimae* in raccoons. General grossness." He held up three fingers. "And I'm sure I could think of more reasons not to use a dumpster. Why can't we use a car?"

Raum rolled his eyes. "The documents are extremely specific."

"What documents?" Forcas said.

"*The Civil Rules and Procedures for Angel Binding and Unbinding*—which I tracked down after reading that article—explicitly states the conditions for safely egressing a prison by means of a mobile garbage bin."

Gaap made a face. "Oh, gross."

Chapter Thirty-Five

They Couldn't Tell if the Cockatrice Was Insulting Them

As **Kelly followed the bald man through downtown** Pothole City, she noticed birds dropping out of the sky. Moving steadily alongside the buildings on her right, she turned her head in short motions, eyes shifting in a figure eight pattern to pick out signs and to place the bald man contextually. She studied the bald man's shape—broad shoulders, slightly pronating walk—and noted the regular spacing of surrounding objects: newspaper boxes, posts, alleys, bus stops, and shadows cast by the buildings.

The bald man stopped at a high-rise office building and pushed through the revolving doors. She noted the address and made a quick stop at her apartment in the former Special Situations HQ to check on the SPs and get some food. After grabbing a bag of cheese crackers, she followed a strange sound to the pneumatic tube room.

"Mehiel!"

The angel who protected professors, orators, and authors was curled up in the corner holding on to the plastic tube. She lifted the end of his shirt and saw a wound leaking mint-colored fluid.

She ran to her bag to get a number she had scrawled on a lollipop wrapper. Af's number. Unlike Murray, Af was easy to reach on the phone. But since he was physically bound to Amenity Tower, she would have to bring Mehiel to him. But there was no answer.

She carried Mehiel down the fire escape, wishing, not for the first time, that the elevators worked. She anchored her feet and lowered him to the ground from the ledge, thinking that out of all the ways to get someone off a fire escape, this was probably the worst, short of just dropping him to the ground like a sack of mulch.

She unlocked her bike and told him to hold on to her, then rode to the condo building, dropped her bike, and met Af at a side door.

"Who's this?"

"Mehiel. He's injured."

Af checked the wound, then went through the mail area, Mehiel on his back. They looked like a shark and one of those tiny parasite fishes.

On the way to the elevator, they passed a resident walking a death worm with a small pink bow on its head. To her surprise, Af smirked at the worm. "Owner taking you outside to do your business? How's that going?"

"He hates that," Af said in the elevator. "And I enjoy it very much. The one vice I allow myself."

Noting her expression, Af continued. "He came here around the same time as I did, and assumed he could escape in the vessel of a death worm. He couldn't."

"How can you tell which one he is?"

"I just know."

They got into the high-rise elevator behind a cockatrice carrying a large insulated pizza box carrier. The cockatrice pressed a different floor and said, "Cluck."

She couldn't tell if the cockatrice was insulting them, or giving them a polite greeting.

The digital sign in the elevator reminded residents about the annual death worm audit: All death worms must be registered with the management office; only unit owners could have death worms; and guest death worms were not allowed.

"We have a death worm problem here," Af said. "They make a terrible shrieking sound you can hear floors away."

The cockatrice got out two floors lower than Af's floor. "Cluck."

"Have a good day," Af said.

"Cluck!" Kelly said to the Cockatrice, hoping she got the tone right. She stared at the box with longing as the doors closed.

"That pizza smells really good."

"We can order one."

"No time. I have to find the rest of the SPs. I got in trouble with Don, but don't really care. What's the worst he can do, start the apocalypse? Give me a bad recommendation?" Heat prickled her forehead as she realized she said too much.

Af frowned. "Don? Don who?"

"It's nothing. Never mind. I got in trouble at work, but the SPs are more important to me." It hadn't occurred to her until she said it out loud. Usually her work took precedence over everything else, not that there *was* much else.

"They're usually at my place, but Mehiel is the only one I've located." And she had a few questions for her so-called handler, Murray.

"Let me help you, then."

"Don't take this the wrong way," she said, "but you can't leave the building."

"True," Af conceded, "but I could help from here."

"Such as?"

"Ordering pizza, for one," Af said.

When they reached Af's floor, they heard a noise outside and she looked out the hallway window down at Pothole City. Af hoisted Mehiel up on his back and stood next to her.

From this wide southern view of downtown, more than forty floors up, they watched as birds dropped out of their migratory paths, and monsters of various shapes and colors dive-bombed office windows.

A small slug monster slammed into the window in front of them, suctioning onto the glass. A tooth-lined rectum yawned open and lightning shot out, melting a tortilla-sized area of the window. Af staggered back, but the glass held. The slug monster flew off.

Kelly blew air through her teeth in frustration. She had just washed that window.

"I saw this earlier. If the birds are dropping from their migratory paths, it means that Anpiel isn't on his post." At Af's expression, she added, "Protecting birds."

Af looked confused. "I thought Tubiel protected birds."

"No, Tubiel returns small birds to their owners. Anpiel protects birds, which includes migratory paths. Let's get Mehiel to a bed."

Before they turned to go back down the hallway, they glanced down at the street. Cars, buses, cabs, double-decker buses, and fire trucks skidded and caromed off one another. The sky turned dark, then light, then dark again. The lighted windows on the office towers somehow coordinated to read 'WTF.' Toward the east, the lake blazed with fire, and a gigantic sea monster emerged from the burning water.

"Hmm," Af said.

She shrugged. "That lake is so polluted, it was only a matter of time."

At his apartment, Af took the sleeping Mehiel to a guest room and lifted the bottom of Mehiel's shirt to check the wound. "Almost closed up," Af said.

"That was fast."

"There are advantages to his status."

"What about *your* status?" she asked.

"I have no status. But, hey, if Raum's plan actually succeeds, then I can have any board seat I want. Of course, my HOA fees will equal the GDP of Panama." Af paused and frowned. "What happened to him?"

"I have no idea. I just found him like this. Maybe it was a burglar, but I didn't see that anything was taken. Can you watch him for a while?"

"Where are you going to be?" Af asked.

"I have to go see about some evidence in a hell lodge."

"Pick up a matchbook for me, would you? I collect them now."

Chapter Thirty-Six

The Jackal Flailed in the Deep End

Af swam his usual fifty laps in the pool, then sat on the side, legs dangling in the water. He put his goggles on top of his head.

Raum strolled into the pool area wearing hibiscus-patterned board shorts, a *Pothole City Cares About Soil-Transmitted Helminthiasis 10K* t-shirt, and a towel around his neck, and carrying an espresso machine.

"Hello there, Af." Raum waved. He spotted an outlet behind the lounge chairs and plugged in his machine. "C'mon, sit over here. Have a macchiato. It's not like we have to worry about losing sleep tonight."

Af took a chair near Raum. The espresso machine whirred, chugged, and spurted out a tiny coffee.

"You seem pensive," Raum said. "Human vessel getting you down?"

"Yes, actually."

"Oh, it's wretched, isn't it? I wake up in the mornings feeling like I was cast down all over again! Okay, bleak face: spill. Not that you need to give me a reason for that lugubrious expression." Raum stretched out his arms to indicate everything in front of them. "We're all trapped here, in this prison, and by prison I mean this building and these vessels. Can you believe these bodies don't just dissolve in the pool? I was afraid to go in at first."

Af furrowed his brow. "You should take care of your vessel. We don't know how long we'll be here."

"Not long, buddy. Between you and me, I'm desperate to get out of here. We deserve it. We've been betrayed, abandoned, and rejected."

"Not to mention the hellspiral of committee meetings," Af muttered.

"Are you joking?" Raum chuckled. "Those meetings are the only good thing we've got. Is that what's keeping you down?"

Af leaned forward to look at the bottom of the pool. "I hired a dental hygienist to make a house visit for a cleaning, and she told me that my vessel has genetic periodontal disease."

Raum patted Af on the back. "That's the kind of problem that lends urgency to our situation. We have to get out of here now and get back into our true forms."

Af put his goggles back on.

"Not that it'll be easy to get everyone organized," Raum said. "The whole escape sub-committee has breathed in some kind of fungus that makes them forget why they're there. I've tried everything: slides, semaphores, charades, you name it. There's no more time. We have to try this loophole now."

Af turned to Raum. "Wait—what loophole?"

Raum rolled his eyes. "Maybe if you had bothered to come to the meeting, you would know."

"Don't be petulant."

"Fine." Raum spoke behind his hand in a stage whisper. "I'm almost certain that we can leave in a dumpster."

"You mean one of those bins in the ground level where the trash goes?"

"Yes, the loophole is to leave passively in a container that takes us out of the building."

"Why a dumpster?"

"That's what the documents point to."

"Which documents?"

"*The Civil Rules and Procedures for Angel Binding and Unbinding*. Also, the dumpster is big enough for all of us, and it's picked up on a consistent schedule."

"I hope the board renewed the waste management contract, considering how carelessly you all tended to the building. When are you doing this?"

"We need to be ready for the dumpster pickup tomorrow at 6:00 p.m. I need three other angels, though more are welcome."

"Do you really think you can get them into a dumpster?"

Raum tossed back another espresso. He threw his towel onto a chair, went over to the pool, and lowered himself into the water. "I'll tell them whatever it takes to get them in there. I presume you'll be joining us?" He gave Af an expectant look, bobbing.

Af shook his head. "I prefer to stay."

"What? Af, you're talking crazy. Why would you do that?"

"I like it here, Raum. I'm a calmer person here."

Raum put on his goggles. "Af, you're not a person. You're one of the most powerful angels of destruction there is. You're a ruler—"

"Over the death of mortals. I know."

"And a Prince of Wrath. That's a big deal, Af. How could you possibly not want to be that?" Raum almost seemed sympathetic for a moment. "You know you can't stay here, buddy."

"You seem to be enjoying the pool."

"For now." Raum flashed a tight smile. "I have a lot of work ahead of me. But then we'll be free."

"And after that?" Af asked.

"We'll be free." He raised his hands to say 'what else matters'?

"What are you going to do after you get out?" Af asked.

Raum grinned. "Destroying this prison, first." He winked. "Then Pothole City. Totally obliterated. Then, yeah, everything else I see. I don't want to leave one human, old friend. Not one. I'm going to go all out, full scale. The elliptical is not cutting it for me, know what I mean?"

A fearful Emim giant stuck his toe in the pool and retreated with a shiver, then hurried to the hot tub, fitting just his foot and ankle inside. The water spilled over to the patio.

"You're not excited?" Raum asked. "You're not totally psycho'd to leave?"

"I believe the term is 'psyched'. Psyched to leave."

Raum reached out and grabbed a float in the shape of a donut with sprinkles. The Jackal yelped in protest at the sudden loss of his float until Raum glared at him.

"Yeah, okay. Well, aren't you psyched?" Raum positioned himself in the float as the Jackal flailed in the deep end, trying to keep his thick, glossy hair above water. "Let's be serious for a second."

"I've been serious this whole time," Af said.

"Ohhh, right. Well, hey, guess what? You won't need this vessel anymore. You'll be back in your true form and won't have to worry about your perio-whatever. Destroy the whole world if you want!"

"I have an appointment tomorrow."

"Cancel that nonsense, Af!" Raum jiggled the float in Af's direction. "You know, I can't help feeling a little offended that you don't think I can do this."

"It's not that, Raum. If anyone can release them, it's you."

Raum grinned and puffed out his chest with pride. "Yes, that's true."

"But I want to stay." Af stood and set his cup on the table.

Raum struggled to get in the donut float. He pulled it over his arms, tried to pull it down, then gave up and tossed it to the side, hitting the Jackal in the head. "You can't stay."

"I can, and I will. It's my choice." Af gathered his things and headed for the door in the glass wall.

"It's the wrong choice."

"I guess we'll see."

The Jackal grabbed his float and paddled furiously to the deep end of the pool. Raum waded through the shallow end and pointed.

"You'll be collateral damage, Af. You understand me? Anything, anyone left in Amenity Tower will be obliterated as soon as I get us out. Even you, if you stay in your vessel."

Af paused, his hand on the door. Raum was right—he would still be in his vessel. His fragile vessel, with its need for maintenance of all kinds.

"Why are you being so stubborn?" Raum yelled from the pool door. "You can't even leave the building! Is it that great here? It's just demented! Why am I the only sane one left?"

Chapter Thirty-Seven

Best Putting Stroke

I don't have much time," the bald man announced when he shut the employer's office door.

"Take a seat, have a sandwich. My favorite show is on."

The bald man sank into a tufted black leather chair and picked up a crystal globe with an engraved plaque: *Hell Lodge Golf Club, Destroying Angel of the Apocalypse, Best Putting Stroke.*

Don, dressed in his usual hibiscus-pattern shirt, stayed focused on his flat-screen TV. He laughed uproariously at Roger chasing ducks around the studio and wiped tears from the corners of his eyes.

"Out of all the shows of this type, this is the best. I hope he wins this year. So"—Don swiveled to face the bald man, but swiveled too far and grabbed on to his desk to pull his chair back in—"what do you want now?"

The bald man leaned back in the chair on the other side of the desk, legs open and arms out to the side, to show that he felt no need to protect his sensitive parts in this room.

"We have a problem."

"No, you have a problem." Don jabbed his finger in the air.

"We both have a problem."

"It has always been *your* problem."

Don deflected his intense gaze from the bald man and unwrapped some kind of burrito from wax paper.

The bald man waved his arm to the side. "You wouldn't even have this—this sinecure if I hadn't fixed who knows how many damn problems that you created."

Don took a sip of his iced tea. "I admit that your services have been useful to me."

The bald man checked his phone for messages. "I'm so glad. Now, speaking of your problem, let me set the scene for one auspicious day. Most of the paperwork on that day pertained to those pesky fallen angels who were assigned or reassigned to a brass pot, a coffee cup, an arcade machine, a parking meter, whatever. But it was just so much *work.* Not only did you have to fill out all those forms—one per angel—you had to translate every word into Sumerian before securing final approval. Tedious."

Don made himself a drink from the bar cart, muddling mint and sugar at the bottom of the glass.

The bald man stretched back, arms at his head. "It would have been a whole lot easier to just bind all the naughty angels to Amenity Tower, Pothole City's Finest Luxury Condominium Building." He extended his arms, palms up. "And now, all of the fallens are together, in the same building. *The same building.* That is some gnarly stuff waiting to happen, Don."

Don sipped his drink. He did not offer one to the bald man, who noticed the blatant oversight. "First of all, I don't see what the big deal is." Don set his drink on his desk blotter. "So they're all in the same place. What's the worst that could happen, they change the bylaws? Besides, *he* is in there. I routed him with all the rest. Do you have any idea how dangerous he is? If he gets out of that condo and wreaks worldwide chaos and destruction—"

The bald man raised a brow.

"It would be bad," Don said. "For, you know... people."

The bald man laughed. "You can't stand people. Why would you give a—ohh, I see."

"What?"

"You don't want him to take all the credit." The bald man stood and slapped his palms down on the desk.

Don wheeled back.

"That's it, isn't it? You two have been at each other's throats for epochs. It must curdle your caustic bodily fluid to think of him escaping and stealing your thunder. Because you're lazy. You'll intend to cause total destruction, but you'll just keep putting it off to play golf or to watch another episode of *What's On Your Mind, With Roger Balbi*. You don't have the project management skills. Those angels are going to pull together as a team and figure out how to escape the luxury condominium building you assigned them to, and *then* they're going to make you look bad."

"How could they possibly do that?" Don sipped his drink, eyes wide and blinking in a show of innocence.

The bald man took a book from the desk, opened it to the middle, and set his wet drink on the paper. Don watched in dismay as the ring spread and soaked through.

"Those angels are supposed to be bound for a thousand years or more." The bald man wiped his hands on his pants and sat. "And you were in charge of processing that paperwork. I wouldn't even have to make an anonymous tip. Anyone in charge could easily trace the mess back to you."

Don's expression indicated that he knew better. "What is it to you if they run roughshod over the planet?"

"I know it's hard for you to understand, but I have certain interests here."

Don leaned back. So did the bald man. Don shifted uncomfortably.

"I got blamed for your first colossal mistake," the bald man said. "I took the fall for your incompetent minion, but I will not be collateral damage for another screw-up. Leave her alone, and stop trying to compete with him. He's not competing with you."

Don shot forward. "Did he say something? What was his exact tone? Defeated, dejected, bitter? All three?"

The bald man rolled his eyes. "You're a middle manager. You're not in the field anymore, and you've caused enough trouble. Just let it go."

After the bald man left, Don picked up his red phone.

"Get in here now."

He practiced his chip swing by the east window until the door opened.

"At your service, boss."

Don chuckled, ignoring his visitor's subtle sarcasm. "That's why you're the star in my pocket that I save for a rainy day. For example, a day in the forest."

"The forest job again? Why do you have to bring that up every single time?" The visitor shuffled papers on the employer's desk.

"Because your mistake affects me."

The visitor straightened. "Is that how you see it? You tell me where to go, what to do, and when to do it. If things aren't exactly how you like it when I get there—"

"Exactly how I like it?" Don thumped a hand on his desk. "You mean, if I want two people dead, and only one of them happens to be in the house, and you don't check to make sure all of your targets are there, then I'm the unreasonable one for blaming you?"

"They were *both* supposed to be in the house." The visitor flicked his gaze up to the ceiling.

"And I don't allow you the latitude to compensate for extenuating circumstances? For contingencies?" Don waited.

The visitor stood and paced, stopping briefly by the south window to fix a crooked framed certificate.

"Look, you tell me that you want something done, and by a certain time." The visitor dusted the bottom of the frame. "You tell me they're both going to be in the house in the window of time you gave me. It's your responsibility to get the situation right so I can do my job. My directive was to torch the place at sunrise, not verify the number of occupants."

A moment passed before Don asked, "Have you ever tried taking initiative?"

The visitor glared at him. "I took initiative once, at the Chamber of Peacekeeping and Water Sports General Session. I didn't hear the end of it for months. Eighty-seven voice mails the first week ripping me a new one for going off course. For taking initiative. So no, I wasn't motivated to do it again."

Don laced his fingers and pressed his thumbs to his mouth. "Perhaps I've been inconsistent. You're an enterprising employee. Finish the job I gave you by the end of the week, and you will be... rewarded."

"There are complications," the visitor said, reluctantly.

Don pulled his chair closer to his desk. "She's the last of the Driscolls, and I want her gone, one way or the other. With her out of the way—"

"What about—"

"Oh, my intelligence sources tell me he's out of commission for good. And with her out of the way, I'll finally be able to shut down production of the Cluck Snack products, so those creepy silent angel-things will stop getting in my way. No offense. And I need to be sure that Af is in Amenity Tower. I want that building destroyed, preferably with both of them in it."

Chapter Thirty-Eight

The Protection of Fungi

Kelly noticed that a few of the SPs had quietly returned to her building without any explanation of where they disappeared to earlier—or where the rest of the SPs might be found.

Standing at Mr. Black's desk, she spread out the train map she nicked from Murray's bag, placed an orienteering competition paperweight on the top left corner, and the pen base at another. The filaments of tracks were dense and complex. Maybe too complex to navigate.

"Kermit!"

In a few seconds, Kermit jogged into the office wearing his usual oversize high-tops and faded Iron Maiden shirt.

"Take a look at this. Does it make any sense to you?" Kelly stepped back a foot so Kermit could stand behind the desk. He tilted his head one way, then another.

She handed him a magnifying glass. Kermit held the glass up to the paper, looked closely, and stood straight.

"This diagram reminds me of a fungal structure with fruiting bodies in a fairly mature stage," she said.

Kermit blinked.

"I used to see them on logs in the forest."

She took a step closer to the desk and Kermit did a little skip to get out of her way. "I think it's an elevated train map." She tapped the paper with a finger. "This hyphal net, the mycelium, appears to be the route map. And the train itself could be the sporiferous hyphal tubes. The cytoplasm flows toward the tips of the hyphae, so maybe that provides the motion. Oh hell, I'm not a mycologist." She straightened and sighed. "It could be something entirely different."

Kermit bent over again with the glass, from the side of the desk.

She placed a fingertip on the end of one of the veins and traced it back to a large shape. "These blobs"—she moved her finger over the paper indicating blobs of different sizes and colors—"are probably the fruiting bodies of the mycelium."

Kermit nodded, his feathered hair bouncing.

She leaned in a little farther over the map, tracing a line on the map to one of the blobs. "And I think... perhaps... the fruiting bodies are the train stations. You can see that the sporophores—the stations—vary in size. Why, I have no idea. If the trains only go to hell lodges, then maybe the size of each station on the map indicates the importance of the corresponding lodge." She looked up at Kermit, who gave her a goofy smile.

"I need to find the station by Don's office. Murray took me there before, but I need to get there without him. If I can see the train, and get on the correct one, I can disembark at the right station, find Don's office, then search it for the evidence I know he has."

She tapped a knuckle on the table to each of the last four words. "And then, I hope, get back here."

Kermit gave her a dubious look.

"Don't worry. I'm not going to get stuck."

He took his sketch pad from his jeans, and sketched something for her.

"You're going to get a Cluck Snack Steamie Pocket," she guessed from the drawing. "Go for it."

Kermit loped out of Mr. Black's office.

She rubbed her forehead in hard circles then went back to the mesh network on the map. Some of the threads on the map were thicker than others, and the paths weren't named or marked. "Those lines must be used more frequently," she said to herself. "It's bananas, but think I can find it."

Kermit came back with a Steamie Pocket and another SP.

She checked his ID bracelet. "Firiel. In charge of the protection of fungi. Favorite food: Cluck Snack Salsa."

"Needless to say, Firiel, you're coming with me." She folded the map. "If we get stuck forever in a hell lodge, then at least we'll be together."

Firiel drew on his sketch pad and held up the page so she could see a frowny face with one tear.

Kelly looked at Kermit. "I don't know if he's referring to the 'stuck forever in a hell lodge' part or the 'living with just me' part. Either way, that's fair."

Firiel clutched the canisters of old-fashioned oats he took from the pantry while peering down the tracks at the station. Kelly's pea coat flapped against her thigh.

Snot dripped from Firiel's nose down to his mouth. She plucked a tissue from her pocket and swiped it against his upper lip. "What's with the oats?"

Firiel sniffled and blinked his tearing eyes. She dabbed his eyes with the tissue, since he had a death grip on the oat canisters.

"When is this thing going to show up?"

Firiel shrugged, then a glistening tube shot down the tracks toward them, the tip morphing into a train shape. It halted with a toy-like squeak, not the grinding metal screech of the regular train. A fissure opened in the side and turned into a double-door. They stepped on and the opening closed behind them. Fluid flowed through pipes attached to the ceiling.

A taciturn server in black pants and short jacket appeared beside their table.

"Two milks," she said. The server nodded and glided away.

Kelly took off her coat and folded it up on her lap. The server returned with their milks and seemed to expect something. She shrugged and reached in her front pocket for some cash, but Firiel handed the valet the canisters of oats.

"Thank you, sir. It's much appreciated." The server bowed, and left again.

"What does he do with the oats?"

Firiel sipped his milk through a bendy straw and drew something on his sketch pad. She considered the sketch: a network of fuzzy blobs, a cord that led to a flat-screen display, and then a stick figure.

"I think I get it. He's another persona of the fungus."

Firiel smiled and drew on the sketch pad again. One of the fuzzy blobs devoured a canister of oats.

"And he eats oats."

Firiel gave her a smile. He took the sketch pad and added some dots. She held it and didn't say anything for a moment.

"Spore ejections?"

He waved his arms around, flicking out his fingers from his thumb repeatedly. He drew more dots and lines.

"Lots of ejections," she said.

He turned his hand palm up and moved it up. More.

"Hundreds—no, thousands of ejections," she said. "Creating an air jet."

Firiel grinned.

"So that's how the train moves."

He hugged his sketch pad and shrugged.

Half an hour later, the tube made an opening and Firiel stepped out first. They walked through a tangled mesh of filaments to another door that led to a station.

When she saw the chicken egg fortune machine, she recognized the same stop as before, but a new machine flanked the egg fortune dispenser: a softly glowing Buddha encased in glass. The slot was marked '10 Baht.' She pulled a quarter from her pocket and held it next to the slot to see if it would at least fit, but the shape and color had changed into a ten Baht coin.

"I've got a magical pocket." She placed the coin in the slot and smiled when the Buddha's eyes flashed and cycled through colors. The automata made a cacophony of kitchen-appliance sounds, then ejected a fortune. In Thai.

She tried the chicken automata. A golden egg dropped and she reached past the tiny hinged flap to get the egg. Inside was a tiny plastic monkey.

"As useful as my high school guidance counselor. Maybe I can get Don to replace these with drink machines."

Firiel raised an eyebrow.

"Cluck Snack drinks, of course."

Chapter Thirty-Nine

Don's Bottomless Pit: Hell Lodge #6

Kelly and Firiel walked on silver sand to the lodge she remembered. Lizards skittered underfoot. A pot of red geraniums hung from the porch roof over two Adirondack chairs.

She held Firiel back with her arm. "I have to make sure he's not in there. One of your colleagues told me he was at his downtown office tonight."

She ran in a crouch to the side of the lodge, stopped under a window, and peeked over the sill. After a moment, she walked around back in a crouch, came around the other side of the lodge, and hurried up the porch. She waved at Firiel to come over.

"Wait here, out of sight. If anyone shows up, hide. Okay?" He ran across the porch and knelt behind a post.

The lodge served as Don's main office, she suspected. She didn't know where he lived, but it wasn't in this lodge, unless he slept at his desk, and Don didn't strike her as a workaholic.

From the outside, the lodge looked like a hunting cabin or a ramshackle summer house. Inside, it was one long room. A massive desk, weighed down with precariously-placed stacks of paper and files, dominated the left side.

To one end of the desk was Don's end of the pneumatic tube, positioned where he could reach it from the chair. "That's where the magic happens," she muttered.

Bookshelves stuffed with black binders lined the wall behind the desk. Aside from the binders, the shelves were a haphazard mess.

She started her search with the papers on the desk. When she finished with one stack, she checked on Firiel, who huddled in the corner of the porch, watching through the slats. A blackbird hopped up and down on his left palm.

As she rifled through the next stack, she got the impression that Don did careless work, made frequent mistakes, and spent most of his time getting other people to cover up those mistakes.

Moving on to the shelves, she bent to the side to read the labels on the binders. They were arranged by year and went back decades, centuries. She pulled out the binder from 1985 and flipped through the papers, seeing nothing of interest until reaching a document from September of that year.

By the time she finished reading it, she was so angry she wanted to split off a new personality and have *her* deal with it.

She put the 1985 binder back in its place on the shelf. A bowl of matchbooks held up the binders on the shelf to the left. She picked one, *Don's Bottomless Pit: Hell Lodge #6,* and put it in her pocket.

The September document was all she needed, but she took several more papers just to be sure. It was overkill, like strangling someone, then feeding them digitalis. But she would definitely get a grim satisfaction from presenting her findings when she had the chance.

Chapter Forty

His Coma Score is Higher Than Three

Af sat in the periodontist's chair, fidgeting with his shirt cuff. The young, doe-eyed assistant clipped a pink paper napkin around his neck. The off-putting hygienist appeared on his left and applied the topical anesthetic. A few minutes later, the hygienist held up a syringe appropriate for tranquilizing a Kodiak bear, and without speaking, inserted the syringe in Af's jaw.

After that, they left him alone. He tried to make himself feel better by thinking of the small pleasures he enjoyed at Amenity Tower: taking his product photographs and writing the accompanying reviews, reading the paper while drinking coffee, making sandwiches in his panini maker. Getting his mail. Riding the exercise bicycle in the fitness center while watching interdimensional monsters fly into windows and slide down the glass.

His relaxation technique didn't work. His heart beat faster than usual and his stomach fluttered. The right side of his jaw was numb all the way up to his nose. He felt desperate—to leave, to ditch his stupid vessel, to flex his real muscles.

The periodontist stepped up to the chair. "Numb?" He asked the assistant to pull the x-rays. "All right, Mr... Smith." He tapped his finger on the screen in front of the chair. "Even after this treatment, it's very possible that you will need surgery."

Af went cold. The cells in his vessel's body felt like they were being crushed by one of those locusts at the fitness center.

"Based on your good oral health and care, I'm strongly inclined to believe this is a genetic condition," the periodontist added.

More and more, Af considered his body a disconnected vessel. Why had he ever thought this could work?

The hygienist returned and laid out the tools.

"May I see those?" Af asked.

"See what?"

"Those tools."

"The curettes?"

"If you say so. But it doesn't mean they're not tools."

The hygienist held out her gloved hand with the curettes displayed on the rubber.

"What's that one?" Af pointed to one of the curettes with a thick hooked end.

"That's the sickle. It's used for cleaning between the teeth."

"Between Godzilla's teeth?"

The hygienist sighed. "The tooth has four surfaces, and each of these curettes cleans one of those surfaces. Now, if you don't mind, I'm going to get started."

"What will you be doing, exactly? I've seen similar set-ups from the Spanish Inquisition."

The hygienist rolled her eyes. "You don't know why you're here?"

"Above all, to bask in the pleasure of your company," Af said. "Secondarily, to see what barbaric, superannuated treatment you're getting at least some ignorant fools to pay you for."

"The anesthetic has obviously set in," the hygienist said in a dry tone. She began scraping Af's teeth. Af heard a voice from the reception desk and relief flooded through him.

"His name is *Af*. How is that possibly a difficult name for you? If I knew his last name, I would have mentioned it. Look, I know he's here. He's tall—not Michael Crichton tall, but he's up there—eyes the color of my favorite mushroom, typically very calm, but gets cranky when he can't do specific things at specific times? Does that seem familiar at all?"

A muffled response, then Kelly's even louder retort. "Look, I know he's here and I need to see him right now."

Af smiled around the sickle. Kelly pushed her way through a gauntlet of receptionist and assistant to get to the side of Af's chair.

"May I help you?" The hygienist said in a condescending tone—a tone that won her a buffet coupon at the *12th Annual Dental Office Support Staff Association's Condescending Tone Contest*.

Kelly put her hand on the chair next to Af's leg. "Af, I need your help." Then, upon a closer look, "You know that you could walk out of here right now like this" —she raised her arms straight out in front of her and took on a blank, slack-jawed expression—"and people would think it's the end of days." She dropped her arms. "Wait, *is* it the end of days?"

Af made a sound that resembled "izzdayureer?"

"No, that's not why I'm here. Do you think I'm the type of girl who gets hysterical over something like the end of days and seeks comfort from a former—"

Af widened his eyes.

She caught herself. "A former polymer engineer?"

The periodontist angled his head into the room from the corner. "I'm the periodontist. Can I help you?"

She stepped back from the chair. "You've got a problem with your floors, doc." She pressed the toe of her boot against the wood slats.

"My floors? What do you mean?" The periodontist came around to the other side of the chair, concerned.

"See how there's give under here, how they sag when you press your shoe on them?" She put some of her weight on her right foot and showed him how the slats were bending compared to the other sections nearby. "I noticed areas like this one in the hall. The laminate floor material is too thin and the padding is too thick. After a while, gaps will form around the slats."

The periodontist seemed on the verge of tears, giving her a frisson of pleasure.

"This office looks new," she said, "so if I were you, I would call the GC and have him redo it while it's still under warranty. And if the GC won't cooperate, get another flooring person in to check it out, and plan on bringing your lawyer to the party, too."

"Oh my." The periodontist rubbed the back of his head and frowned.

Af smiled on the one side of his face for the second time since Kelly came in.

"Okay, Mr. Smith," the hygienist said, as she had Af rinse into a paper cup attached to a suction. "Don't chew anything until the numbness wears off, or you could bite your lips, tongue or cheek."

"Does Mr. Smith look like an imbecile to you?" Kelly asked. "Why would he want to chew anything, anyway?"

The hygienist went on in a rote monotone as though she hadn't spoken. "Don't drink hot or cold liquids. You won't be able to tell how hot or cold they are."

"His coma score is actually higher than three," Kelly said from beside the window, arms crossed.

The hygienist kept going. "Take the antibiotic after breakfast and dinner, on a full stomach. The bottle will instruct you to take it on an empty stomach, but eat something beforehand. I like angel."

"Mr. Smith is not in the habit of taking instructions from bottles or any other inanimate object," Kelly said in an absentminded tone while looking out the window at a construction site. A moment later, she realized what the hygienist said. She turned her head toward the chair in time to see the hygienist's head split in two and a crack erupt down her torso.

"I *knew* it," Af said in a slurred voice, then rolled out of the chair and onto the floor.

The halves of the hygienist's shell fell to the shoddy wooden floors with a thud. The frazzled periodontist slapped his hands to his mouth in horror and keened a little. She knew he was reacting to the floor damage, not to his employee revealing herself as a giant crab-like creature with overlapping plates and seven pairs of segmented legs that terminated in gleaming, super-size dental tools.

The hygienist grew more than ten feet tall in a lightning-fast succession of molts as her exoskeleton split off and regrew with a sound like aluminum foil being crushed into a ball.

The drop-ceiling tiles cracked over the hygienist's head, which itself had four segmented arms over the mouth. Her tailfan twitched and knocked over a large piece of equipment by the chair that housed the water scaler.

"My floors! My ceiling! Everything's falling apart," the periodontist said from the hallway.

"Your floors were a lost cause," she yelled over the commotion. "Next time, get some engineered hardwood, a competent GC, and a *human* support staff who don't morph into giant crab things."

This was the second time in a week she had to deal with demons working under a human facade. She didn't like that trend.

The periodontist crouched behind the x-ray machine and cried.

"Also, your sprinklers aren't up to code, so when you continue your barbaric services—"

"That's what *I* said," Af said in a slurred voice.

"—in a new office, get the fire department's consulting services during build-out, okay? Jerk."

A sucking cup on the end of one of the hygienist-monster's fourteen legs caught her hair and a sickle cut Af across the left shoulder. Another arm shank sprayed the dental assistant across the knees with a stream of water.

Kelly pulled her hair from the suction cup, picked up the tiny assistant, hoisted her onto her back, and carried her through the office, setting her down in the waiting room by the coffee machine. The assistant yanked open the door and ran screaming down the hallway.

"You're welcome!"

Af impaled a piece of the hygienist's abdomen with a super-sized bottle of mouthwash, and yellowish, bubbling pus oozed out of the hole in one of the sausage-like sections of its belly.

Af and Kelly guarded themselves behind the reclined patient chair and threw anything they could find from the cabinets behind them.

"At least she finished your treatment," she said.

"They didn't, but I think I'll look for another option with a new periodontist who wasn't trained during Scotland's witch trials. Perhaps there have been advances in the field since then." Af lobbed a package of tissues at the hygienist, who struggled to maneuver out of the space in the corner by the window.

"Ahm, this seems to be an ineffectual defense." Af held up a bottle of mouthwash.

"I didn't think I needed an RPG case to visit you at the periodontist," she said. "How did you manage to leave Amenity Tower, anyway?" She peeked around the chair at the hygienist demon. "Never mind—just fill me in after we get out of here."

The hygienist lunged at the periodontist with hairy snapping jaws and legs ending in drill heads and probes. He screamed as the hygienist gouged and flayed with dental excavators and chisels before spewing caustic digestive juices that bound the doctor in a corrosive, sticky web.

After some sniffing, the hygienist devoured the web-bound periodontist in five bites.

"He doesn't have to worry about his floors anymore." She waited until the blood-engorged hygienist faced toward the window as it tried to slither out from behind the chair. Time to end this now and clean up fast before someone investigated because of the noise or the window.

She ran to the back of the chair and pushed a cart into the hygienist and crushed it against the wall, leaving yellow smears. The hygienist regurgitated blackened chunks.

"What *is* that?" Af curled his lip in disgust.

One of the hygienist's shanks landed on the cart, which set off a dental laser.

She yanked the fire extinguisher off a nearby wall. "At least the doctor, and I use that word loosely, had *some* fire compliance." She pulled the pin and aimed it at the hygienist.

Af shielded his eyes.

The hygienist looked like a crustacean dipped in marshmallow fondue, its flailing legs flicking off white blobs. Kelly took advantage of the hygienist's lack of sight and frantically glanced over the selection of knives on a tray table.

"They're tiny, yet somehow more menacing," she muttered. She grabbed a knife and sprang onto the chair, using both hands to thrust the knife between the hygienist's eyes.

Finally, the hygienist went still. An unmoving, smoking husk. She prodded it and waited. She hit it upside the head with the lamp and waited. Stabbed it in the thorax and waited.

When she was pretty sure it was permanently out of commission, she dropped the knife and pushed the lamp out of the way.

"Any other appointments today?" Kelly jumped off the chair, then staggered back, astonished.

Af took up the entire high-ceilinged room with his massive, hulking, blood-red, black-winged, ram-horned form.

"I really didn't like this experience," he said in a voice like a Ferrari engine. He furled and unfurled the tips of his leathery wings. "I don't think I can do this anymore. This human thing. Maybe I should stay like this."

She tried to calm herself down enough to speak, and ignore the hammering in her chest. "It kind of sucks, doesn't it?"

He snorted fire and rolled his huge black eyes. "Kind of? Listen, thanks for killing that thing. Sorry I didn't change, you know, beforehand."

She shrugged one shoulder. "It worked out all right."

Af stepped toward the window, caving in the floor, and crashed through the wall, reminding her of the old Kool-Aid ad. She watched, incredulous, as Af tackled a construction crane and swung it around to the window. He flew back and gripped the side of the building. His body rumbled, and radiated both heat and cold.

He blinked at her. "I just wanted to let you know that you won't be in any danger from me."

She gave him a wry smile. "Thanks. Maybe I'll see you around."

He extended a giant, muscular arm and presented a pitch-black claw in a delicate gesture. She shook it, marveling at the weight and sharpness of it, and then he was off. The building trembled in his wake.

Chapter Forty-One

A Very Expensive Loophole

Kelly looted the samples drawer, scooping up floss, toothpaste, and a handful of toothbrushes before heading out. In the reception area, a man stirred sugar into a coffee and read *Billing Fraud Weekly*. "This coffee is actually kind of decent," he said.

"*Now* what?" She was running on energy reserves and feeling like she lost something dear to her.

He held out a hand and put the magazine on the serving table. "Is that any way to greet Af's ferryman?"

She raised her eyebrows at him in a gesture that said 'And?'

He bowed at the waist. "Owing to my services, Af was able to temporarily leave the prison to which he's bound and entertain the hilariously preposterous notion of mortality, here in this dank, shabby warren. I am a very expensive loophole."

"You're *some* kind of hole."

He flashed her a licentious smirk. "You're delicious. I want to soak you up like water through the dragon's blood tree."

"Whatever that means, but... gross." She poured herself a cup of coffee and glanced at the magazine's feature story: "115 Ways to Overbill." Number one was obvious: invoice for services the patient didn't actually receive.

She wondered if Af would be receiving a bill for the full appointment, even though it ended rather abruptly. Then she remembered that the periodontist had been eaten alive by his employee, and probably wouldn't be catching up on billing anytime soon, but she'd have to call and make sure.

"Look." She put the magazine on the table and crossed her arms over her chest. "I just disposed of a dental hygienist-turned-giant-monster-mite, and Af just reverted, or turned, or transitioned, or fell off the wagon or whatever the hell you call what he did. I'm not in the mood for you."

She guzzled the coffee then tossed the paper cup and grabbed the door handle. "Why are you still here? That was your cue to leave, in case you're oblivious to body language."

"Af invoked me to accompany him on a time-limited trip, to and from his destination. He reserved my time."

"As you might have noticed, Af isn't here anymore. So you can go."

"Can I come with you?"

"No. Go home, or back to the river, or whereever you came from."

As they went out the door, the ferryman's hand lingered on her shoulder. She reached up and touched his hand. He smiled. She twisted his finger to the edge of breaking. He gritted his teeth and made a muffled groan.

"I like you," he said, still in pain.

"Never touch me."

The streets around the periodontist's office jutted out at odd angles like an enormous creature tried to emerge from underneath the pavement.

Pothole City's emergency warning siren whooped in undulating scales. A sea of Exchange workers in vests of red, gold, blue, and other colors poured out of the giant smoky carport, and ran wild in the streets, climbing over cars and into windows, seizing other workers in a berserker rage. Bankers and money managers streamed out of buildings, stabbing other bankers with their metal pens.

The ever-efficient Pothole City Streets & Sanitation snow removal trucks, some of them tiny plows, methodically drove through the streets and scooped up some of the lunatics.

Kelly ducked into an alley and took out her phone. A shabby poster for *Sharktic* covered the entire alley wall.

"Ooh, I heard about that movie," the ferryman said. "A mutant arctic shark terrorizes a cruise ship in Greenland. Or maybe it was Norway. Anyway, we should go see it together." He grasped her shoulder, enthused.

"What are you doing here?"

"I need protection!"

She shook him off and turned away, tapping a number on her phone. She waited while it rang, then left a message.

"Murray, I've left you so many messages that you probably won't even get to this one. But listen, we're near the Exchange and your traders are losing it." She clicked the phone shut and deflected a slobbering, pinstripe-suited, stapler-wielding banker with a solid kick to the groin.

"You know," she said to the ferryman, "I thought Murray had an easy job. I had to switch disguises and skill sets multiple times a day, while all he had to do was go out once in a while and stop one of his invokers from doing something stupid. Kind of like a family lawyer. But he was doing more than I realized."

Each of the SPs had probably been doing more than she realized, given the current circumstances.

The ferryman cowered into the alcove, holding his arm in front of his face and jabbing his keys into the air with his eyes closed. "Can we keep going, please?" Something sprayed him with blood and a thick chartreuse-colored substance, and the ferryman screamed.

She tucked her phone in her pocket. "Hold on, I see a falafel stand." As she gave a cart vendor cash for a paper boat of falafel, a dark-suited finance worker ran screaming out of a bank and barreled straight toward them wielding an overstuffed black binder.

“Hold short.” She stopped the ferryman with the back of her hand and gave him the falafel boat for safekeeping. The ferryman touched her hand. She yanked her hand away and smacked him on the chest.

The finance worker raised the binder and brought it down from over his head, and she pushed the ferryman, pivoted on her heel, and shoved the ferryman to the gutter as the binder thwocked her on the back and knocked the breath out of her.

As the banker’s momentum carried him forward, she tripped his left foot. A city bus lumbered up to the nearby bus stop, brakes squealing. A full-wrap ad covered the side of the bus, depicting a cockatrice posing with a wife and two well-groomed cockatrice children: *Cockatrice Food Delivery & Catering -- A Family Business. No Biting, Or Your Delivery Is Free!*

Af landed on the bus, crushing the top of it down to the sides. He smiled and pointed at the cockatrice ad. “We’re using him as a vendor. I love the anchovy and poisonous egg pizza.”

He gripped the corner of the bus, shattering the windows with the tips of his black claws, and locked eyes with her. “Are you okay? Do you need anything?” He batted off a vulture-headed water bug the size of a mature St. Bernard.

“Nah, we’re good here. Just enjoying the day.”

Af flew off again.

“Thanks for visiting,” she muttered.

She pushed the ferryman to get him started down the sidewalk again.

“What’s the big hurry? Let me take you to a movie.”

“I need to get back to Amenity Tower, invertebrate.”

“Why, is there an amenity you like?”

“I don’t use the amenities. I have to find the SPs, see if maybe I can prevent the building from being destroyed, and have some words with my handler.”

“But you have time for falafel.”

“First, that vendor was fast, and second, do you want me to pass out from hunger along the way? Unlike you, I run on calories from food.”

Even though the financial workers were mostly confined to the area around the Exchange, every other kind of worker overran the streets, from professors in bow ties to kitchen workers in white aprons to insurance workers in blue collared shirts, all losing their minds.

White earthworms, bigger than oil pipelines, crawled up the Bank of Pothole City Hotel and Corporate Center, and amassed on the east side of the huge building, where they proceeded to gnaw on the exterior.

Kelly and the ferryman ran from cover to cover, into alleys and under store canopies. The ferryman panted. "Can we"—he swallowed, and panted again—"Can we hide out somewhere, like that off-track betting place I saw down the street?"

"Keep moving, don't look anyone in the eye, and look crazy. If someone gets in your way or touches you or speaks to you or even gets too close to you, snarl at them like you're the alpha wolf and they're the beta who approached the carcass before you did."

Then the flying leeches came, in flocks that sounded like an old steel fan. A densely packed flock swooped down so close that she felt their wings beating against her.

"Get it off me! Get it off!" The ferryman frantically pulled at her arm, signaling to his back. One of the leeches adhered to the ferryman's upper back and beat its veiny wings on his shoulders.

"It'll fall off on its own in about an hour."

"An hour?" The ferryman's voice had raised in pitch. "This isn't exactly a normal leech. How do you know it's not killing me right now?"

She narrowed her eyes. "You're not exactly mortal. What does it matter?"

"*Pleeease* just take it off." His voice caught with a hiccupy, pre-panic sob, so she rummaged through her many pockets and came up with a packet of Cluck Snack Lem'n Jüc ("Discourages Leeches"). She ripped off the top and poured the Jüc over the leech, who harrumphed, turned and vomited on the ground before flyijng off.

The ferryman exhaled and put his hands on his knees. "Thanks."

She watched the leech rejoin his flock, or whatever the plural noun was for leeches in flight. "It was polite of him to not vomit in your wound. He didn't have to do that, you know."

"Great. Remind me to send him a thank you card."

She handed him a bandage and darted across the street, glancing at a peeling, pitted billboard exhorting the viewer to get their vampire hunting certificate at Pothole City Online College ("As Seen On TV!"). "Oh, *come* on."

The ferryman followed her to an alley while trying to apply the bandage under his shirt. "I hope this isn't a shortcut, because I'm still on the clock," he said.

She stopped in front of a set of dumpsters and he stumbled into her. "What did you say?"

The ferryman rubbed his forehead. "The deal was to accompany Af to his appointment downtown and then back to his prison. Just because he reverted to the angel of destruction and just because the apocalypse seems imminent doesn't mean I'm not going to charge him. Given the nature of my work, you can understand why I don't include a force majeure clause in my standard contract."

"*I'm* the force majeure." Kelly bored into him with her stare. "You'll charge half your rate."

"Yeah, yeah. Half."

The sky vacillated between TV-static gray and a glittering dark purple. A pudgy man on the corner screamed, "The Angel of the Abyss will be a contestant on the next season of *Cheesemasters: Pothole City*!"

The ferryman paused and Kelly pulled his arm. "False prophet. Probably. C'mon, we gotta go."

As they rounded the corner and passed by a department store, a massive shadow blocked what remained of the sun's light. A moment later, Af crashed through the roof of the department store building, shattering the centuries-old glass rotunda.

A Heavy Milkshake Snow Coated the Streets

Kelly pulled the ferryman through the nearest department store entrance, which led to an empty women's accessories section. Af's hulking figure rested by the cosmetics counter and a rack of women's hats. When he spotted her stalking toward him, he held out a claw. "Can I do anything for you?"

"Thank you, but no," she said.

He scooped up a pile of cosmetics from the destroyed counter and let them slide through his claws like pirate's treasure. "Pretty."

She waved a hand in front of his distracted black eyes. "Did you tell anyone about the ferryman loophole?"

The ferryman wrapped scarves around his head. "Is that all I am to you? A loophole?"

"Why don't you go over there"—she flicked her hand at a convenience store across the street—"and buy yourself a carbonated beverage. And Af? I'm not on a leisurely schedule. I have to find the SPs."

Af's attention skipped to hats on a rack. He selected a round straw resort hat with a wide brim and attempted to place it on his head, which required piercing the brim with one of his horns.

"No, I definitely did not tell anyone about the ferryman loophole." Af adjusted the hat until he destroyed the top. "Wait—um, no."

"No? Think hard," she said.

"Ah—"

"What?"

"I might have mentioned something in the pool area."

"And?"

"May I help you find anything?" A petite saleswoman approached them, unaware or uncaring that she was the only person left in the store. Her ink-pot hair, unevenly applied red lipstick, and ghastly pallor reminded her, unpleasantly, of her high school French teacher.

When she spotted Af, the woman put a hand to her throat and opened her mouth like a fish then retreated, thick heels clicking on the marble floor, skipping and skidding as she broke into a run.

Af unscrewed a bottle of blue nail polish. "I think I said something to Raum while we were using his espresso machine by the pool. And then again in the mail area."

She ignored the safety issue of plugged-in electronics by the pool. "Who is Raum?"

Af mumbled something unintelligible.

"What?"

Af cleared his throat, which to Kelly sounded like accidentally shifting the Ferrari back into first gear while going ninety miles an hour—something a car-stealing ghoul bounty did in Georgia while she chased him in a 1977 Corolla SR5.

"The angel of death and the prince of evil," Af murmured.

"I didn't quite get that. Raum is who again?"

Af flashed her a sheepish expression as he painted one of his claws with the nail polish. "The angel of death and the prince of evil. Also, the destroyer of cities."

"And at the time, you didn't think, 'perhaps I shouldn't inform the destroyer of cities about the loophole that lets me out of prison for *as long as I want?*'"

The ferryman ducked in between them like a vaudevillian, fedora in hand. "For as long as he can *afford*. Very important."

Kelly batted the hat out of the ferryman's hand, eyes fixed on Af.

Af painted the rest of his dinosaur-sized claws on one hand.

"Af, I'm in a hurry. Tell me exactly what you said. This was part of what I was hired to do. Even though I already resigned."

Af considered her over his bison-like shoulder. "You quit the job?"

"I haven't told Don yet, but that's what I've decided, because I recently suspected who his fugitive was."

Af planted a giant hand on the marble floor, which cracked all the way to the door.

"And I saw that he misrepresented you." She paused. "Tell me what you said to the prince of evil."

"I had some DVDs to return, so I was in the mail area," Af said, mentally retracing his steps. "I told Raum that I'd made an appointment and couldn't go to book club with him. Raum is very social; he needs to be around people. He likes company, as long as it's not human."

"That's it?" Kelly exhaled. "Maybe it's not that bad, then."

"No, it's just as bad, because that would have been enough for Raum to figure it out." Af wrapped a necklace around his tree-sized ankle.

"How?"

"He would have remembered our conversation by the pool, when I mentioned scheduling a dental procedure. He found it outrageous that I, an angel of destruction and prince of wrath, would undergo periodontal treatment. And he would have put the two comments together. Are you sure you're OK?"

"I'm fine."

The ferryman snorted and rolled his eyes. While not appearing to move at all, she pushed in the ferryman's knee from the back and he collapsed to the floor.

"When will you learn?" Af said to the ferryman, and admired the shiny bauble around his ankle in a low mirror. A moment later, he propelled himself up and out.

Kelly and the ferryman left the department store and walked into a snowfall. A delicious one. The ferryman raised his face to the sky and closed his eyes. When the snow fell on his face he tasted it. "Milkshake."

A heavy milkshake snow coated the streets and awnings. People stopped in their tracks and opened their mouths in ecstatic delight.

"Hard to think of a more effective way to subjugate everyone in Pothole City," she said. "No one fights or gets anything done because milkshakes are falling from the sky. Diabolical and brilliant."

The ferryman didn't respond. He, like everyone else, faced the sky.

Two people rushed out of an advertising agency building, brows furrowed. They opened their mouths and closed their eyes.

"Mark was right, it *is* milkshake!"

"But the TV and radio ads haven't run yet!" the other one said.

"Great. The best promotional idea I'm ever going to have," the first one said, "and I'm getting fired for it."

She turned to the ferryman. "No one's getting subjugated. Not on purpose, anyway. It's just a promotional stunt. C'mon, milkshake zombie. We're running the rest of the way."

Chapter Forty-Three

Removing This Coyote Requires a Permit

They headed to an intersection where the rusted-out elevated train tracks made a ninety-degree turn. "I can't reach Murray. I have to go to his place and see if he's there. Maybe he knows where Tubiel is." She bounced on the balls of her feet while glancing north, the direction of Murray's loft. "Decide right now if you're coming with me."

The ferryman nodded, eyes wide. Kelly paused outside of a Mexican restaurant as the packed commuter train labored around the curve.

Though it seemed to move in slow motion, the train howled and screeched at a deafening pitch. Dozens of interdimensional monsters pressed up against the doors and side windows, while others clung to the roof and sides of the train.

"Maybe they're leaving town," the ferryman said.

Af came out of nowhere and smashed down on the tracks, rendering them impossible for any train to use. He hopped to the ground, crushing newspaper boxes and a solar-powered miniature trash compactor, which she knew cost Pothole City five thousand dollars each.

"Just so you know," Af said to her, "I'm not actually trying to destroy the city. It's just hard to observe a safe turning radius when you look like me."

She chuckled. "If Pothole City gave you a bill for the building window, the bus, the glass rotunda, that marble floor, those newspaper stands, the solar-powered trash cans, and the elevated tracks, you'd have to cash in a lot of bearer bonds."

The ferryman made a zipping motion across his mouth to indicate that he wouldn't tell.

"I'll send a big I.O.U. to the mayor's office," Af said. "I'm just trying to protect you."

"Who me?" the ferryman said.

"Um, no." Af gave him a look.

"Maybe you could stay in the air? This guy's expensive enough without the collateral damage." She jerked her thumb at the ferryman.

"I provide a valuable service!"

She noticed a rhino-sized coyote roaming under the elevated tracks, with scales covering the hump of its back and two huge horns curling out of its brow. It raised its snout and snatched a pigeon that flew out of its roost under the scaffolding, crunched down and swallowed.

"Excuse me for one second." She held up a finger to the ferryman. "Do not go anywhere."

She reached into her pocket and took out her vial kit. The coyote took a break from its pigeon snack frenzy to lick itself. A man in olive green pants and shirt stopped in front of her, barring her path.

"Who are you?"

"I'm a wildlife biologist with the Natural Preserve District of Pothole City."

"Ooh, that's a good one." She noted his uniform and accessories.

"Were you about to apprehend this coyote?" the biologist asked.

"Are you serious?" She patted down her pockets. "Oops, forgot my coyote cuffs."

"Then what's that in your hand?"

"Cluck Snack Krispy Baked B'nana Bitz for Dogs and Ferrets. Want one?" She popped one in her mouth while holding on to the vial in her other hand.

"Uh, no. Now look, I don't know what your purpose is with this animal, but if a coyote gets in trouble, he is the property of Pothole City, just like all wildlife except for migratory birds."

"I know some folks who would take issue with that." She walked closer to the coyote, which had pigeon legs sticking out of its mouth.

"Removing this coyote requires a permit," the biologist said, raising his voice. The coyote looked displeased with the legs and spit them out.

"And a forklift." She wanted him to go away. Pothole City was falling apart and this park bureaucrat was bickering about his jurisdiction over a monster coyote.

She held out her left hand and pointed up with the right, above the biologist's head. "Look, an ivory-billed woodpecker!"

He whirled around and stared at the sky. It would take at least a minute for the biologist to determine it wasn't there, considering all the other creatures occupying the airspace. She held out the vial and the coyote funneled into it. By the time the biologist turned back around, the coyote was gone.

"What—where's the coyote?"

She shrugged. "It heard there were bigger pigeons down the street."

"Which way did it go?"

She gestured south, and the biologist ran off. A refrigerator-sized water bug hopped off the train, unable to resist a snack. It grabbed the biologist with its forelegs, sank its pointed beak into him, then guzzled up the liquid inside.

Kelly winced. She waited for the right moment then waved at the ferryman to follow. They sprinted across the street, and she took a second to swipe the biologist's badge.

"This could come in handy." She frowned at the dead man. "Sorry you didn't make it."

Chapter Forty-Four

I Still Have Nightmares About the Robo-Badgers

They ducked swooping creatures and falling debris the rest of the way north to Murray's apartment. Kelly pried open the door, scurried through, and shut it behind them.

"Hi." A youngish guy watching TV on the sofa raised a hand from a plastic bin of Cluck Snack P'nut Butt'r Chunks ("For Ferrets, Not Dogs") in a tentative wave.

"Hi?" he said again, as though they knew each other.

The ferryman started forward, but she stopped him with a forearm in the gut. "Oof."

She took stock of the loft, but everything looked intact, and aside from a general messiness that would have made Murray apoplectic, nothing was out of place or missing, indicating he hadn't been home.

"And who are you?"

"Uh, that's kind of hard to explain..."

She crossed her arms. "I'm kind of in a hurry and I'm losing my patience."

"I'm a friend of Murray's. In fact, I lived here for years until just recently." He picked up the snack bin and held it close to him as though for protection.

Only one thing made sense to her, though it didn't actually make sense at all. "You're not Stringfellow Hawk, are you?" This apocalypse was getting to her. There was no way that—

"Yes! I am! How did you know?"

He *was* Murray's pet that he lost. "You're the ferret?"

The ferryman held out a hand and frowned. "Wait, *whaaat?*"

"Wow, that saves me a lot of awkward explaining." Stringfellow collapsed back on the sofa, smiling.

"How?"

Stringfellow nodded. "It started back at the Conservation Center. Some old comrades of ours. Long story."

"The Conservation Center?"

"It's kind of a halfway house between captivity and reintroduction. I spent a few weeks there." He gazed off into the distance. "I still have nightmares about the robo-badgers."

Yvonne the cat wound around her ankles and she went to the kitchen to open a can of cat food. "How do you know Murray?" She filled Yvonne's bowls.

"Murray and I served together as deputies of the four o'clock a.m. hour. It was a tough schedule to maintain; it takes its toll on anyone, even angels. So when Murray got promoted to protector of bankers and traders, I switched over to protector of small animals: ferrets, hamsters, hedgehogs, things like that. I even had employees, if you can believe that."

The ferryman snuck into the kitchen behind her and looked in the cabinets. He selected a can of Cluck Snack Ravioleee ("Not for Ferrets or Cats") and opened it by the tab.

"But our supervisor was a vindictive jerk who took Murray's transfer as a personal affront," Stringfellow said. "He took it out on me and made some modifications to my paperwork that turned me into one of the animals I was supposed to be protecting. But I was lucky—real lucky—that Murray found out. He took me in and even got me all these ferret toys and snacks."

Stringfellow gestured to the cabinets that held the snacks, and at the tents and things around the sofa.

"Your supervisor," Kelly said in a dry tone. "He wouldn't happen to be a duplicitous agoraphobe named Don, would he?"

"Yeah, how did you know?" Stringfellow said.

"Lucky guess. By the way, that Ravioleee isn't for ferrets or cats."

"Oh," Stringfellow said.

The ferryman froze, fork at mouth. "Is it approved for ferrymen?"

She made an exasperated noise. "Does it say it's not for ferrymen? Then yes." She turned back to Stringfellow. "How did you turn back to this form?"

"My only guess is that Murray fixed it, even though I haven't seen him lately," Stringfellow said. He took the Ravioleee from the ferryman and tossed it in the tras, but the ferryman swooped in and caught it before it got there. "I guess he reversed whatever that jerk-off supervisor did. I should find another job now, though."

The ferryman shook some Cluck Snack P'nut Butt'r Chunks ("For Ferrets, Not Dogs") onto the Ravioleee and dug in with a fork.

Kelly went back into the center of the apartment. The ferryman followed her, then wandered around, stopping at the record cabinet.

"You haven't even spoken to him lately?"

Stringfellow shook his head. "I've been here like this"—he gestured at his body—"since last night. His voice mailbox is full."

"Yeah, I know." She opened the front door. "Well, good luck, and thanks for showing me the pellet." She hesitated. "Why *did* you show me the pellet, if Murray's been so good to you?"

Stringfellow ate another handful of P'nut Butt'r Chunks, chewed them for a while, and cleared his throat. "I saw some things around the apartment." He swung out his arm. "Things that made it clear Murray was not on your side. I just thought you should know, and the pellet was the best method I could find for getting the message across. Also, I'm no fan of Don's."

The ferryman rifled through the cabinet of record albums, perplexed. "What the—? They're all the same!"

"You must be relieved," she said. "To not be a ferret anymore."

"Aw, heck. Being a ferret wasn't bad. It was fun to be that small.

Everything was a toy, you know? Something to play with. And for some reason, I needed a lot of toys, not to mention a lot of grooming aids. I was like a little miss ferret pageant contestant."

"Welcome back, anyway."

Chapter Forty-Five

10% Off Any Ferrying Service

In another alley, a few blocks from Murray's apartment, a rat the size of an otter scampered over the ferryman's shoe and left a present. The ferryman shrieked and kicked his foot back and forth. "I can't do this anymore. I'm out."

"There's been a lot of that lately." Kelly hoisted her bag to a different place on her back.

"But don't worry," the ferryman added. "As we agreed earlier, I'm not going to charge Af for the trip back. And here's a coupon for 10% off any ferrying service, including concierge."

With that said, the ferryman saluted and popped out of the world.

"No one says thank you." She flapped the card back and forth on her hand.

The electric lavender of the sky rolled into bright blue and progressed toward Dijon mustard yellow as bolts of lightning flashed. She didn't hear buses or cars screeching to stops or crashing into newspaper boxes. She didn't hear anything except rumbling thunder and the furtive scrambling of rats.

Kelly pictured Tubiel and Kermit and the rest of the SPs and ran to the mouth of the alley.

Pothole City exceeded the promise of its name. Giant potholes and ruts in the pavement radiated out from huge, broken-off chunks of Pothole City's buildings, blocking her off.

She sat on one of the chunks and pictured Jay Vanner sitting on the granite blocks across from her, wavy hair askew in the wind, crow's feet crinkling around his wise, squinting eyes. He would tell her, "Kelly, you need to separate yourself, mentally and physically, from this adverse situation. If you can't change things to your liking, just send the reminders of the past on their way."

She pictured all of the thoughts and images in her head as paper origami. She tossed them into a fireplace, doused them with lighter fluid, and flicked a lit match onto the pile.

With that taken care of, she squeezed between the intricately carved signature of a haberdasher's office and the granite snout of a gargoyle. The stone scratched her shoulder and one of the gargoyle's teeth hooked her bag.

When she got out, she found only an obliterated expanse of slash-and-burn landscape, with a strange glowing box right in the middle.

A lone taxicab drove down the four-lane street. She recognized the realtor advertised on the cab's topper: *Untraditional Spaces for Untraditional Clients. We Go to Heaven and Back to Help You Sell Your Condo.*

The glowing box looked like a vending machine. She headed toward it, crunching debris under her sneakers. The wind roared viciously, carrying a gritty smoke in its wake that stung her eye.

A colorful and brightly-lit Cluck Snack-branded machine stood alone in a bleak landscape, and she trudged toward it.

It didn't have a bill acceptor or any other way to pay for the merchandise. She shook it. Nothing happened.

The vast majority of the SPs were missing, and she suspected they were being held in Amenity Tower, but she needed one with her to consult.

She stepped back from the machine and thought about how this kind of thing worked. Something occurred to her to try, but she didn't expect it to work. "Oh no, my small bird is missing. What if I never see it again? How can I get it back? Gosh, I wish there were an angel who—"

Tubiel popped into the space next to her, wearing the clothes he was wearing when she first met him.

"That actually worked?"

Tubiel smiled, but she was furious.

"Then why did I have to drive you all over downtown Pothole City to return those birds if you could just pop in like this?"

He shrugged. She let out a long breath. Murray must have manipulated it that way, must have wanted her distracted then. Why? What was he doing that he wanted to get her out of the way?

She slapped her palm on the machine. "Can you operate this snack emissary that flew in from planet Cluck Snack?"

Tubiel touched the window and the machine glowed brighter. One of the metal coils extended and a snack dropped to the tray. Tubiel reached in and pulled out a Cluck Snack Drinkable Cake Flav'r Pudd'n Pack ("Not for Hamsters or Dogs"). He split up the pack, giving one container to her and keeping the rest for himself.

"Now what?" she asked.

Tubiel shrugged. He pushed the straw in the foil opening and drank the Cake Flav'r Pudd'n, and she did the same.

"Are the others with you?"

Tubiel nodded.

"Are they OK?"

Tubiel took out his sketch pad and wrote something on it.

"They're playing ping-pong?" Kelly said. Tubiel held up some fingers. "Some of them are. Then where are the rest of the SPs?"

He shrugged and made a face that said, 'I wish I knew,' then waved an arm around them to indicate the others were scattered.

She peered into the machine. "Can I get the Cluck Snack Pizza Gum?"

Tubiel put his fingertips on the machine. It pulsed and ejected the gum with a short electronic melody.

"Help me drag this machine back to Amenity Tower."

He turned back, took hold of the machine, which his arms barely got around, and pulled, to no avail.

"Just kidding, Tube."

He let go and smiled. "I'll be at Amenity Tower in a few minutes. I'll find the others."

He tapped the glass on the machine and something dropped into the bin.

Kelly retrieved the item and examined it. "Cluck Snack Meal'n a Box Totez—Take Your Cluck Snack With You'). This is exactly what I need."

Chapter Forty-Six

Just This Morning I Gave Someone Directions

On the roof of Amenity Tower, the wind gusted to near- jet blast force and the emergency warning siren whooped continuously. Kelly cursed Pothole City as she verified her rappelling tools and ropes were still under the window washing rails.

An angel with glossy blue wings alighted on the corner of the roof and said, "Oh, sorry. Thought you were someone else." He took off again, staying close to the building.

A creature with a wasp body and the head of a seal flew at her, barking. It snapped at her head and circled back around, jaws wide open. With a fast draw, she let her knife fly, and the seal-wasp dropped with a soft crunch in a mound of snow. She pulled her knife from the creature and wiped it off in the milkshake snow, scooping up a ball of it to eat.

"I really have to close that air handler," she muttered.

"You always had great aim," a voice said behind her. "You could try that on me, but both of us know it wouldn't work."

She raised the knife again at her shoulder and with a gentle flick of the wrist and sent it flying, a strip of orange tape trailing off the handle. It landed in his chest, right where his heart should have been. He smiled fondly at her, pulled the knife out of his chest with a sucking sound, and wiped the knife off in the snow.

"I know how you are about your weapons." He tossed the clean-ish knife to the ground between them. "Fastidious." He took a step toward her.

"Don't come any closer."

He put his hands out. "I'm not the demon you think I am. Just this morning I gave someone directions."

Incredulous, she said, "You burned down my house with my family inside, you demented vulture."

The bald man put his hands in his pockets. His tie flapped in the wind like a salmon spawning upstream. "Isn't it funny that I found you here, instead of the other way around? You caught up to me so many times. You were so ambitious, so focused—even as a child."

"My mother was great at her job. The best." She was annoyed with herself for being flattered and wanting to hear more, even from the angel she had been trying to kill for almost twenty years.

The bald man gave her a strange look. "She did big jobs—museums, high-end jewelry stores—but did her own canning and sewing. Where do you think all that money went?"

The wind howled.

Kelly tucked a piece of hair under her wool cap so a strand would stop whipping her in the eye. She had looked, but never found it. "I have no idea. Now stand still so I can kill you again. Or run. It doesn't matter."

"You probably see this is as one-sided relationship," he said. "I mean, you've been finding and killing me over and over for years. I propose that we move from the provisional acceptance of a de facto recognition to the formal ties of a de jure recognition."

"You don't have a provisional acceptance from me."

"You didn't return the gift basket I sent," the bald man said. "That was consideration you accepted. Wouldn't that be provisional acceptance?"

"No, because I gave it to a bear."

"Do you know what else?"

"I'm going to push you off the building?"

"That's posturing. Your heart's not in it anymore." He walked towards her at the pace of an uncurling fern crozier. "You did your duty to your mother and that thieves den of an ad hoc family, what, a hundred times? It's just your bad luck that I can't be killed, and that you've been after the wrong angel all this time. Ironic, considering your chosen career."

Kelly sat on the building's davit.

"You know it wasn't me, don't you?" The bald man asked quietly. He waited a moment. "Is this how you want to spend your life? Alone and preoccupied with the past?"

She opened a snack packet of nuts and popped some cashews in her mouth. "Maybe."

"Isn't it enough that you've devoted decades to avenging her? You're like a machine that's programmed to repeat the same task. When you've finished the task, you shut down. Am I close?"

"You're close to getting pushed off this building."

"I like you, Driscoll. You've lost yourself along the way, but you keep working, and that's something. When you were that girl of ten, you put any so-called avenging angel to shame. The rod of God couldn't have done any better than you. I mean that.

"Then," he said, "over the years, as you've tracked me down and attempted in vain to end my life, I couldn't help but notice that you got perfunctory and detached. Maybe it was that Mennonite Butler job. That must've been a real kick in the area."

"Speaking of detached—"

"Yeah, I know, that's what my head is going to be, right?" He laughed. "Love it."

"I'm so glad." She drew her second knife and realized he was closer than before.

"I'm the closest relationship you've got, Driscoll, so if I get nosy about your non-existent personal life, I think that's understandable."

"We don't have a relationship," she said, disgusted.

"Again, what about the gift baskets I sent you? The one with the scorpion fish, sacks of flour, and the Sig Sauer P229?"

"Yes," she said. "I got that one. And the Cheeses of the Midwest and the Candy of the Ottoman Empire. Don't send me any more."

"I already sent the crab variety pack."

"The what?"

"It's a medley of orangutan, porcelain, and boxer crabs. With a pound of coffee beans."

"Fine, but one more gift basket doesn't mean we have any kind of relationship, or that I agree to stop killing you."

He put his hands up in a complaisant gesture. "If you say so. But Driscoll, after all those times you stabbed me, blew me up in my car using common baking materials, strangled me in a matinee, and poisoned my bowl of pasta with death cap mushrooms, I almost feel like we're friends. Maybe one day," he said, looking almost plaintive, "we could be. But I'll always be your guardian. Unless you want to submit the paperwork to replace me—"

"My *what*?"

The bald man put his hands on his knees. "Your guardian. I'm a watcher. One of *Those Who Are Awake?*" When he didn't get a response, he added in a tired voice, "I'm bound to this form for seventy generations. And feeling every single one."

She got in his face, inches from him. "You're telling me that you're my guardian angel?"

"Yes. And that's why I was there that day, in the gas station."

She put up a hand. "You want to lay this on me now? Today? Wow, you are the worst guardian angel ever. You say you didn't set that fire, but then you just sat in a gas station watching possums become roadkill while I lost everything. I hope that pre-wrapped turkey sandwich at least gave you Norovirus."

"There was nothing I could do."

"So what if you didn't strike the match? You didn't help. What's the point of you?" She turned to leave, resenting the unexpected burden of knowing that she had tried to kill her guardian angel dozens of times since age ten. More weight to carry, on top of everything else. And whoever torched the house and her family was still out there.

"And no more gift baskets," she yelled. He hadn't helped her. He hadn't even tried to tell her the truth until now. Had he?

She thought that Jay Vanner would say she was a pathetic human being who had failed in every possible way.

As she started back to the building, a man screamed from the roof of the hotel next to Amenity Tower, his hands forming a megaphone around his mouth. "The four diabolical angels are escaping from their hellish abyssal prison! End times are imminent!"

The bald man made a call, guarding the mouthpiece from the sound of the wind.

"Hello, Pancakes Plus? I need to cancel an order." He took out his wallet, flipped over several plastic-covered photos of Kelly and her mother, and read off the last few digits from his credit card.

Chapter Forty-Seven

His Carefree Life Would be Bludgeoned by This Assignment

Kelly's family had celebrated her tenth birthday and the successful heist of a diamond necklace on the same day. Their cabin, nestled deep in the Allegheny forest, was raucous with drunk thieves and sugar-pumped fifth-graders.

The handmade cherry-wood dining table was slick with fruit punch and bourbon, slammed enthusiastically in jelly glasses to punctuate a frequent toast. At the center of the table sat Kelly's gigantic cake.

While her quasi-friends swarmed upon a pinata in the corner like a vigilante mob, ballad-singing thieves held her up under their arms and passed her from person to person. They spent the night playing guitars, singing and drinking, and the next morning, her mother made her eggs, then returned to bed before she went off tracking.

Three miles into the forest, she stopped at a tree and dropped her pack, almost certain she had forgotten her compass. A moment later, while rummaging through her pack, she smelled the smoke. She ran to get to the cabin, but it burned in big swooping, crackling waves of flames.

She tied a bandana around her face and ran as close to the cabin as she could, but struggled to breathe, and staggered back. She ran to the cover of trees and fell into the leaves. Her vision narrowed, colored dots in a splotch of dark, and lost consciousness.

Just when she despaired of finding any sign of who had been there to start the fire, she found a man's boot print masked under leaves.

The top sign pointers above the ankle were contradictory, which meant that someone was here within the last twenty-four hours and bent the tall grass, indicating a different direction of travel.

She sketched it in her notebook and wrote "first footprint" above it, along with the date, time, terrain, and weather, then studied the leaves around the print, picking up every single one before examining the soil itself, noticing a transfer—an insect wedged in the nubs of the boot and one not commonly seen in that part of the forest.

A few twigs next to the print, a few of them green, had been snapped recently. A faint smell of sap told her that her quarry had been to the cabin not more than four hours ago.

To find her quarry, she followed the underside of leaves, broken twigs, scuffed logs, moist worms and soil, ants, rotting trees, bruised roots, and a strange etched pellet under pine needles.

A broken cobweb got her pulse racing. It was a sign that could tell her how far away he was and when he had passed through. She took four careful steps toward the web that broke at her quarry's head.

She stood alone in the forest, listening, glasses held at her side.

At a paved road, she reassessed. At other times, she would have to tune in all over again to this change in location, but she felt confident enough to isolate the track and move ahead. Across the two-lane road was an old gas station with a logging truck parked by the orange sign.

A food counter faced the road. One man, probably an employee, walked inside; not him A second man, probably the driver of the truck, selected food from a rack, but wasn't the right height and weight.

A third man—tall and stocky and bald—sat at the counter, wearing a windbreaker over a turtleneck.

She zoomed in on the entrance of the gas station. Sliding prints in the dust indicated that someone, maybe her quarry, was too tired to pick up his shoes high enough.

As she looked through the binoculars, the light changed. The air smelled of ozone, something metallic. The clear post-dawn light around the gas station darkened and turned into the midnight blue and soft pink and yellow of a Hubble photo.

The colors swirled over the gas station, the midnight blue turned even darker, and with a start, she remembered her quarry and crossed the empty road to the gas station.

When she sat on the swivel stool next to him, the bald man jumped a little.

"You look like you just crawled out from under a log." He picked a leaf out of her hair and she slapped his hand away. Her weird light gray eyes, ringed with black and set in a face caked with dirt and soot, reminded him, for some reason, of a moth with deceptive eyes on its wings.

"You killed my mother."

The bald man sighed.

"I followed you here."

He almost laughed. That cabin was so far back in that huge forest it might as well be in the center of the earth. He drove out, quite some time ago.

Faster than even he perceived, she withdrew a hunting knife from across her back and thrust it cleanly, masterfully, into his heart.

He cleared his throat. For the moment, he left the knife in his body, because it looked badass. To impress her a little more, he took a bite of his sandwich and chewed contemplatively.

"That should've killed you." She shook her head in disappointment.

"I can't be killed." He plucked a napkin from the dispenser and dabbed at his mouth.

"Why not?"

"Because I just can't."

"I'll figure a way."

"Maybe you'd be doing me a favor."

"Don't care. I'm gonna follow you and figure out a way. Rest of my life, that's what it takes."

"Like I told you, I really cannot be killed."

She thought about this. "The next best thing, then."

"You're too late." He put money on the counter. "I'm being punished enough."

"Meantime, I'll be watching. Then I'll sneak up on you and you won't know when."

The bald man rubbed the hollow of his temple with a fingertip. His carefree life would be bludgeoned by this assignment, and on top of that, he had to be the fall guy. But with what he supposed was a masochistic mindset, he also kind of looked forward to it.

Chapter Forty-Eight

You Can Get Ladybugs by Mail

Raum, Forcas, Crocell, and Gaap huddled in the dumpster.

Forcas gagged. "This is a bad, bad idea."

Crocell pushed Gaap. "Would you fold up your wings, please?"

Gaap groaned. "I'm in some gastrointestinal distress."

"Why do I let you talk us into this stuff, Raum?" Forcas said.

"Shh!" Raum said. "This is going to work. This is the loophole. The *only* loophole. And once the garbage truck shows up, which it will probably do sometime in the next six hours, we'll be free. First thing we do is destroy this building. The quality of life has really gone downhill with these monsters rubbing their mucous cocoons against everything. Then we can level the city, destroy the rest of the humans, and spread out from there, to all cities, all humans. This world will be ours."

Gaap yanked one of his wings from under Forcas. "Hey, get off my wing!" He examined his wing for damage. "Listen, Raum, I don't know about this plan."

"It's too late. The plan is in motion," Raum said.

"Being bound here isn't so bad," Gaap said. "We've got an indoor lap pool, a fitness center, a diligent maintenance team—"

"You should have seen Dragomir with my dishwasher last week,"

Crocell said. "He took it apart and put it back together in under an hour. Very impressive."

"Yes, he's a wonder." Raum clapped his hands together. "All righty. Everyone get on their game and remember what you are. We may have lost our grace, but who needs it? It was only holding us back."

"Being bound here is holding us back," Forcas said.

"Shut up, Forcas," Raum said. "Being *bound* is holding us back."

Forcas made eye contact with the others and expressed incredulous frustration. "Isn't that what I just said?"

Raum continued as though he hadn't noticed. "Now, the truck is going to pick up the dumpster and hold it upside down." He shined a laser pointer at a drawing of a dump truck and a bin. "Do not be alarmed. We're going to fall into the garbage truck, which will drive away from the building and out of the radius—and then we'll be free."

"Dammit, I forgot to pick up the mail today," Crocell said.

"So?" Forcas said.

"I ordered a box of 1000 ladybugs," Crocell said.

"Why?" Raum said.

"Why not? "

Raum was silent. "Anyway, who cares about the mail? In just a few minutes, we'll be powerful again! Why are you thinking about insignificant human matters?"

"Because you can get ladybugs by mail. What a world! Also because I'm in this human vessel and can't help it," Crocell said.

"Oh, please," Raum said. "You're bigger than that!"

"I was," Crocell said. "Now I'm someone who gets unreasonable enjoyment from picking up the mail and from the holiday decorations that just magically appear in the lobby."

"Now we wait," Raum said. "The garbage truck should be here anytime now."

Chapter Forty-Nine

She Turned on the Revolving Chicken Head

Kelly checked the real-time feed for the Cluck Snack street van. The van was close, only five blocks away. She grabbed her bike and rode standing, careening around dazed and despondent traders, bankers, and professors until she came to a smoking halt, scattering a queue of customers at the Cluck Snack counter window.

The whatever-it-was in the chicken costume clucked in surprise and consternation as she opened the back panels of the van.

She tossed in her bike. "I am commandeering this vehicle pursuant to section 9-302-020 of the Pothole City Municipal Code." She put her hands against the feathery back of the chicken and gently pushed him out the door until he hopped onto the street.

With a curt "Sorry" to the murmuring would-be customers, she sat in the driver's seat of the van and examined the controls. The pedals and clutch were much farther up than normal, so she slid the seat back as far as it would go and felt around for the gearshift, which wasn't in the center console or to the side of the steering column.

"Where—?"

Eventually she found the gearshift, which resembled an old Simon game. She pressed the green triangle and peeled out.

At the first light, she turned on the revolving clucking chicken head on top of the van. That didn't seem official enough, so she clicked on the flashing lights, too.

If the Cluck Snack street van didn't bring the SPs out of hiding, nothing would.

Kelly wove the van around large debris in the street, at one point hopping a tire up on the curb to get between a fat, naked, screaming man and a deserted city bus. Lightning stabbed down from a shimmering red and silver sky. Thunder rumbled, reminding her of Af's angel form.

She headed east on a relatively uncrowded street, closer to Amenity Tower and her apartment, hoping the stray SPs would hear the Cluck Snack jingle and come running. Two of them did, by the library with a crash-landed airplane on it. Moments later, the two SPs contentedly nibbled Cluck Snack Krispy Baked B'nana Bitz for Dogs and Ferrets.

Then more SPs came, entranced by the siren call of Cluck Snack.

"Is that everyone?" She craned her head and looked behind her. "Wait, where are Mefathiel and Zack?"

Rochel drew a map on a paper menu, showed the map to the others, who nodded in approval, then handed it to Kelly. She turned the map upside down, then to the side... and back up. With a sigh, she slapped it on the wide dashboard.

"Why would Zack be—OK, let's try it."

Iggy and Tigg, long-suffering and often bored angels of the future, glared at each other across identical desks in a modest office in what was once the third-tallest building in Pothole City.

Iggy cleared his throat. He held up a picture of a death worm in a fruit peddler costume. He shook it and the paper rippled. Tigg cocked his head, opened a drawer, and presented a photo of the SPs in an RV.

Iggy scoffed. He slid a photo of Murray over to the other desk and smirked. Tigg crumpled up a piece of paper and threw it at Iggy, who smoothed out the paper, a photo of Af in jail.

Zack, the missing SP, padded over to Tigg and whispered something in his ear. Tigg grinned, and Iggy stood, his chair clattering to the floor.

By the time Kelly arrived at the office of the angels of the future, papers were fluttering down to the floor and the water cooler was spewing filtered water on an acrylic painting of a lighthouse.

The angels of the future turned to look at her. Correction liquid dripped off Tigg's hair.

"Don't tell me I have to find all of your pencils."

Zack ran over to her and clutched the side of her pants. Tigg shook his head, spattering droplets of corrector fluid on his dark wood desk.

"Thanks for watching him," she said, to neither angel in particular.

Zack proudly held up a purple and yellow device.

"And for the, uh, label-maker," she added.

Tigg shot a withering look at Iggy.

Zack pressed some buttons and the device whirred. He handed Kelly a small white label. "Cluck," she read. She peeled off the label and stuck it on the back of her hand.

Chapter Fifty

Is That the Empanada Truck?

As they left the two agitated angels, Kelly knew she would have labels stuck all over her by the end of the day, and made a mental note to tell Zack he shouldn't wander into random offices.

A line had formed at the Cluck Snack van.

When she got close enough for the people to hear her, she pronounced, "This is an official vehicle of the Pothole City Division of Infectious Disease. If you're here as a volunteer tester for a new strain of a viral hemorrhagic fever that we're investigating, then please stay in line to receive your synthetic dosage."

The line cleared out in seconds and Kelly and Zack got in the van. She sat on the center console, facing the SPs.

"Now that I have you rounded up, I want to talk strategy. Since you've been off your posts, the city has pretty much fallen apart. The bound angels in Amenity Tower are planning to escape today, and the king of the demonic locusts is unhappy with my job performance. But most important, you're all in danger."

Tubiel scribbled on his sketch pad and held up a drawing of a small bird with big eyes and an open beak.

"That's an irrelevant objective. But an adorable one."

Tubiel smiled. Kermit held up a sketch of a clock.

"We need to define our objectives more closely."

Dave held up his drawing, a water insect, and pumped his fist in the air.

"I love water insects as much as anyone, but let's not use past experiences as a crutch."

Morris showed his drawing of a series of ducts and equipment.

"And that seems like a private objective."

They watched her expectantly. She held out her hand and made a beckoning gesture. The SPs handed her their drawings and she shuffled through the papers.

"You're right," she said. "And I didn't see it. We use your talents to get into that building and stop the bound angels from getting out." She thought about it for a minute. "OK, listen up. We're going to do a Key Hole recon patrol—hey, wait, is that the empanada truck?"

She stood in a half-crouch and tucked the keys in her pocket. "I'll be right back. Some of us can't live on Cluck Snacks alone."

When she turned the corner with a bagful of hot baked empanadas, the Cluck Snack van was gone.

"Motherclucker," she said, and ran to Amenity Tower, eating a spinach empanada on the way.

Chapter Fifty-One

Apparently, Your Ferret is Also a Notary Public

W***hat's On Your Mind, With Roger Balbi*** **was in** session in the management office's studio.

On the monitor in the reception area, Kelly watched a woman with red hair and a manic look in her eyes hold a squawking goose on her lap. The goose quacked and flapped its wings, while snapping its beak in Roger's direction.

"Shamanically speaking, Roger—" the woman started to say.

Roger abruptly turned to the camera and spoke over her. "We've got some surprise guests for you today, so just bear with me for a moment. We'll be right back."

He waved frantically at Kelly to come into the studio and ushered the woman off her chair and out the studio door.

The woman sideswiped her with her ample chest and jammed a piece of paper down her shirt.

Kelly fished the card out from her shirt. "Shamanic and Psychic Animal Services," she read. "Specializing in Fowl. This card good for 15% off any thirty-minute session."

She ripped up the card and stuffed the bits in her pocket as she entered the studio. They could take their ferrying and shamanic services and cram them in their—

"Let's get started," Roger said, all business.

Feeling violated, she took one of the seats in front of the camera. "This isn't a good idea."

Roger gave her an encouraging, close-lipped smile, eyes crinkling at the sides. "Just be yourself." He checked his Databank watch.

"You don't want that. Isn't there someone else for you to interview?" she said through clenched teeth.

"Of course there is," Roger said. "I have to turn down guests all the time. But I get the impression that you and my surprise second guest have a few things to sort out."

"Surprise second guest?"

"Here's a hint: he protects bankers and traders."

"Murray." Her tone was bone dry.

"Yep."

She gave Roger a cutting stare. "If we did have anything to sort out, it would not be on your show."

"Why not?" Roger held up his palms. "*What's On Your Mind, With Roger Balbi* is a good show. It's won the *Conseil d'Administration* Award from the French-American Building Manager's Association, Pothole City Chapter, for three consecutive years. It also won the Trailblazer Award, presented by the Amenity Tower Community Committee, this year *and* last year."

"Impressive, but any sorting out Murray and I have to do will be done in private."

They looked up at a knock on the door. Murray leaned in with a piece of paper. "Is this the studio? I received this invitation." He blinked in surprise at Kelly. "What are you doing here?"

Roger led Murray into the other chair, then straightened his tie and performed a few bizarre vocal warm-ups. His camera operator raised a forearm and held it straight up. A moment later, the operator brought his arm down to point at Roger.

"From Amenity Tower in Pothole City, this is *What's On Your Mind, With Roger Balbi*, on local access channel nine. I'm Roger Balbi.

"*What's On Your Mind, With Roger Balbi* is brought to you by Clucking

Along Holdings, Inc., the makers of Cluck Snacks. '14 Million Chickens Can't Be Wrong.'

"Today, we're proud to feature the band *Hot Room of Miscellaneous*. We're also going to play some Rock Paper Scissors with a speleologist vs. a serologist, give Dragomir the Turkle test, and build a cloud chamber. But first, I'm thrilled to have with us today two very special guests: Kelly Driscoll, vampire hunter, and—"

"I'm not a vampire hunter, Roger."

"And Murray, who's in charge of the protection of bankers and traders."

"Oh, you should think about that," the camera operator said to Kelly, peeking around the camera body. "My cousin's fiancée just got her vampire hunting certificate from that online school on late-night TV, and she's raking it in—they just bought a new house in Crisis City with an infinity pool and wine cellar."

"Owen," Roger said, with a smile and a tone that said, 'I'm going to fire you and you'll miss out on Secret Santa.' "We're live. I'm sure our guests don't need any advice from us."

Roger turned back to her. "We've established that you are *not* a vampire hunter. I'd like you to tell our audience a little about yourself. You work as a—" He raised a brow to prompt her.

"Squirrel expert."

"Right, right. Well, tell us something we don't know about squirrels."

"Sure, Roger." She straightened in the chair and twined her fingers. "Squirrels can be charming and ingratiating, but they're much more deceptive than you might think. For example, a squirrel will dig a hole, pretend to push an acorn in that hole, and then cover the hole while keeping the seed hidden in its mouth.

"They call this behavior"—she turned her head to look steadily at Murray—"'deceptive caching,' which could be considered tactical deception. It was previously thought to occur only in primates."

Roger nodded enthusiastically. "Fascinating."

Murray shifted in his seat. His body signaled it was ready for flight.

"Isn't it?"

"And Murray. Tell the audience about what you do."

Murray opened his mouth then closed it again. "Uh."

Roger smiled. "Take your time. Working memory is a limited resource."

Murray squinted at Roger, and settled into his chair. "I wish I could say that I have an exciting job like Kelly's, but I have a very boring mid-level corporate position. If I elaborated, your eyes would glaze over."

She snorted.

"Kelly, you have a comment?" Roger asked, momentarily distracted by the residents gathering outside the studio window and inside the door.

"Hell yes I have a comment," she said. "This betrayer killed my mother, burned down our house, and took my family from me, all before I turned eleven. He then employed me under false pretenses and pretended to be my colleague and my friend." She paused, glancing at the audience of residents. "And he killed his own kind."

The residents gasped, cawed, and hissed, depending on their form. Something blue splattered on the studio window.

Roger looked down as though to focus his thoughts, then at the camera, then at Kelly. "You are familiar with Amenity Tower, yes?"

"I've worked undercover in Amenity Tower for several days now, as a window washer, an elevator inspector, and a grief counselor. I've also been here as an FDA Criminal Investigations agent, and as a member of the Fugitive Apprehension Task Force."

Roger intertwined his hands and tilted his head like Charlie Rose. "And what were you looking for?"

"I was looking for a red herring, when my real target was working alongside me the whole time."

A flame-colored dragonfly buzzed under the studio door, popped out to three times its size, and took a chunk out of Murray's arm before flitting out again.

"*Ow*! What the hell!"

Kelly stifled a laugh.

"What's your response to that, Murray?" Roger asked, fingertips together at his chin.

"It hurt, obviously. I think I need stitches."

"No, your response to what Kelly said."

"Completely untrue and unprovable." Murray casually leaned back in his chair, but his face took on a pallor unaided by the brown suit.

She took some papers from her bag. "I have an employment contract, signed by you. It says that Murray, the employee—and here's an attached head shot of you—'will release, indemnify and hold harmless the employer, his supervisors and co-workers from any liability arising from employee's actions in the performance of his job, regardless of whether said actions were requested specifically by the employer.'"

The crowd of residents, both in the studio and watching in the reception area, listened attentively as she piled on the accusations. A few of them hissed and booed at Murray. Tom the water scorpion brought up his ukulele to play a quick instrumental song for the onlookers, while an Enim giant tapped pensively on a bowl containing a fighting fish.

"'These actions," she continued, "include: locating and eliminating all members of the Driscoll family, viz. Anne Driscoll, daughter Kelly Driscoll, and Anne Driscoll's work associates; sabotaging the manufacturing and distribution of Cluck Snack products; kidnapping, starving, or otherwise eradicating all single-purpose angels in Pothole City; golf caddying; plant watering; technical support; and Pothole City tax auction attendance in my stead.'"

The residents looked at one another and murmured. Murray wiped the sweat off his forehead with his sleeve then locked his hands together in his lap.

"'Pursuant to this contract," she continued, "you certify, as the employee, that you will not hold anyone else liable for any harm resulting from the performance of your duties, i.e., the immolation of the Driscoll cabin at the end of Rural Route 3 in the Allegheny Forest and the confirmed death of all residents.'"

Roger recoiled, eyes wide, and shook his head at Murray.

Kelly held the contract at the top and showed it to Murray. "The contract is notarized in blood with a paw print. Apparently your ferret"—Kelly raised a hand—"Excuse me: former ferret, Stringfellow

Hawk—is also a notary public. I compared the prints."

"That doesn't necessarily incriminate me." Murray rubbed his nose. "I could have passed the job to a colleague. There's nothing to prove I actually did it myself."

Roger leaned forward. "It kinda does incriminate you, Murray."

"I also have"—she pulled out more papers from her bag—"a reimbursement form for a rental car and two nights in the Allegheny Forest Furry Friends Lodge that correspond to the dates of my mother's death.

"Additionally, I have an Employee of the Month award for you, signed by Don. There's also a photo of you and the telepresence robot, and a handwritten note that reads 'Murray, thanks for your great work on the Driscoll job, sincerely Don.'"

Murray scratched his head. "We might have had other work to do there. Natural gas drilling. Taxidermy. Meat curing."

She pulled out a glossy 8x10 photo. "Here is a photo of you, posing with a whitetail buck you killed—accidentally, I want to point out—with our cabin on fire in the background." She pointed. "There."

Roger took the photo from her, glanced at it, then gave Murray a look of disappointment.

"Where did you get this?" Murray's face reddened.

"Don's hell lodge. And finally, I have something I found in your apartment." She rolled the pellet between two fingertips.

Murray gaped. "What—How—Where did you get *that*?"

Kelly smirked. "Your notary public."

"Murray," Roger asked, with the serious tone of Charlie Rose interviewing a high-profile dictator, "Kelly mentioned you killed one of your own, too. How did you manage that?"

"Mikriel," she said. "His favorite food was Cluck Snack Sweet n' Savory Breakfast Syrup."

Murray looked at the residents, pressing their faces against the studio window.

He stared at his shiny oxfords.

"*Grace Zabriskie Sings the Ferret Hits*," he said after a protracted silence.

She came to a horrified realization. "All those record albums."

Murray nodded. "There's a hidden track at the end of the record. Only one of them was ever produced that way. I bought as many as I could find over the years. Hundreds of them." He met Roger's eyes as though unable to look away. "Until I found it."

Roger gestured at him to continue.

"I invited Mikriel over to my loft to fix my record player."

She rested her elbows on her knees and covered her face with her hands.

"Why Mikriel?" Roger asked.

"He's—he was in charge of audio equipment," Murray said. "He came over. I played the record. He leaned in with his stethoscope. Then the hidden track played, at 179,000 Hz. Mikriel started to vibrate, and then—he dissolved."

Kelly got up and paced around the studio, hand over her mouth.

"I felt terrible." Murray stood. "I haven't been able to sleep. I've lost my appetite. My work performance has degraded. I lost three traders."

She lunged at Murray. He tried to run out of the studio, but an impassable and encroaching wall of bound angels, interdimensional monsters, and a giantpicked him up and took him down the hall.

Roger sighed and tilted his head at the reception office. "They'll take care of Murray. Don't worry—I've trained them to maim, not kill."

Roger turned to the camera with a wide smile. "And that's our show. Tune in next week for our special guest, a resident of the twenty-first floor and the person responsible for his company's edible decorations. Please join us again."

Roger handed the microphone to his assistant. "And that's a wrap. Kelly, thanks for being on the show. I hope you get the revenge you deserve."

"Thanks, Roger."

Chapter Fifty-Two

AngelRoute Pro

Roger, I need to use your computer."

Kelly went with Roger from the studio into his office.

"Do you need to check your email? Isn't that what the business center is for?"

"I have to use your specialized software."

"Here, I'll log in for you."

"No need." She quickly typed in the username and password.

"What the hell?" Roger put his hands on his hips.

"I might have been here before. And it really wasn't hard to figure out." She opened a software application called AngelRoute Pro, went to the toolbar, and chose 'View History' from the menu.

"Don hates to work," she said. "Normally, someone in his position would be in charge of assigning bound angels to their respective prisons. But in order to route hundreds of bound angels to different prisons, you have to fill out a lot of paperwork. When I saw how much dust was covering the piles on Don's desk, I realized what he had done."

She typed for a moment, focusing on the screen.

"The way Don arranged it, instead of having to fill out hundreds of individual forms, and setting the route for each individual prison, there would be just one form for all bound angels."

"A route that led to my building," Roger said.

"Yep." She stared intently at the screen. A moment later, she said, "This part is..." her brow tightened with a vertical furrow. "Delicate."

She cross-checked the routes to the building with the list she made from the paperwork. "Here's the problem."

"There's a problem?" Roger put his hands on the desk.

"Ideally, the modifications I'm making will reassign any angels who have not already been routed to the building, so new ones won't keep getting routed here. But there is a risk that *all* current Amenity Tower angels will be reassigned, even if I don't specifically reassign them. This is tricky software—I've been reading the manual and it may as well be written in Sumerian."

Roger flashed a conciliatory smile. "I never needed to use it. The program was just there, like that Minesweeper game. I tried using it once or twice but could never get past the first level."

She moved the cursor from one side of the screen to the other, pausing after each motion to double-check her work.

"So." Roger looked over her shoulder. "No more angels would be bound here."

"That's right. No new ones."

He flashed an amused half-smile. "You're going to send them all to Murray's office, aren't you?"

"Yep. Bound angels who aren't here already, and the hitchhiking interdimensional monsters that follow them, should start arriving at Murray's office presently."

It was a small action, but one that would cause mind-blowing amounts of inconvenience for Murray. Maybe she would have time to do more later.

Roger exhaled, stretched, and cracked his neck. He went and sat in the corner chair by the rubber tree and under a motivational poster for 'Planning.'

She tilted an Amenity Tower floaty pen. "As for the monsters destroying what's left of the city, I'll have to think up a different solution, since your copy of AngelRoute Pro doesn't include the

Interdimensional Monster Add-On Pack. Ha."

Roger clapped his hands once and kept them together. "Fair enough. But why not route them to Murray's apartment, instead of his office?"

"He'll be spending much more time in the office."

"It's just too bad we can't see it," Roger replied.

Her smile curved up one side as she tapped on the keyboard and cocked her head to get him to come over to the desk. "But we can. First, though, I'm really craving a coffee and a rhubarb pie."

Kelly left Roger's office and headed to the automat where she lucked out: two slices of the rhubarb sat in the same space behind the door, and the stick-monster working the counter gave her the second slice for free.

She reconvened with Roger at his desk, where she tossed him a wrapped slice of pie, keeping one for herself.

"The suspense is killing me." Roger attacked the pie. "Do you have a secret camera hidden away at Murray's office?"

"Do you host a show? Two cameras inside, two outside."

They watched the black and white feed. Murray, already hobbled from the beating he took earlier, perused Don's paperwork.

A light flashed in the center of the room and Murray jerked his head up. A giant angel with hundreds of eyes in the shape of a wheel appeared.

The many-eyed angel looked everywhere at once, turning to one side then another. When it spoke, it sounded like a mountain decided he had something to say. "Is this Sheol? Perdition? The Gates of Death? The Gates of the Shadow of Death? Silence? The Bilge? The Lowest Pit?"

"It's my office," Murray said, standing.

"I am to be bound here for seventy generations," the angel said in a deep grumbling rasp. "Where is your bathroom?"

Murray sat with a resigned thud. "There's only one bathroom. Down the hall."

In the management office, she rubbed her hands together in glee. She couldn't even remember feeling this jubilant before.

Roger stepped back from the screen. "You ported all incoming monsters and bound angels to Murray's office—but can't he just leave?"

She beamed. "No. I bound *him* there, too."

Chapter Fifty-Three

Get Your Poop Shields On

Kelly left Roger's office and pressed the elevator button for the top floor.

Tom the giant water scorpion bowed slightly and smiled. "Manicure? Latte? Shoulder massage?"

She smiled back. "No thanks, Tom. I'm good."

The elevator cab stopped on the next floor and the Jackal stepped in, wearing swim shorts, a towel around his neck, and holding a burning bush. Tom pressed the button for forty-eight.

The Jackal glanced over at the bush. "Why are you in a poopy mood?"

"I'm not in a poopy mood." The bush flamed a few inches higher.

"You're going to have to get your poop shields on," the Jackal said to Kelly behind his paw.

"Don't say things like that in front of other people," the bush said, blazing a stronger reddish hue.

"Weekend guest," the Jackal said, rolling his eyes.

The elevator stopped at forty-eight. "Have a nice day," he added, stepping out of the cab.

When the elevator reached the top floor, she sprinted up the stairs to the roof, where the air felt crisp and cold, and the sky glowed with a menacing purple hue.

There was also nothing left of Pothole City as far as she could see.

The building where she lived, the former headquarters of Special Situations International, was still intact. But beyond Amenity Tower and the SSI building, Pothole City was nothing but razed earth, rubble, and flying monsters circling overhead.

"It's just one big pothole," she said into the wind.

Right above her, the sky cracked and blackened in a fissure and she stepped back. A pair of muscular brick-red arms with glossy black claws gripped the edges of the fissure. Af jumped out and landed on the roof, glossy black wings unfurling, muscles flexing.

She turned her back to him and walked to the edge of the roof, putting a boot up on the embedded bolt where she had secured her window washing ropes. "I'm disappointed that you haven't changed back yet."

"The Af you knew was trapped, weak. A moth flapping its insubstantial wings against the glass."

She scoffed. "More like a moth riding the elliptical, reading *Lodge & Camp,* and buying applesauce cake from the building's automat. More accurate, less poetic."

Af cleared his throat and pressed on. "Imprisoned, and sentenced to attend board and committee meetings."

"Brutal."

"Those things can go on for hours," he said in protest. "You wouldn't believe how much time they spend on the most inconsequential thing. And there's always a guy who asks questions about every single item on the agenda. I'd like to see *you* handle it. Not well, I'd imagine."

His voice in this form took some getting used to.

She pushed at her bag with her toe. "If you ever see me at one of those meetings, feel free to chloroform me." She pushed off the rail and came closer to him. "What are you doing? Didn't you kind of like this whole almost-human thing?"

Af cocked his head and gave her a sidelong glance. "Do you remember what you said to me the day we met? It wasn't exactly a rousing endorsement for Pater's 'splendour and brevity' of the human condition."

"I was much younger then."

"That was the other day," Af said.

"Maybe I would change the tone of it now."

He smiled. "It was the SPs, wasn't it? They got to you."

"They're fine. Stop making this about me. You were the one who had the tantrum."

He held up his palms. "It's just what I do. If I were an angel of accounting, then I would go fill in a ledger. If I were an angel of aquaculture, I would build an artificial swamp habitat."

"If that's the case, why not go all the way? The only destroying you did was accidental."

"Because you could have been anywhere." Af spread out his arms to indicate a swath of space. "You were in and out of all of those alleys. Did you *want* me to do more? I made sure that your building" —he gestured to the Special Situations HQ—"and Amenity Tower went unscathed."

He tilted his head at the city below them. "Also, you're giving me way too much credit. Those monsters that flew in from the interdimensional portals did most of the damage. I was just enjoying my true form. What does it matter to you, anyway?" he asked.

"It *does* matter."

He flapped a wing back and forth. "It matters to you that I go back to my human form?"

"Yes. But there is a small chance you could be rerouted."

"What? I can't be rerouted!"

"The interdimensional monsters that got in through the air handler are putting an angel of destruction to shame." She gestured at the chaos below. "They're flying or taking the trains out of the city to destroy everything else. And all you care about is staying in Amenity Tower?"

"I don't want to be transferred to a bottle of gin or a mastodon skeleton or a deep fat fryer for a thousand years. Not again. Not after meeting you."

"I'm almost certain you won't be rerouted," she said, feeling oddly happy and not quite recognizing it.

Af gouged a line in the roof with the tip of a claw. "I'll be sure to send you postcards from the tumbleweed I get assigned to." He braced his arms and closed his eyes.

"Hey. Why don't you change into something more comfortable, like your human vessel. We'll stop the prince of evil from leaving in the dumpster. We'll get that air handler closed and stop any more of those monsters from getting in. And we can find the SPs then get some peanut butter sandwiches on raisin bread at the automat. Sound good?"

Af smiled.

The door back into the building slammed shut. Roger strode toward them, shiny red tie flapping in the breeze. He stopped in front of Kelly, brushed dust off his black suit, and cast a look of moderate surprise at Af.

"My promotion to Regional Manager will be official in—" Roger checked his Databank watch. "Right about now. It's been a pleasure knowing both of you. Best of luck in your future endeavors."

"What about *What's On Your Mind, With Roger Balbi*?" Af asked.

"The show was my test of worthiness," Roger said. "The property management corporation I work for doesn't give Regional Manager to just anyone. This took a hell of a lot of planning. The crap I put up with managing this place would make you shudder, so I'm relieved to move on. Now, if you'll excuse me. I think it's starting."

Roger stood still, hands loose at his sides, eyes closed. A moment later, his body shuddered and cracked open and expanded up and out.

"Huh. What do you think that is?" Kelly asked as they watched Roger's transformation.

"Hard to tell," Af said. "A tegu? A pterosaur?" He craned his neck to the side with a quizzical squint.

Roger's body expanded rapidly. Sharp spikes protruded from his back and he howled with the pain and effort of it.

"It's hard to get used to," she said. "He's always been so thin. How much do you think he weighs now?"

"More than eight short tons."

Roger gave one last, piercing shriek, launched off the roof, and became a distant speck on the horizon.

"Definitely some kind of iguana-monster," she said.

"I have to wonder what kind of buildings he's going to be supervising from now on," Af said.

"Wait." She picked up Roger's watch and key ring. "Who's going to be manager of Amenity Tower?"

Af sighed and changed back while she watched a monster devour monster mid-flight.

Chapter Fifty-Four

Cluck Snack Cluck

Clementine did a double-take at the building entrance from behind the front desk. She set down a binder and put her glasses back on. "Now what the hell is that? I don't need this kind of day again."

Kelly was just heading back to the package receiving area, but stopped and looked with Clem as a giant chicken head rolled up into the carport, beak opening and closing. It braked to a stop with an emphatic "Cluck!" from the speaker.

Af came up to the desk with his mail in hand and exchanged nonplussed looks with Kelly and Clementine.

Five man-sized chickens, wearing yellow leggings and big chicken feet, hopped out of the Cluck Snack mobile street van in unison and ran to the revolving door.

The first one got a chicken foot stuck in the door, and had trouble maneuvering his comb. The two behind him learned from his mistakes, but still had trouble moving through.

Clementine put her hands on her hips. "If this is some kind of heist, they're not gettin' through me."

"Cluck snack cluck snack cluck snack cluck!" the chickens yelled as they spilled into the lobby. One went up to Clem with as much of a businesslike attitude as was possible in a chicken costume, while the others ran loose by the seating area and fireplace.

"Your manager will be happy to receive us," the chicken said. "He has been inviting us to his studio every week for many months."

Clem shook her head. "Uh-uh. Well, your friends better not be initiating courting over there. We just had those carpets cleaned."

After further negotiation with the chicken, Clem let the group through. The lead chicken high-fived a fan and another chicken skipped in a circle in front of the desk.

They paraded around the lobby, tossing Cluck Snack gum and chewable vitamins to excited residents, singing:

"Cluck cluck cluck cluck cluck cluck snack

Snack snack snack snack snack snack cluck

Cluck snack cluck snack cluck snack cluck

Snack snack snack snack snack snack cluck!"

Residents pressed their backs against the wall, leaving colorful smears and streaks, as the chickens passed through the open door to the elevator vestibule. Some residents followed the chickens, and some scurried away into stairwells or behind plants.

"I'm going to go look for the SPs," she said. Clem and Af gave her vague gestures and murmurs in response.

She took the stairs up to the second floor. As she walked down a hallway with unmarked doors, a faint sound grabbed her attention. She halted, took two steps backward, and opened the door to a huge storage room.

Most of the SPs were playing ping-pong at a regulation-sized table. A few others tinkered with the objects they pilfered from the resident storage lockers, including a waffle maker and a laminator, which they tried to combine into a single machine. Tubiel watched the ping-pong game while humming the Cluck Snack song.

"Hey guys. Can we get out of here now?" She didn't want to let on how relieved she was to find them safe.

She noticed that the chickens had moved into the management

office reception area and took the SPs there. They grinned and jumped up and down, ecstatic to be in the middle of all of the Cluck Snack excitement, and see the chickens performing live in the studio with the camera operator.

"It's too bad Roger ascended," Af said to Kelly. "He's been desperate to get the Cluck Snack chickens on his show for the longest time. This would have been the highlight of his entire life. Except for, you know, ascending. I suppose."

"Of course the chickens showed up *after* his ascension."

The SPs pressed up against the glass of the studio window. The door opened and they crammed into the studio.

"Meet me by the dumpsters later," she told Af.

One of the chickens came out of the studio and into the main management office. He went right up to Af and whispered something in his ear.

Af pressed his eyes shut and nodded. The chicken went back into the studio and shut the door to the noise.

Tears ran down Af's cheeks onto his shirt.

Chapter Fifty-Five

Pothole City Dumpster Task Force

One half of the dumpster lid flipped open. Four angels, like four surprised raccoons, blinked at the sudden light and at the woman who hoisted herself up on the corner.

"Pothole City Dumpster Task Force." Kelly held a fake badge with one hand and a vial in the other. "Get your fallen butts out of the dumpster, right now."

"My butt has not fallen a millimeter," Gaap said. "It's as taut as it ever was."

Forcas raised his eyebrows. "I had no idea the Dumpster Task Force was so elite."

Raum agreed. "I underestimated how seriously the city takes its dumpster enforcement." He hoisted himself out and sat on the edge of the open lid. The others grumbled and brushed trash off themselves.

"All of you," she said. "Out."

"Or what?" Raum asked, holding out his arms to the side.

"Or you'll end up in these vials." She showed them her case of vials with a smile. "And you'll be sent back."

"Really?" Forcas said. "Where?"

She shrugged. "Could be a chafing dish, a coffee mug, a stuffed animal. Could be wherever you came from. Not my business. Or you can get out of the dumpster, forget about the end of days and go back to your apartments."

The garbage truck backed up to the loading dock, beeping loudly, engine and brakes roaring. It inserted its prongs into the slots on the dumpster. The angels bent their heads in a huddle and spoke softly, and a second driver, supervisoring the lift, gave a halt signal to the driver.

What's the hold-up?" the driver yelled.

"Dumpster Task Force." She flashed her badge to the driver. "We have a situation here that I'm working to resolve, so hold steady."

The angels spoke amongst themselves while she waited next to the dumpster.

"We should stay," Crocell said. "If we leave, we're just going to get bound again, and I can pretty much guarantee you that wherever that next prison is, it won't have the amenities that Amenity Tower has. What are the chances we'd be put in another luxury condominium?" He popped up and looked at Kelly. "We don't want to go back."

"Then get out of the dumpster and let these guys do their jobs."

"It's true. You can't go home again," Raum said, his normally upbeat countenance downcast.

"I need to check my mail," Forcas said.

"Fine, we'll stay, for now!" Raum grabbed the edge. "But don't come complaining to me later."

The angels hopped out of the dumpster. Crocell fell onto his side with an "Oof."

"Please don't put us in those vials. Look how glorious we are." Gaap's wings unfurled to their full width, dropping eggshells, banana peels, and candy wrappers. "And check out this butt." He patted a cheek. "See how firm? I've been training."

Raum brushed wilted salad leaves and coffee grounds off his sleeve. "What about Af? I know that Af is no longer Amenity Tower Af: product reviewer, committee member, coffee drinker. He's an angel of destruction, a prince of wrath and a ruler over the death of mortals. I know he's out there, destroying everything as we speak, because that's what he does."

They turned their heads at the soft thud of shoe heels. Af rounded the corner into the loading dock. She let out a relieved breath, and Raum's looked disappointed.

The garbage truck driver yelled impatiently. "C'mon, lady! I got eighteen more dumpsters to pick up today!"

She waved to the driver. "Go ahead, you're all clear."

The driver waved back. "Give the mayor my regards."

The four angels trudged back to the building. Raum patted Af's back and showed him a spiral notebook. "Say, Af, since we're staying, would you mind taking a look at my book-in-progress? It's a thriller. I call it *Sixty Floors of Wrath*."

"I don't really have the time right now, Raum. Get Vassago to read it."

"Vassago has food poisoning."

"Then ask Roger," Af said, not bothering to tell Raum that Roger ascended.

Chapter Fifty-Six

Amenity Tower's Nastiest Engineering Problem

Kelly ushered all of the SPs into the mechanical room, past a wall-mounted breathing apparatus. The cavernous room vibrated with the whirring, rumbling, and motorized sounds of the equipment and the high-pitched whistling of the air intake. A giant Barry Blower motor grumbled aggressively in the far corner.

"Is beast. Runs all the time. Sucks air." Dragomir stalked up to her, scowling.

"That's your best feature," she said, referring to the scowl.

"Why you bothering me? Very, very busy."

She maneuvered an SP named Morris in front of her. "Take him to the air handler. He's going to fix it, permanently."

Dragomir pointed a finger at the four-foot-tall, pajama-wearing, label-making creature in front of him.

"I do not like children."

"I'm not a big fan of shrieking germ farms, either. But he's not a child. He's child-*like*."

"He wears pajamas with attached feet and plays with child's toy. I do not see the difference."

Morris made eye contact with Dragomir and handed him a label.

Dragomir rolled his eyes and handed the label to her. It read 'Velocity.'

"He's been obsessed with that label maker ever since his friend lent it to him. But it doesn't matter. He can fix the stack."

Dragomir laughed, a hand on his stomach. "This child, he fix Amenity Tower's nastiest engineering problem, the one that gnaws on my—"

"That's right," she said. "And he's usually extremely busy, so you're damn lucky he carved out the time for you."

Dragomir crossed his arms. He sneered and smiled at the same time. "This may be, but handler cannot be fixed. Building must get redesign from square one. Many consultant have reach the end of professional... abilities in this building."

"You killed them?"

Dragomir waved his hand, scrunching up his face. "No, I did not kill them. What I try to say is, the turbulence on roof"—he made a swooshing gesture with his arm—"that rips through air handler is phenomenon these so-called experts have never seen before, not ever, in whole career."

Morris placed the label-maker on the floor and reached his arms up to Kelly, who hesitated just a second before hoisting him up on her back.

"Why do you care what they think?"

Dragomir squinted at her.

"No one knows this building better than you. So help Morris do his thing."

"Give me one reason why child can fix nasty problem, hm?"

Morris applied spit to her hair, twisting strands until they stuck out from her head.

"Because Morris is the angel in charge of HVAC systems."

Dragomir snorted. "Where was he when I start this gypsy-cursed job?"

Chapter Fifty-Seven

Excess Velocity

Kelly gestured to the doors of the air handler room. "If this is where the monsters get into the building, wouldn't you have a problem with chunks?"

Dragomir snorted. "No chunks. Monsters enter with the excess velocity, the extreme turbulence. Small chunks left on mesh." He shrugged. "We sweep off. Wind make bad situation even worse."

He thumped on the first of three heavy, submarine-style access doors, all in a row. "Static pressure with door closed is zero-point-fifty." He tilted his head at the gauge by the door. "When you open door—"

With one deft move, Dragomir pulled the handle open, revealing the louvers, mesh filters, and coils of the air handler. A solid blast of cold air made her stagger back a step.

"Static pressure decreases. Is fun, no?" He kept the door open and raised his voice over the howling wind. "Monsters do not enter building as solid form," he said, loudly, as one creature entered, followed by another. Dragomir seemed unconcerned. "Air and creatures are filtered, heated or cooled, then go out through ducts and to the resident floors."

A jaguar-thing with shiny yellow wings took form from a cloud of particles and roared at her.

Dragomir continued, unfazed. "Monsters egress through hallway vent on each floor, under apartment door, and circulate in apartment. Maybe go out through bathroom vent, maybe not. Maybe stays in apartment and eats whatever it finds. This why no humans left in building."

She grabbed the power screwdriver on the side of Dragomir's tool belt and distracted the jaguar while she vialed it with the other hand.

She pocketed the vial and focused on two other creatures. One, a weasel with a tiny walrus head, leapt on her.

A tusk pierced her skin as she struggled with it, and when she managed to push it off her a few inches, she wrenched it out. The monster writhed, and she stabbed it with its own tusk.

Morris made an ad hoc bandage from a piece of sketch paper, some Cluck Snack Pizza Flav'r Gum, and his saliva. Morris taped the bandage down on her shoulder. It soothed the pain in seconds.

"Filters too close to louvers and louvers too small," Dragomir said. "If building was redesigned from ground up, they could make louvers larger. This increase space between louvers so velocity would not increase, and bring in more monsters. But is impossible to fix."

Morris pulled out his sketch pad. He drew a bottle with a spray nozzle, a milk jug, something small and tree-shaped, a chicken with a word bubble that read 'Cluck,' and a dollar sign.

Kelly held up the pad. "I knew there'd be a quiz. OK." She tapped her finger on the nozzled bottle. "You want the Cluck Snack Sweet n' Savory Breakfast Foam Topp'n." She glanced at Morris, who raised the corners of his mouth in approval.

"And..." She raised her chin and closed her eyes, translating the sketch, searching her memory of Cluck Snack products. "The Cluck Snack Gummi Milk Bott'l with Liquid Center."

Morris nodded and lowered his eyes to a spot of oil on the concrete.

"What is it?"

Morris drew a bubble around the two objects on the pad then connected it to a third, empty bubble.

She guessed. "There's a third Cluck Snack product. And you don't know which one it is."

He flashed his eyes wide with a touch of defensiveness, as though to say he didn't know everything and she shouldn't expect him to.

"The two things you have already are liquids, right?"

He shrugged one shoulder.

"Maybe you need something solid. Give me a sec." She paced to the other side of the huge room, walked in a circle, and came back.

"The Cluck Snack Chewable Vitamin: Tree Edition," she said.

Morris raised an eyebrow.

"*Not* for Dogs and Ferrets."

Morris clapped. She dispatched Af by phone to round up the products they needed and meet her as soon as possible.

Dragomir removed his glasses and rubbed his eyes. "What is this Cluck Snack? Is the only thing cat will eat."

"I have no idea." She waved the sketch book. "Let's wait until Af gets back with these."

"You are going to use *snack food* to fix air handler?"

"You'd be surprised at how versatile this snack food is."

Dragomir walked off, holding his head in a vise grip and cursing under his breath.

Chapter Fifty-Eight

How's the Swarming Going?

As Af entered Amenity Tower Grocery, the Jackal stumbled toward him with a bag full of Cluck Snack Meal'n a Box Totez ("Take Your Cluck Snack With You"). His thick, lustrous hair was held back in a band. "They're half off!"

Af wasn't familiar with the layout of Amenity Tower Grocery. He had zipped in and out a few times to get a single, overpriced item—a spice, a corkscrew, some cream of tartar—but for the most part, he ordered his food through the mail.

He referred to his list. The Cluck Snack products would probably be dispersed all through the store, in every category. The Cluck Snack Sweet n' Savory Breakfast Foam Topp'n would likely be in the breakfast aisle.

There seemed to be a hundred subtle variations of every product, and the Cluck Snack brand was no exception.

Several agonizing and bewildering minutes later—thinking about how earlier that day he was in his majestic, glorious angel form and was now staring blankly at an aisle of snack food—Af spotted one lone, dusty box of Cluck Snack Sweet n' Savory Breakfast Foam Topp'n, half-hidden behind the instant breakfast drinks.

The breakfast aisle was a challenge, but the other sections were even worse. Af nearly gave up on finding the Cluck Snack Gummi Milk Bott'l with Liquid Center. What did 'gummi' mean? He looked for the Bott'l in the breakfast aisle, in the milk cooler, and in the baby aisle.

The store's few employees rushed past him with boxes. Finally Af went to the front to flag down someone to help him while the wind beat against the side windows like a crazed ex-lover.

A wheezing produce aisle stocker lumbered through the store with Af. Each regular step seemed to take the employee three or four tedious motions, with the slowness and the swiveling. Af balled his hands into fists and gritted his teeth as he followed the stocker into the candy aisle.

He searched frantically for the product, now that he knew how it was shelved. "Gummi Milk," he muttered. "Gummi Milk, dammit, Gummi Milk!"

"What's that?" the stocker asked.

"Nothing," Af said. After what seemed like the length of time he was bound in the arcade game, he located a bag of the Cluck Snack Gummi Milk Bott'l with Liquid Center. As he triumphantly held the blue and white bag in his hands, Af was overcome with relief and elation. "This is what being human is like!"

"I know," the stocker said, shambling off. "Livin' the dream, right?"

Running on the endorphin high of procuring two of the three Cluck Snack products that could stop the Apocalypse, Af hurried to the vitamin aisle and found a Cluck Snack Chewable Vitamin: Tree Edition ("Not for Dogs and Ferrets").

But then he tried to pay for the items.

And he waited. And waited. A locust was dominating the lone cashier's time with a cart-load of Cluck Snack Meal'n a Box Totez ("Take Your Cluck Snack With You").

Af drummed his fingers against his leg.

When the locust took out his coupons, Af nearly lost it. He remembered he was still an angel of wrath and destruction, and considered his two choices: revert back to his original form and start by leveling this store. Or stand in line. Because he was falling for Kelly, he stood in line.

"Could you go faster?" the locust asked the cashier, who was scanning the items at a glacial pace. "We're making swarms to form a plague, and of course they sent *me* on the food run." The locust held up one of the boxes. "I have sixty of these. Can't you do one scan for all of them?"

"Sorry," the cashier said, "but it's our policy to count everything by hand."

The locust rubbed his wings together in impatience, making a creepy whispering sound.

"How's the swarming going?" The cashier asked in a cheerful tone.

"It's going all right, I guess," the locust said. "We've been practicing our rolling motion for the end of days, so I hope we can—"

Af tossed a wad of money on the cashier's station and rushed out of the store. He returned to the mechanical room with a bag full of Cluck Snack products.

Chapter Fifty-Nine

Clean Showers and Good Coffee

Morris ripped open the packaging, cradled the Foam Topp'n, Gummi Milk Bott'l, and the Chewable Vitamin, and toted them to the first access door by the louvers.

Dragomir started forward. "If silent creature makes miserable job worse than is now, I make him chewable vitamin."

Kelly flashed Dragomir a warning look to discourage him from interfering.

Another monster came through the louvers and out the coils, its particles cohering into a giant flounder with two eyes on the side of its head, and, incongruously, burly bear arms.

Dragomir took a broom, opened the heavy door, then swiped the bristles against the mesh.

The monster swung out an arm, swiped the bottle of Cluck Snack Sweet n' Savory Breakfast Foam Topp'n, and put it in its mouth. But the bottle was an awkward shape and the flounder-thing seemed at a loss. It looked like a seagull with a hoagie bun in its beak, unsure what to do next.

After she speared it with Dragomir's power screwdriver, the flounder spat out the bottle and she vialed the monster, wondering what Don wold do with all those vials.

"It's a good thing you got that bottle back," Af said, "because it was the last one they had."

"Let's hurry. This is getting painful."

Morris put a vitamin in a squishable rubber bowl he kept on him at all times. He sprayed the Foam Topp'n on the Chewable Vitamin. The vitamin changed shape and color, expanding into the size of a cake. Then Morris took one of the Gummi Milk Bott'ls, bit off the top and squeezed the liquid contents onto the vitamin, dissolving it.

Dragomir laughed. "Ha! Science project complete failure! I told you fixing handler not possible. Now please let me return to purgatory of daily life."

Morris took the bowl and poured its now-liquid contents into the empty Breakfast Foam Topp'n spray bottle. He waited a moment for the wind to stop gusting, but still couldn't even get across the access door. Af put his hands on Morris's back to guide him the rest of the way.

Morris used the nozzle bottle to spray the mist onto the louvers and filter. The mix of three Cluck Snack products came out of the bottle and formed a lattice structure around the air handler.

Kelly stepped around Morris to get a closer look. "Looks like the stinkhorn mushroom."

Dragomir wiped the tears off his cheeks. "I have not laugh this hard since *What's On Your Mind, With Roger Balbi* have those circus cats."

Morris came back into the main mechanical room and sketched something for her. She nodded and he sketched something else, then she took the pad again and looked at the drawing for a few seconds. "Mm-hm. OK.

"Here's what Morris did," Kelly said to the rest of them. "After the Angel of the Bottomless Pit, aka Don, assigned all of the bound angels to Amenity Tower, the energy turned the building into a truck stop for dimensional flotsam and jetsam—like the Jackal and your scorpion elevator attendant. The monsters were probably attracted here by the clean showers and good coffee, then got sucked in the rest of the way."

Dragomir and Af looked at her blankly.

"Or to look at it another way, Amenity Tower is like a highway off-ramp with a diner in the shape of a giant donut. The monsters can't resist taking that off-ramp."

Dragomir scratched his ever-present stubble. "But building does not have donut on it. I would know."

"It's figurative," she added.

Af took the sketchbook from her. Morris's latest drawing was a stick figure angel with a huge head, big eyes, and wings; a lighthouse; a can of Red Bull, a margarita, and a vacuum.

"How did you get all of that from this?" Af asked.

She shrugged. "Isn't it obvious?"

A few moments later, a comforting *purr* replaced the high-pitched whistling of the air intake.

Chapter Sixty

In the Interest of Succession

Kelly narrowed her eyes at Roger's week-view calendar like she was The Man With No Name staring down Ramón Rojo in the climactic showdown. She crossed out meeting after meeting with a black marker, and marveled at Roger's energy. He managed a sixty-story building until six or seven in the evening, spent the whole night doing situational offense with an all-fallen angel board and committee members, and still made time for his local access show.

But now Roger was free. His Facebook status said 'Ascended.' And now *she* was the idiot who received a mysterious call from Claw & Crutty, the property management company that employed Roger, and agreed to work at Amenity Tower as interim manager.

They said Roger suggested they talk to her. She didn't know what to believe, but it didn't seem that much less weird than working for the Destroying Angel of the Apocalypse.

The most vocal of the fallen angels and the dimensional monsters that remained in the building gathered outside her door. They wanted many things, but most of all, they demanded the continuation of their beloved local access show, *What's On Your Mind, With Roger Balbi.*

Clementine, recently promoted to front desk supervisor, pushed through the crowd of residents and brought a large wooden crate to her office.

"Finally, that vampire I ordered."

The return address on the crate read *6th Lodge*. She cut the plastic cover, and pulled open the front of the crate. Inside was a telepresence robot just like Don's. When she finished the assembly, it stood five feet tall with a display screen and camera, on wheels.

The note read, "Walk a mile in the Destroying Angel of the Apocalypse's shoes. *This* is how you manage people. See attached photo and mementos from robot's Maui vacation (sorely needed). Best, Don."

She held up the photo of Don's telepresence robot on a Maui beach, a lei draped around its screen. The card read, "Don—Wish you were here."

"I don't know how he got out, but that guy really knows how to relax vicariously through his robot," she muttered. She made a mental note to add Don to the list of fugitives she'd track down after surfacing from her current morass of managerial busywork.

She sat in her swivel chair and put Don's note to the side. On her left was a teetering pile of that day's mail, and on top of the pile was a disc in a transparent cover. She picked it up, glanced over it, and put it beside the pile.

Af knocked and opened the door. He sat on the other side of the desk, glanced at the disc, and held it up. "What's this?"

"Don't know. It was in the mail."

"Let's watch it in the studio."

They elbowed past the shouting crowd, shut the door behind them in Roger's studio, and closed the curtains. Af put the disc in the player and sat next to her.

In the video, Roger leaned forward on an orange plastic chair, positioned in front of a paper-craft backdrop consisting of orange, growling-faced lions; an ocean; Ben Franklin; and a smiling giraffe.

"I'm Roger Balbi, manager of Amenity Tower, Pothole City's Finest Luxury Condominium Building, and host of the award-winning local access show, *What's On Your Mind, With Roger Balbi*. My planning and preparation has finally paid off. I'm being promoted next week, so I'm recording this special segment for my replacement in the interest of succession." He held up his calendar and grinned.

"Oh God." Kelly pressed in at her temples. "What did I agree to?"

"The first thing you should know is that you will have to deal with the politics and personalities of the board, who are all cast-down angels. You'll also have to field constant complaints from the residents, most of whom are interdimensional monsters. The board members will expect special treatment, but you have to remain objective. Here's a tip: the cleaning crew are a well-read, elite fighting force, and the most mentally stable people in the building."

Af nodded. "That's true."

"There are some things you should watch out for, like people who attempt to infiltrate the building under the guise of a local official."

She looked sideways at Af. He shrugged.

"Specifically, a woman in her late twenties—"

"Late twenties? Still got it."

"—who has accessed the building as seemingly every task force official in the city. But I have cameras everywhere," Roger said with a devious smile, "including the hallways and in every residential unit."

"*What*?" Kelly and Af said simultaneously.

"But she's cute," Roger said, "and frankly, I don't care what she's doing. Amusement is worth its weight in gold around here. If it bothers you, you can always stick her in lockup." He jangled a set of keys.

She expelled a long breath. "Lockup? Amenity Tower has more amenities than I thought."

"I don't know if that should be considered an amenity," Af said.

"Finally, the show." Roger leaned forward and clasped his hands. "I know the residents must be losing it over the interruption. First, feel free to change the name. I've ascended. My ego is no longer attached to the show. Second, refer to my manual and checklists, as well as my address book of vendors, suppliers, and potential guests. I have my shows arranged weeks in advance, so the first few sets of guests are already lined up. Also, a note for the new board president: I recommend a scorched-earth policy. Good luck. You'll need it. Sayonara."

The screen turned black. Kelly removed the disc from the player and they locked up the studio.

They ran into Dragomir in the management office, smiling, to the extent of showing his teeth, and Kelly found that perturbing.

"I thought air handler was lost cause: can't redesign it, so just have to put up with it, like human body or family. And louvers only weather-proof, not storm-proof or monster-proof. So when your little person here"—he slapped Morris's back, sending him stumbling forward a few steps—"put that Cluck Snack spray on mesh, I laugh and laugh forever. But it worked!"

A huge grin stretched across Dragomir's face. "Can you believe, because I can barely believe. Only one creature show up so far, a giant tongue with turtle shell, covered in algae. Had to brush off mesh."

Kelly high-fived Morris.

"Morris work with me now as consultant," Dragomir said, "for HVAC, pipe, and duct jobs. Also Owen, for small appliances, Jonah, for large appliances, and Fef, for elevators." Dragomir looked giddy. "Life almost bearable now!"

The engineer left with Morris, who waved to her as he shuffled away, and Af went with her to Roger's office.

"I'm kind of thinking the monsters should have included Amenity Tower in their wave of destruction," she said, "because I'll be interviewing for permanent managers all day. I don't want this job, and I'd like to try being just me for a while. Which could be an embarrassing, miserable failure."

Her desk phone rang. She answered.

"Open the video I sent you," the bald man said.

She checked her email, saw the email from him, then played the video. Af stood behind her and Tubiel pored through Roger's stuff. From his hell lodge office, Don watched his telepresence robot enjoy its vacation (on the screen within the screen, the robot stood awkwardly under a palm tree and held an elaborate tropical beverage it couldn't drink).

Murray frantically made coffee drinks for rerouted angels and monsters, crammed full in the room. Then she jumped an inch when

Don ignited in a white blaze that shrunk to a dot in a split second, like an old TV set turning off.

Coffee sloshed on Murray's hand when the bald man appeared out of thin air next to him. He touched Murray on the back, and Murray disappeared the same way, but with a green flame instead of white.

The bald man gave her a thumbs up. "See you around, Driscoll. You can thank me later."

The video ended there.

"What *was* that?" Af asked.

"Just someone doing me a favor. Even though I don't deserve it."

She made a quick call to the bald man and left a message on his voice mail. "I appreciate the gesture, but I'd rather take care of Don and Murray myself. So if you could undo their conflagration, as amusing as it was, that would be great."

When she hung up the phone, Af said, "Can I make you dinner? We could watch a movie after," and she thought that maybe she'd stay in Pothole City for a while.

Chapter Sixty-One

Clucking Along Holdings

Kelly interviewed several potential managers, and then stopped at Af's apartment with Tubiel in tow. She poured herself a coffee and wandered over to the telescope. Besides Amenity Tower, the Special Situations International building was one of the few structures left standing downtown, thanks to Af's efforts.

She looked past the razed earth to the flattened industrial outskirts of Pothole City. She passed over a building with a fuzzy light, went back, and adjusted the focus.

The telescope was powerful; she could make out the glowing white lettering on the lone remaining building outside of their three block radius: "Clucking Along Holdings: Makers of Cluck Snacks. A Driscoll Family Company."

A Taste of...

the Last Donut Shop of the Apocalypse

Nina Post

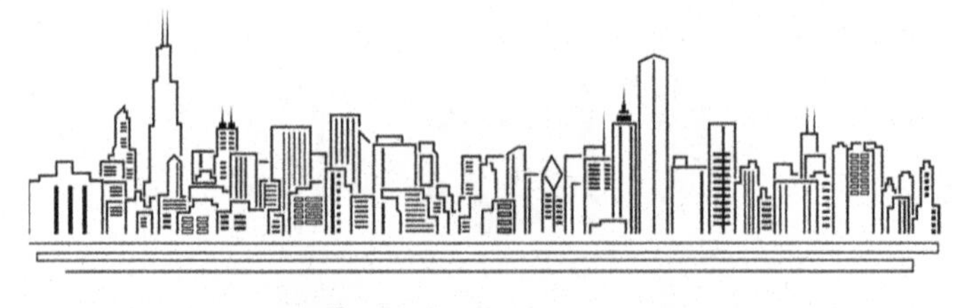

Chapter One

As a formerly successful and then not-so-successful bounty hunter, Kelly Driscoll hated working as herself. After gaining access to Amenity Tower as an elevator inspector, hamster grief counselor, FDA criminal division agent, and various city officials, she had somehow been named interim manager of the building. These days, she showed up to work as herself.

Being Kelly Driscoll meant that she winced when anyone in Amenity Tower, Pothole City's finest (and only) luxury condominium building, recognized and greeted her. It felt wrong to not radically change her eye color, her skin, her facial shape, her hair, her clothing, her body type, her occupation, her name.

But she didn't mind being herself at home, which for weeks had been the top two floors of a 1920s-era art deco high-rise a couple of blocks from Amenity Tower in downtown Pothole City.

She gathered her ash-blonde hair in a bun and went into Mr. Orange's office, packed full of small, single-purpose angels, or SPs as she called them.

They had all moved in before the destruction of the city with the notion she could protect them. After she sent Murray—the corrupt angel who killed the SP in charge of audio equipment—to indefinite retirement in a hell lodge, the rest of the SPs stayed with her, and now she worked a steady job with benefits to keep them in Cluck

Snack products.

This time, her employer wasn't the Destroying Angel of the Apocalypse, who begrudgingly paid out expense forms after a few months, and it wasn't a Jackal who wanted to steal a painting from an ex—it was a shadowy property management conglomerate who paid for health insurance.

The small angels sat in a group in Mr. Orange's office wearing pajamas, eating cereal, and watching *Clucking Along Holdings Presents the Cluck Snack Weekday Cartoon Adventure Hour*, with animated and live-action segments.

"Back at five," she said.

They waved with spoons that flicked droplets of milk and bits of cereal across the room and on the marble floors. She grabbed her bag and a phone rang the minute she started out the door.

"Where is there a *phone*?" she said, to an empty hallway.

It kept ringing.

She did a U-turn and went into Mr. Black's office, thinking it was one of the two landline phones, one black and one red, on the massive metal desk, though they had never rang before.

But the ringing was farther away.

She went back into the center of the floor and listened. The call was definitely coming from inside the house.

It sounded like it came from the pneumatic tube room, even though it didn't have a phone, but to her surprise, when she unlatched the casing of a red metal box she found a ringing phone labeled *Answer: 'Special Situations International: We're Usually Awake*.

Kelly shook her head, wondering how she'd missed that, unhooked the receiver and put her own spin on the instructions. "SSI, You Won't Catch Us Napping."

Special Situations International once had their headquarters in the spacious top floors where Kelly now lived rent-free. As far as she knew, Don, the Avenging Angel of the Apocalypse, had used it for out-of-town guests, but no one ever bothered her about it. The company's origins and purpose remained a mystery to her, but she knew that Mr.

Black—a former SSI executive whose office she occupied—used to be an elite orienteer, evidenced by the photos on his wall.

"Yeah, this is Jerry Shanks," said the loud voice on the other side of the call. "I'm a bail bonds agent with Shanks Brothers Bonds down on Locust Street."

Kelly held the phone a few inches from her ear. His voice would carry up to a passing airplane.

"My client failed to make his court appearance," Jerry said. "This is the number he gave me as a contact."

"What's the name of the client?" She got a pen and memo pad.

"Driscoll," Jerry said, practically yelling at her. "Archie Driscoll." He pronounced it *AH-chee Dris-kul*.

She sat on the one small chair in the tiny room and saw an SP zip by on a modified sled.

Archie Driscoll? Probably just a coincidence he had the same last name. No shortage of Driscolls out there. Sure, one of them had to be her father, but not this one. She never thought she would ever meet her father, and had no doubt that would remain the case. In her mind, she put the thought in a tiny jar, gave the jar to a salamander in a canoe, and watched him row away into thick fog.

"I need to recover that money," Jerry said. "I'm responsible for the bond payment. Hello? You still there?"

She knew full well how his business worked. "Yeah, I'm here. Did this Archie Driscoll give a company name?"

"C-A-H. That mean anything to you?"

Because of his thick accent, she said, "Charlie-Alpha-Hotel, right?"

"Yeah."

Clucking Along Holdings, a Driscoll Family Company. One of the last buildings standing after Pothole City was obliterated. Maybe she had a living relative. Or maybe this had nothing to do with her. It was probably just some random Driscoll who knew someone from SSI or any other company that used to be in the building, or who used to work in one of those companies.

She didn't know SSI was supposed to do in this case, but that wasn't her concern. Regardless, she may as well try and pick up some extra money.

"You need him apprehended?"

"Yeah, sure," Jerry said. "That'd be helpful."

Taking a side gig could interfere with her work at Amenity Tower, or taking care of the SPs, or her relationship with Af, if that really was anything. But she could handle an additional job, and it would be good to have a project that took advantage of her talents rather than constantly reminding her of her limitations, and didn't involve running a condo building.

In her head, Jay Vanner told her, *Kelly, invest energy in your natural talents and seize the opportunity to show them off. In one job, you may feel like a failure, but in this job, you can achieve something.*

"Give me the info, then."

"What, are *you* going to do this?"

"I'm more than qualified."

She took down some notes and by the time she hung up, had a job—the kind of job she could do well, and the kind of job she liked. But she had resolved to make an effort to be herself, to be the real, accept-no-imitations Kelly Driscoll.

No reason she couldn't do both, right?

Just as she closed the door to the tube room, the phone rang again. For a phone that hadn't made a peep since she took up residence, it was disconcertingly active.

One more call, but then she would really have to leave. She had to film an episode of *What's On Your Mind, With Roger Balbi* before meeting Af, the former angel of destruction she spent way too much time thinking about as of late.

"Special Situations International," she said on the red phone. "We're Excessively Caffeinated."

Tubiel, the single-purpose angel in charge of the protection of small birds, and the SP she was closest to, came in and held up a Cluck Snack cereal box. He wore his usual outfit of shiny black patent sneakers with a mirrored metal letter on the sides; jeans with a large mirrored metal brand sign; a puffy black nylon jacket zipped up to the top; and mirrored aviator sunglasses, on the top of his head.

"This is your client," a male voice said over the phone. Confident, and with an undertone of urgency. "Institute Code Cluck Snack immediately."

Her client. Right.

She checked inside the phone case to see if it contained instructions or a code. It didn't, but she would start with the basics.

"I'm actually new here. Which client?"

"Your *only* client."

"I don't have any clients. I just got my badge." As far as she knew, no badge was involved with working for SSI, but then again, maybe it did.

"Clucking Along Holdings. SSI's *only client*!" He let out a frustrated breath. "This is Hamlet Gonzalez, Clucking Along Holdings' Vice-President of Snacks and Flavors."

Kelly recovered. "Of course. I meant that we, the elite team here at Special Situations International, *share* you as a client." She had no idea what SSI did or what kind of special situations they handled or if they were an elite team of anything except orienteering, but covered for her ignorance. "As much as I have to be reminded since they took my employee photo, I realize I don't have an exclusive relationship with Clucking Along Holdings. Though it often feels that way."

Kelly wanted to uphold SSI as a functioning entity because she wasn't paying rent. They were technically squatting in the building since she'd stopped working for Don, King of the Demonic Locusts.

Clucking Along Holdings was SSI's only client? If Clucking Along Holdings somehow owned SSI, as a subsidiary or division, and discovered that the SSI executives abandoned the company, they could kick her and the SPs out on the street.

If that happened, she would have to steal and take temporary residence of the Cluck Snack street van, and then just like that, she'd be running the mobile Cluck Snack operation whether she wanted to or not.

Hamlet sucked in a breath. "Since you're new, I'll lay it out for you, but then do yourself and SSI a favor and learn the codes. Code Cluck Snack is the top emergency level, the top priority. It means that you drop everything and find our missing president. We would like to handle this discreetly. Clucking Along Holdings has never held a press conference and does not encourage media visits to its plants, so do not inform the press about this."

"If you insist," Kelly said, humoring him. "You have a code for finding your missing president? How often does he go missing?"

"Not often. Not for this long, anyway. Don't you have a guide or a legend or a manual or anything like that?"

"We have a manual, but Mr. Orange dropped it down the laundry chute and it got stuck."

"Yes, that *is* like Mr. Orange," Hamlet said in a thoughtful and slightly critical tone. "May I speak to him, or your supervisor?"

"I'm sorry, but everyone's out for Founder's Week."

"SSI takes a whole week to celebrate their founding?" Hamlet sounded incredulous. "We take only one day at CAH."

"Oh, SSI takes our founding very seriously."

"I'll have to take that up with Mr. Orange," Hamlet said. "They left you in charge, by yourself?"

"I'm the only one who can lift the water jug for the cooler."

Hamlet Gonzalez didn't know that Special Situations International had vacated their headquarters without leaving so much as a forwarding address, and what he didn't know wouldn't hurt him..

"Tell me more about this missing president."

Kelly closed her eyes as a fallen angel with curled-up black lycra wings leaned over and patted her face with powder. The giant water scorpion, normally the elevator attendant, applied color to her lips with one arm and brushed her hair with another.

Restless, she shook off the angel and the scorpion and sprang out of the chair. "I have a small window of time for these two interviews. The accountant is meeting me in twenty minutes." Those two sentences summed up why she felt like a mastadon in a cat carrier.

"Smile more!" The camera operator gave up on her with an exasperated sigh, then gave her a pleading look next to the monitor. "Ask yourself, 'What would Roger do?'"

She smiled, but not in the way the operator would likely want. "Roger would transform into an iguana the size of a whale and ascend to the higher form of regional manager."

"Ha ha," the camera operator said. "OK, our first guest is on in five, four, three, two, one." He pointed a finger at her, indicating she was live.

"This is *What's On Your Mind, With Roger Balbi*, the award-winning local access variety show out of Amenity Tower—Pothole City's finest, and only, luxury condominium. I'm your host, Kelly Driscoll."

She glanced out the window at the waiting area outside the door, where residents started to gather. "You may have seen our first guest eating a power breakfast of coffee and angel claw at his new favorite restaurant, Pothole City Donuts, located right here in Amenity Tower."

Smiling with strained cheerfulness, she added, "'Pothole City Donuts: We Fill the Potholes of Your Soul with Fried Goodness.'"

After a deceptively short second, in which she took in the scope of her life thus far and wondered how, exactly, fate and her choices had put her in Roger's studio chair, she continued. "Or you may have seen him installing and personally trimming sculpted hedges in the shapes of Pothole City business leaders. It's the mayor of Pothole City, Whip Whipson."

The mayor strolled onto the set, displaying a Pothole City Donuts-loving girth, pasty skin, and a blue, elbow-length, elastic-sleeved blouse. Looked like a minor demon.

"Hello, Roger, it's good to be here." He eased himself into the chair and let out a tortured wheeze.

"My name isn't Roger," she said, though she wouldn't have minded pretending to be Roger for the show. It would make things easier.

The mayor turned to check with his assistant, a movement which seemed to take much longer than it should have. "Isn't this—?"

"*What's On Your Mind, With Roger Balbi*? Yes," she said, "but I'm not

Roger Balbi."

"Well, we can't all be Roger Balbi, can we?"

"No, we certainly can't." Kelly smiled. "Mr. Mayor, can you compare the condition of Pothole City a mere three weeks ago to its condition today?"

The mayor, his forehead already sweating, put on a serious expression and steepled his bratwurst-sized fingers, which didn't have the 'master of reason' effect he was probably after.

"Yes, Roger."

She didn't bother.

"After the loss of nearly twenty-thousand buildings in Pothole City, only three structures remained: first, the building we're in right now, Amenity Tower." He paused to catch his breath. "Second, the former headquarters of Special Situations International, just across the street." Break for extended wheezing, and to blot his forehead with a tissue. "And third, the current headquarters of Clucking Along Holdings, makers of Cluck Snack products."

The mayor shifted in the chair and adjusted his elastic cuffs.

Outside the window, a butterfly-like monster with orange-slice wings and a white-furred head zoomed around the management office to the obvious consternation of a monster with a smooth, cyndrilical body crowned with hundreds of wildly swishing feathery tentacles.

The mayor continued. "Our city is very fortunate that Clucking Along Holdings took the lead on the rebuilding efforts. New buildings are sprouting like shoots from the rubble. Within just days after the conflagration, entrepreneurs started businesses on any platform they could find. In fact, new business formation is at an all-time high, as entrepreneurs from all walks of life have set out to meet the needs of our population during the rebuilding process."

"Such as the vice and bootlegging entrepreneurs who are taking control of the city and dominating illegal markets with the assistance of the city's so-called business leaders?" Kelly said evenly.

The mayor's assistant, standing by the door to the studio, shook his head as if trying to shake off a spider. The mayor coughed into his hand, which resembled a cinnamon roll.

"The mayor's office and the Relief Society are doing everything in their power to restore authority," the mayor said.

The popularity of Amenity Tower had skyrocketed since the apocalypse turned the city into ruins, and she got grumpier by the day. Interviewing the mayor did not help, and dealing with the Amenity Tower board of directors gnawed at her soul.

But she needed to wrap up the interview and storm through the next one so she could get on with her work.

Not for the first time, she wondered how in hell Roger got by. What was his secret to keeping his sanity while he worked at Amenity Tower as manager: Meditation? The black magician suit? The bright red tie? Diplomacy? Sorcery?

No, the tie. It had to be the tie.

"What are you doing to rebuild a semblance of government in Pothole City after the previous apocalypse?" she asked.

The mayor cleared his throat, a sound that reminded her of the faulty carburetor in the sidecar motorcycle she had used to drive Tubiel around returning small birds to their many different owners, all over the city.

"After the destruction, I signed a proclamation and assigned administration of the relief initiative to the Pothole City Relief Society," he said.

"And who are the members of the Pothole City Relief Society?" Kelly asked.

"The city's most prominent business leaders." The mayor puffed out his chest.

"Who exactly are the business leaders in the Relief Society?" She wouldn't have asked if she didn't already know it was a short list.

"The Pothole City Relief Society includes the founders of United Donuts Co. and Pothole City Donuts," the mayor said, "as well as the president of Clucking Along Holdings; the Chief Executive Officer of Claw & Crutty; the founder of Pothole City's leading garbage disposal company, Pothole City Waste; and several attorneys."

Pothole City Donuts was the new donut shop leasing space on the first floor of Amenity Tower, and their business was doing gangbusters compared to United Donuts. Kelly didn't know why the founders of two donut shops were in the Relief Society. But then, the number of available business leaders in Pothole City was limited.

"And finally, Mr. Mayor, how would you classify the mood in the city right now?"

The mayor intertwined his fingers in his lap. "I would characterize the city's mood as understandably fearful and uncertain, but also hopeful. And dare I say, *exhilarated* over the prospect of change, of moving forward. I think people are focusing on the small things."

At the moment, Kelly was exhilarated over the prospect of having a snack.

The show's second guest, a wiry man with a mustache and an amused expression, passed through the studio lights to take the seat across from Kelly.

"Why don't you introduce yourself to our viewers," Kelly said, giving the man what she hoped was an encouraging smile, and not a menacing snarl.

The camera operator gave her a thumbs up.

The man leaned forward slightly and kept his hands flat on his thighs. "Sure. My name is Sugar Montana, and I'm the Pothole City Transportation Commissioner."

"Thanks for taking the time to appear on *What's On Your Mind, With Roger Balbi*, Mr. Montana."

"Call me Sugar." He nodded, and flashed a smile so fast it qualified as subliminal.

"I'm sure our audience is keenly interested in Pothole City's deteriorating pothole situation," she said.

Sugar cleared his throat and darted his gaze at the camera. "Of course they are."

In the management office, the butterfly monster thudded against the window and the tentacled cylinder had hopped up on the reception desk. A third resident, a monster resembling a smallish volcanic crater with feathery appendages, huddled, trembling and nonplussed, by the supplies closet.

Sugar sat up a little straighter. "The residents of Pothole City have probably noticed more potholes this year. This is clearly due to the combination of last year's blizzard, along with frequent freeze-and-thaw cycles, and the demons in the underworld seeking points of weakness in old asphalt. Our revised pavement strategy calls for more so-called 'pothole killer' machines for use in alleys. We don't want to be called *Sinkhole City*." He chuckled softly.

Tom the giant water scorpion herded the butterfly monster and the other two monsters out into the hallway to resolve their conflict there.

In the studio room, Kelly looked intently at Sugar. "Don't you think that the destruction of Pothole City just weeks ago has something to do with the worsening pothole situation?"

At the studio window, Tubiel cupped his hands around his mirrored sunglasses with the side safety mesh and looked into the studio. He waved at Kelly, and put his hand back to the glass.

"Yes, that could have something to do with it." Sugar's mouth quirked, delicately, to indicate his facetious tone. "After the destruction, much of the rubble was swept or trucked away. Some of that rubble was hastily backhoed into the lake, forming an artificial beach of rusted iron spikes and chunks of gravel."

Sugar glanced at the window, presumably to make sure the mayor wasn't listening, though Kelly got the impression he didn't much care.

"This process almost certainly caused more potholes to form," Sugar continued. "Moreover, traffic consisting mainly of Pothole City Cab Co. Livery drivers, city vehicles, and Cluck Snack delivery wagons started flowing through the city before the street-resurfacing program got underway. This definitely worsened existing potholes."

More residents assembled inside the management office. Enim giants, fallen angels, worm-like residents in mucous envelopes, residents with hard exoskeletons, and a couple of SPs watched the monitor screen as colorful opaque wings and membranous wings flapped gently in the crowd to make a breeze. Tubiel jumped up and down at the window, but only saw his head.

"And how many potholes did you fill last year, Commissioner?" Kelly asked.

"Over seven-hundred-thousand street potholes," Sugar said. "Crews also filled more than fifty-thousand potholes in alleys, considerably more than the previous year."

"Wow."

"Yeah, wow is right." Sugar smiled. "Our department would like to be less reactive to the problem."

The third guest, a band called Frog Hotel, clattered into the studio with their equipment as Kelly went out. She wanted to stay and watch, but had the meeting with the accountant about the reserves and the investment accounts, the package she had to put in the delivery drop box across the street, and most important, she needed a snack.

By the time she opened the door leading to the elevator vestibule, she had smears of colored slime and powdery dust on her shirt. She was getting used to it.

About the Author

Nina Post is the author of seven novels, including Danger Returns in Pairs, Danger in Cat World, Extra Credit Epidemic, The Last Condo Board of the Apocalypse, The Last Donut Shop of the Apocalypse, One Ghost Per Serving, and The Zaanics Deceit. She lives in Seattle. To stay up-to-date on new releases and get exclusive subscriber-only bonuses, sign up for Nina's newsletter at http://www.ninapost.com/newsletter/

Thank You for Reading

http://www.ninapost.com

Please visit http://curiosityquills.com/reader-survey to share your reading experience with the author of this book!

Death by Cliche, by Bob Defendi

To Sartre, Hell was other people. To the game designer, Hell is the game. When Damico is shot in the head by a loony fan he wakes up in the worst game of all time. Set on their quest in a scene that would make Ed Wood blush, Damico discovers that he is a creative force in this broken place. First a peasant, then a barmaid, then his character's own father... all come alive. But the central question remains. Can Damico escape, or is he trapped in this nightmare? Forever.

It's a comedy. We swear. Based on a true story.

Going Through the Change, by Samantha Bryant

In this lighthearted, nontraditional superhero novel, four menopausal women in the same town start to exhibit strange abilities: incredible strength, the ability to wield fire, to fly (sort of), and armor-plated skin. Each woman struggles to deal with her changes in her own way, until life throws them together. When the women start to talk, they find out that they have more in common than they knew--one person has touched all their lives. The hunt for answers is on.

Lightning Source UK Ltd.
Milton Keynes UK
UKOW01f2227070817
306875UK00001B/181/P

9 781620 070178